SHADES OF SILENCE

SHADES OF SILENCE

Liz Lazarus

Published in the United States by Mitchell Cove Publishing, LLC.

While this novel is a work of fiction and the agency, "Florida Cares," is fictional,
the information about DMST (Domestic Minor Sex Trafficking) is accurate and
obtained in collaboration with Georgia Cares, a 501(c)(3) non-profit agency
whose mission is to ensure that child sex trafficking victims receive quality care
and services. Georgia Cares' vision is that child sex trafficking is one day eradicated
and survivors are restored and thriving with the help of trauma-informed treatment.
To learn more, visit www.gacares.org.

ISBN 978-0-9909374-5-6

Edited by Evelyn Fazio and Rebecca Faith Heyman
Cover Design & Jacket by Alliene Bouchard of AllieneBouchard.com
Interior by Jill Dible of Jill Dible Design
e-book by BookNook.biz
Author Photograph by Tony Deferia of tdeferiamedia, Inc.
Author Logo by Amber Clark of Wildcraft Designs

Websites: www.shadesofsilence.com | www.lizlazarus.com

ORMOND BEACH NEWS
Coast Guard suspends search for missing Ormond Beach plane
BY GAGE HOLLOMAN

The US Coast Guard announced today that they are suspending the search for Ormond Beach pilot and restaurateur, Michael Sinise, pending further developments. Sinise's plane, a Cessna Caravan C-208, owned by charter company Island Connections, was reported missing on the afternoon of April 9th when he failed to arrive at North Eleuthera, Bahamas, for a scheduled pick-up. According to Miami Response Center, Sinise departed alone from Flagler Airport and indicated no signs of distress prior to dropping off radar approximately two hours into the flight.

Bill Cook, a Lieutenant with the US Coast Guard, directed the search, which began shortly after 5:30 pm on April 9th and followed Sinise's filed flight plan, beginning with the aircraft's last known position. The team employed Coast Guard HC-144 Ocean Sentry aircraft and Navy P-3C long range patrol aircraft equipped with radar, night vison and thermal sensors. Over the course of the next seventy-two hours, hundreds of square miles were covered with no signs of debris or oil slick.

"Thermal cameras were used at night to detect heat from an engine or even a person," said Cook. "During the day, we'd go over the same grid we'd covered the night before, but with the benefit of daylight."

When asked why the search was halted, Cook explained, "We followed the flight path and surrounding area, checked with nearby airports, and tried to locate the plane's emergency beacon but never detected a signal. Should further developments arise, we'll resume the search, but unfortunately, we don't have promising news at this time."

The Coast Guard plans to issue a preliminary report outlining the facts surrounding the search sometime next week. A final report is expected to take several more months. Further developments will be handled by the National Transportation Safety Board. Anyone with information regarding this case should contact the NTSB's Response Operations Center at 844-555-9922.

1. Julianna | Monday, July 5

I poured myself a glass of red wine from an open bottle at the bar and pictured Michael sitting across from me. We were having a nightcap now that the diners had finished their desserts and coffee and were headed home, their tummies full of pasta with homemade Italian sauce. He raised his glass to make a toast—to having me all to himself for a few weeks. I was about to do something I considered reckless: abandoning the restaurant for two weeks to go on vacation in Italy. Before Michael, I'd never been out of the country, much less on a cross-Atlantic flight, but he'd planned our adventure to the last detail. We'd never really taken a honeymoon. I was too worried about leaving the restaurant unsupervised, but he'd finally convinced me to relax. Samantha and Alex could easily handle things while I was gone.

I guess it just wasn't in my DNA to be so carefree, a work ethic I'd inherited from my father. Little by little Michael had shown me that it was okay to have fun. Taking time off for an overdue celebration of our marriage was part of enjoying life. He was a hopeless romantic.

I dabbed my eyes with a cocktail napkin. Now I was the romantic one, clinging to a distant memory. I was also feeling more hopeless—it had been ninety-five days since I'd last seen my husband.

I started to take a sip of wine when I heard a voice behind me.

"We need to talk," she said.

I whipped around to see a woman leaning against the hostess stand at the front of my restaurant. We had closed over an hour ago. My bar manager and chef had just left for the night, leaving me alone to finish some paperwork. She seemed to have appeared out of nowhere.

Her voice sounded like a girl's, but she looked more like a Real Housewife. She wore a tight navy dress with a scooped neckline that accentuated her rounded breasts. Gold bracelets adorned both wrists and her heels were so high that her feet arched unnaturally. Her bleached blonde hair was tousled about her face, and her skin was deeply tanned, the color that came from hours of soaking up the Florida sun.

"We're closed," I said, perplexed that this woman was somehow in my restaurant at nearly 1:00 a.m.

"You're Julianna, right?" she asked. Her eyes squinted slightly.

Most of my customers, even the regulars, called me Miss Sandoval. I couldn't put my finger on it, but there was something off-putting about the informal way she said my first name. Or maybe I was just irritable from a long night. Holidays were always busy, and that night's Fourth of July dinner crowd had been no exception.

"Look, I'm sorry, but we're closed," I repeated. "You'll need to come back during normal hours."

For an instant, I thought about my pistol in the safe in the back office. It wasn't that I felt in danger—she looked more like the type who'd be robbed than someone who'd do the robbing. Still, her presence was strange, especially on the one night when my stepson was out of town, leaving me to close the restaurant alone.

"He's not who you think he is," she said.

I shook my head, trying to make sense of her words. Was she drunk? High? And who was she talking about? It didn't matter. She was keeping me from going home and I was already exhausted. I reached in my jacket pocket for the key to the front door and stepped from behind the expansive bar to escort her out. As I approached, I got a better look at her face. She was heavily made-up, with contoured cheekbones, lash extensions and plumped-up lips. I reiterated that we were closed and she needed to leave.

"You stupid bitch," she sneered. "You don't have a clue!"

I stopped in my tracks. My entire body stiffened. The hatred in her voice was personal, as if she knew me, which she didn't. Before I could respond, I heard a blast outside. Glass shattered like someone had dropped a full tray of dishes onto the concrete floor.

Her eyes bulged and she gasped for air, opening and closing her mouth like a hooked fish. Her doll-like face was now oddly contorted. She stumbled forward a few steps, struggling to maintain her balance. When she tried to speak, blood spewed from her mouth.

I screamed.

She lurched forward, arms outstretched, and tried to grab me.

I instinctively stepped back and watched in horror as she clutched her chest and gasped for air.

Our eyes locked.

She stared at me, terrified. Her expression was the haunted, helpless look of someone who knew death was certain. Then she collapsed face-first to the floor.

I took another step back, turned and sprinted through the open archway toward the kitchen. I continued retreating down the hall to my office and slammed the door behind me. My heart was pounding in my ears. My fingers trembled as I struggled to twist the flimsy bar lock on the door knob.

Only then did I realize that I had no escape. My small office had no windows or other exits.

I frantically snatched the phone and dialed 9-1-1.

"Hurry, hurry, hurry," I chanted into the receiver.

"9-1-1. What is your emergency?"

"A woman," I panted. "A woman has been shot."

I glanced at the space between my desk and the back wall and squeezed myself into the small opening. My desk was made of wood. It wouldn't stop a bullet. Still, I felt safer crouched behind it.

"What is your address?" the dispatcher asked.

"Café Lily. 216 South Atlantic Avenue, Ormond Beach."

"And your name?"

"Julianna Sandoval. Please, send the police right away!"

I listened for any sounds of movement in the hallway. Whoever shot her could be coming for me next. The restaurant was eerily quiet, but that didn't mean I was alone.

"Help is on the way, Julianna. Just stay with me. Where are you?"

"In my office." My voice cracked. I tried to swallow but my mouth was dry.

"Did you see who shot her?"

I blinked, trying to recall the scene I'd just witnessed. I'd heard the gunshot and the window shattering. Why hadn't I looked in that direction? The entire time, I'd never taken my eyes off the woman. Why hadn't I tried to identify the shooter?

"Ma'am, are you still there?" the dispatcher asked.

"I'm here," I whispered.

I eyed the safe on the wall. I'd have to give up the cover of my desk to retrieve my pistol, but I had no choice. A flimsy lock wouldn't hold up against someone determined to break down the door. I stood quickly and pressed the cold metal keypad—0216, my parents' anniversary. Or was it 0212?

My mind went blank.

No, it was 0216.

With a single motion, I grabbed the gun and darted back to my hiding place. I squatted behind my desk with the phone pressed against my ear and my gun pointed toward the door. As much as I tried, I couldn't catch my breath.

"You're doing good, Julianna. The police are on their way."

But what if help didn't arrive in time?

2. Grant | Monday, July 5

By the third ring of my cell phone, I'd rolled over in bed and glanced at the clock: 1:33 a.m. As I picked up the call, I grumbled out loud, "Somebody better be dead."

I had just returned from vacation up north, visiting my aging parents in Jersey City. Let me rephrase: It wasn't a vacation but time away from work, trying to convince the two most stubborn people I knew that Florida summers, while miserably hot, were still better than freezing Jersey winters. The trip was a bust. They weren't budging, and I didn't get any rest.

I fumbled for my notepad and pen on the nightstand as my boss, Police Chief Michele Jamison, relayed the situation.

"We've got a homicide," she said, her voice somber.

My head dropped. The morning had started with a delayed flight from Newark, forcing me to take a later connection through Atlanta. Getting home should've taken a few hours; instead, it took the entire day. I'd just gone to bed and wasn't due back to work until the following morning. I wanted nothing more than a few hours of sleep.

"I need you," she added. "Hall's never worked a homicide so I'm giving this to you. Besides, he's up for vacation."

Summers were always an endless juggling act of trying to fit in everyone's time off, but it didn't matter. There was an unspoken rule that we were always on-call. Technically, this was Detective Chase Hall's case until 7:00 a.m. Monday, but he wasn't ready to be the lead on a homicide.

Chief Jamison didn't mention it, but I was certain there was another factor influencing her decision. She tended to be a few steps ahead of everyone else, a real chess player. If this case ended up going to trial, the last thing she needed was a clever defense attorney asking our newest detective how many murder cases he'd led before. It wouldn't look good.

"What do we have?" I asked.

"Café Lily. The owner said she'd locked up for the night and assumes the victim must have stowed away inside the restaurant. No signs of forced entry. According to the owner, the victim seemed to be there to talk to her, but she wasn't making sense. Then the owner heard a gunshot and the victim went down. It appears to be a single shot in the back, through the glass window. The owner didn't see anyone."

I was scribbling notes as she debriefed the scene. I'd learned over the years that information never came in the purest of forms—you can't remove the human element. It was like that kid's game of telephone. By the fourth or fifth rendition of the story, the facts changed. It wasn't on purpose. It just was. So it was important to write everything down immediately, on first hearing, when it came to evidence and crime scenes.

"Look, Grant, I need you to solve this. Quickly. It's peak season. That restaurant was packed full of tourists a few hours before the shooting. The Mayor has already called me." She sounded tense but still in control.

"I understand," I told her.

Chief Jamison was good at sheltering us from politics. It was one of the things I appreciated most about her. She was level-headed, and too smart for this small town and its petty Mayor.

"I'll see you there," she said and hung up.

I put the pad and pen on the edge of the bed and rubbed my eyes. I'd just taken a hot shower half an hour ago to decompress. Now I needed another one to wake up.

I walked to the kitchen, put a filter in the coffee maker and scooped a few heaping spoons of coffee grounds. Normally, it was already set up, my ritual before going to bed, but vacation had thrown off my routine.

Back in my bathroom, I stripped off my T-shirt and boxers and stepped into the shower. As I splashed water across my face, I could hear my phone ringing. I toweled off and picked it up—two missed calls from Detective Hall. I called him back as I grabbed my department-issued black polo shirt and tan pants.

"Hey," I said. Before I could say more, Hall peppered me with questions.

"Why didn't the chief pick me? I'm willing to put in the hours. I think I should postpone my vacation. I'll call the cruise line."

"Hold on," I exhaled. "Look, I'm trying to get out the door. We'll sort it out when I get there."

In truth, there was nothing to sort out. He and his wife had booked a cruise, their first trip since the birth of their daughter. There'd be plenty of work when he got back. Besides, no way was the chief making him lead investigator.

Outside my apartment, I walked to my usual parking spot where my black Chevy Malibu was slowly rusting in the ocean air. I would have preferred a spot in the garage, but alimony payments didn't allow for extras. I punched the address to the restaurant into my GPS, although I was pretty sure I knew the way. Café Lily was an upscale joint on the main road on the north side of town. Good for a first date, although I always felt you shouldn't set the bar too high. Take her for pizza and beer and see how she reacts. Yeah, I was jaded. Divorce tends to do that to you.

The commotion at the restaurant made it easy to spot: flashing police lights, a camera crew and a small crowd gawking at the scene. I turned into the entrance. Crime scene tape encircled the entire parking lot preventing me from going further. One of our younger officers guarded the front.

"We've had a murder," he said, with a mixture of terror and excitement.

"Yeah, that's why I'm here." I pointed to the tape which he quickly lifted, allowing me to drive in. Hall's identical black Chevy Malibu was already in the lot so I parked next to it.

The chief and the on-duty patrol supervisor, Sergeant White, were standing outside. Jamison was taller than White, even in flats. Her hair was pulled back in a tight bun. The blue lights of the patrol cars bounced off her ebony skin. When I approached, White got in his first jab.

"This shit's following you from Daytona," he said.

"This shit's why you have a job," I retorted.

"Boys." Jamison tilted her head toward the crowd and the news truck. She was right. Some banter was fine in the office, but it could be misconstrued by an outsider, especially the media.

Hall bounded up and rocked up and down on his toes. "I've canvassed the area. What else can I do? Can we go in?"

I raised my right hand above his head. "Hall, you're up there," I said. Then I lowered my hand to his waist. "And I need you to be down here."

Hall dropped his shoulders and stared at the ground. I felt like I'd just kicked a puppy. He didn't deserve my reprimand. He was young and eager, but he wasn't being reckless, not like what had happened in Daytona. I pushed all of that out of my mind and focused on the task at hand.

"Come with me," I said to Hall as I walked to the back edge of the parking lot.

"We're not going in?" he asked.

"We will, but we start here. I need to feel the scene. Our victim's dead. She won't be undead if we get in there any faster."

I surveyed the one-story building on the small private lot. The front of the restaurant was mostly glass, with a thick, concrete border at the top. Cursive lettering in purple neon lights spelled out *Café Lily*. Next to the name, a single white lily with a green stem illuminated the front entrance.

In addition to the police cars, there were two other vehicles. One, a white Mini Cooper, was parked next to the front door. The other, a blue Volkswagen Jetta, was at the edge of the lot. If I had to guess, the Jetta belonged to the restaurant owner. She wouldn't take up prime spots that were better left for paying customers.

A surveillance camera on the roof pointed toward the lot. From what I could tell, it didn't cover the front door, which was unfortunate. I'd have Hall canvass the area for other cameras from nearby shops. Maybe they'd captured a glimpse of our shooter.

Every investigation was like a bag of puzzle pieces. You never had all of the pieces, and some of the ones you did have were from an entirely different puzzle. The key was to collect enough relevant fragments to put an initial picture together.

White strolled over to Hall and me. He stood next to us and faced the building. "This just ruined our streak," he commented. "We haven't had a homicide in three years."

I chuckled. Hall wasn't the only naïve one around here. Murders were always going to happen—it was just a matter of time. Even if you lived in a bubble, bad guys still walked among us. In fact, the nicer the bubble, the better the hunting grounds.

"Jamison is talking to the Mayor," White needled, as if I didn't know.

"Yeah, well, there's a difference between solving a case and solving a crisis," I replied. "Come on, Hall, let's go."

As we approached the entrance, I observed the shattered window to the right of the door. Hall and I scanned the pavement looking for the spent brass, but found nothing. The shooter must have recovered it or he'd used a revolver, which didn't eject its casings. I assumed my killer was a "he"—most of them were, although I knew to keep an open mind.

Detective Hall and I walked to the front door, where Officer Phelps was guarding the scene. Unlike Daytona Beach, where I'd spent most of my career, Ormond Beach was a small town. Within a few months of arriving, I'd met all of the other officers. When Phelps saw us approach, he jotted down the required information into the crime scene log—our names, the date and time, and our reason for entering the building. Hall and I each took a pair of cloth booties and a pair of latex gloves from a box at the entrance. The summer humidity made the gloves hard to pull on.

"Why don't you start with photos and then do the sketch," I told Hall as I took in the scene. The smell of spices, maybe something Italian, filled the air.

Just inside the front door was a wooden hostess stand stacked with menus. Behind the stand was the dining room with white-clothed tables, the larger ones in the back to allow for maximum occupancy without sacrificing intimacy. A bar with mirrored shelves, liquor bottles and glasses covered the length of the back wall. To the left of the bar was an open archway, which presumably led to the kitchen and storage areas. Next to the hostess stand, the victim lay face-down on the floor.

"Do we have ID on her yet?" I called back to Phelps who was still guarding the door.

"Yeah, her bag was on the floor. I pulled out the wallet to get her ID. Everything's on the bar. Name's Brittany Jones. Valid license. Lives in a condo over on Myrtle Street."

Myrtle Street was a nice area of town.

"Did you run a background check?" I asked.

"No, figured you'd do that," Phelps said.

"Called the Medical Examiner?"

"Yep. They're on the way."

As Hall took photos, I approached the body. She was lying on her stomach with her head tilted to the side, her cheek resting on the

shiny gray concrete. The first thing I noticed were her long legs—
toned and tan. Both of her shoes had come off. They were navy
heels with red bottoms. I couldn't remember the brand, but knew
they were expensive, assuming they were real. Her right hand was
tucked under her body and her left hand stretched above her head.
Gold bracelets rested on her knuckles, thrown forward from the fall.
Her nails were painted solid white, a stark contrast to her tan skin.

She had been shot in the back with what seemed like a large-caliber handgun, probably a .45. Whoever did this meant to kill her.
There was barely any blood on the floor, which led me to believe
the bullet hadn't exited her body.

I focused on the task at hand, gathering every piece of information. Still, I couldn't escape the strange spiritual moment I felt
during most murder investigations. A human being, a young woman
full of life only hours ago, was lying dead in front of me. She was
somebody's daughter, sister or mother—maybe all three—and now
she was gone.

I'd worked with cops who pretended not to take a case personally, but they were just lying to themselves. You have to take a certain
amount of this job personally to do it well. The trick is to find the
right balance. If you take too much to heart, you can't do the work
at all.

She was my responsibility now and I needed to find out why
someone wanted her dead. If I succeeded, she'd have justice. But if
I failed, her death would become nothing more than a cold case,
a file folder archived on some shelf in a warehouse. That wouldn't
be right. No matter her situation, she didn't deserve to die like this.
Somebody needed to answer for her murder.

"Hey, look at this!" Hall broke into my thoughts. He was kneeling by her side, pointing to her neck. I took a few steps so that I
was standing next to him. At first it appeared she had a birthmark,
but when I crouched to get a better look, I could see why Hall had
called me over. She had a tattoo of a dagger interwoven with a vine
of small flowers on the side of her neck.

"Make sure you get it when you do your close-up shots," I said
as I stood.

Something was off about this woman. She had fancy shoes, nice
jewelry and perfectly manicured nails. But her hair was bleached too

yellow and the tattoo was kind of trashy—not the artwork, but the placement. Girls trying to be upscale choose the ankle or small of the back, not the neck.

I walked to the bar where her wallet lay open next to her other possessions. Her ID indicated that she was twenty-two years old. The photo showed a much more natural version of the young woman in front of me. Her bag, a medium-sized clutch, had a designer label: Louis Vuitton. I rummaged through the matching designer wallet to find a few credit cards: a Platinum American Express, a Bank of America debit card and a Dillard's department store card. She had $200 in cash, all crisp twenties like they were fresh from the ATM. I expected to find the latest version of the Samsung Galaxy or iPhone, but instead found a Tracfone, the kind you prepay and can't be traced. Made me wonder what kind of trouble she'd gotten herself into.

Sorting through the rest of her bag, I pulled out a makeup pouch with some powder and lipstick and tortoise-shell Coach sunglasses. Then I found the most curious item of all: a small digital recorder. As far as I knew, the only people who needed recorders were journalists and detectives, neither of which Brittany Jones seemed to be.

Hall was peering around my back. His eyes widened when he saw the recorder. I could tell he was itching to play it. I was, too, but I knew better. All evidence had to be turned over to FDLE, the Florida Department of Law Enforcement, to be sure we didn't accidentally destroy it. I'd put a rush on it, though, as I had to believe it would provide useful information.

The last item in her purse was a keychain with three keys: one for a Mini Cooper, presumably the car parked outside, and two silver door keys. A fourth key, dark green and not on the chain, stood out. The blade reminded me of an alligator snout and the hole at the head looked like an eye. We were about ninety miles from Gainesville and the University of Florida Gators. Maybe she went to college there?

I put her bag and its contents into an evidence pouch, sealed and labeled it, and then turned around to study the dining room one more time.

"What do you see?" Hall asked.

I squinted, surveying every part of the room in more detail. It was important to assess the scene and all its evidence before I talked to the witness. Once I spoke with her, it'd be too easy to focus solely on her account of the story, but there was always a bigger picture to consider.

"I'm thinking attempted robbery," he said. "Maybe the perp got spooked when he saw multiple people inside."

I shook my head. For as tech savvy as Hall was—and he was a digital whiz kid—he had yet to develop instincts for a crime scene.

"Look around," I replied. "This is an upscale restaurant. Clients pay with credit cards, not cash. There'd be nothing to rob but paper receipts. And her wallet—it still had cash and credit cards."

"Maybe there was no time," he offered.

"It would have taken seconds to snatch her bag. And why shoot one person point blank and not the other? This wasn't a robbery," I said, and then pointed to the lifeless body. "She was targeted."

"So how are we going to solve this?"

"She's the only person who might be able to tell us, and she's not talking."

Hall grew pensive, a notable change from his typical behavior, which I'd labeled "Energizer Bunny on Red Bull." If he could just learn to be still and absorb the scene, he had real potential.

Chief Jamison had hired me from Daytona to head up the criminal investigations division after the supervisor and another veteran detective retired. She had just lost over fifty years of experience and was short-staffed. My job was to rebuild the team, doing both the recruiting and the training. This case would be a good test of Hall's aptitude and an even better test of my patience.

Once I felt I had a good grasp of the scene in the dining room, I was ready to move on.

"Where's the witness?" I asked Officer Phelps, who hadn't moved from the front door. He was doing an admirable job of keeping extra folks out. People, especially other officers, wanted the chance to be involved. In reality, all they'd do was contaminate my crime scene.

"We moved her to the back office," he replied. "Jenkins is with her. Name's Julianna Sandoval." He pointed to the archway at the back of the restaurant.

"What'd she say?" I asked.

"Said the victim came out of nowhere after she'd locked up. When she told her to leave, the victim started cussing her out. Once she heard the shot, Ms. Sandoval ran to safety."

I nodded and motioned for Hall to follow me. We walked out of the dining area and down a narrow corridor. Wine crates were stacked neatly on the side and a few papers were tacked to a large bulletin board on the wall, showing daily menus and staffing charts. On the other side of the hallway were swinging double doors that led to the kitchen. Jenkins stood just beyond the kitchen, outside the entrance to a small office. I beckoned him over.

"How's the witness doing?" I asked.

"Nonstop questions," he whispered. "Who was she? Can she change her clothes? When can she go home?" He rolled his eyes. "I asked her to pull up video from the parking lot to keep her busy until you got here."

In my experience, people who witnessed violent crimes reacted in one of three ways. Some went catatonic; they completely shut down, barely able to function. Others became hysterical. The rest asked a lot of questions, probably out of a need to regain control. Not that any of the three reactions were desirable, but if I had to pick one, I'd take the third. At least you could get information out of those witnesses.

3. Julianna | Monday, July 5

A man dressed in a black polo shirt and khaki pants, with a sizeable gun holstered at his side entered my office. He had salt and pepper hair, cut in a short military style. His hazel eyes had noticeable bags, yet struck me as kind. He was tan and muscular, the type of man who might like the outdoors.

"I'm Detective Grant," he said, extending his right hand. As we shook, he cupped his left hand over mine. His palms were warm, like Michael's. I quickly withdrew my hand.

"This is Detective Hall," he added. A younger man dressed in a similar black polo shirt and khaki pants, also with a holstered gun, nodded at me but didn't speak.

"Are you okay?" Detective Grant asked.

A nervous laugh came over me.

Was I okay? I was alive, which was more than I could say for the woman in the other room.

He continued, "I know you've been through a lot this evening and I know you've been asked a lot of questions. You're probably exhausted. I just wanted to speak with you for a few minutes and we can talk more tomorrow, after you've had some rest. Would that be okay?"

I nodded and pointed to an empty chair next to my desk. He was the first person to ask if it was okay to question me. I appreciated that.

Detective Grant sat down, putting us at eye level. The younger one, I forgot his name, remained standing like a statue, guarding the door.

"Do you need something to drink? Some coffee? Water?" Detective Grant asked.

"Oh, I'm sorry. I should be offering you something. What can I get you?" I looked at his partner. "Either of you?"

"No, we're fine, thanks," the detective replied. "You're the owner of the restaurant?"

His question surprised me. I thought he'd want to know about the shooting. "Yes. My parents opened it years ago and I took over after they died."

"It must be hard to run a restaurant on your own, especially during peak season."

I tugged the edges of my jacket. His words "on your own" struck a chord.

"Well, I have help. My staff. My stepson." I paused. "And my husband…until he went missing."

The detective's head tilted slightly.

I explained, "You probably heard about it on the news. Michael Sinise. The pilot whose plane disappeared. That was my husband."

A look of recognition came over his face. "I'm sorry," he offered. "I didn't connect the name."

"Sandoval's my maiden name, but when you get married late in life, well…" I paused. "Too many people already knew my name to change it."

The younger detective stepped forward as if he was going to ask me a question, but Detective Grant held up his hand, blocking him. It was clear who was in charge.

"Can you tell me a little bit about your day? What time did you come in?"

I wondered why that mattered, but told him anyway. "I got in around ten. We have a buffet brunch on Sundays, so the menu is easy. I usually come in earlier but knew it was going to be a late night with the holiday."

"What time did you open?"

"Eleven," I replied.

"Who else was working today?"

"Let's see. Our chef and her staff. They were already here when I arrived. And the bar manager and servers came in not long after me."

"Maybe it would be easier if I could have a copy of today's schedule?"

"Of course." I grabbed the shift schedule that was still on my desk and handed it to him.

"Have you let anyone go recently or had any issues with customers?"

I shook my head. "No. No issues. Most of our employees have worked here for years, since my parents owned the place."

"And you took it over from them?"

"Three years ago. They were in a fatal car crash." My eyes drifted to the framed photo of my parents on my desk. They were arm in arm. Mom was looking at the camera, smiling, and Dad was leaning over, kissing her on the cheek. It was my favorite photo of them.

"I'm sorry," he said.

His condolences seemed sincere, not just the obligatory response that comes with tragedy. I shrugged. It sucked. I missed them every day, but the best way to honor their memory was to keep the restaurant going. For them, and for Lily.

"Did you leave at any point today?"

"No," I replied. "Wait, yes. Once. I walked over to Jamba Juice for a smoothie. I know, in a restaurant full of food, I go somewhere else for lunch." I glanced at the empty plastic juice cup still in my trash bin and wondered if he wanted proof. Instead, he chuckled slightly.

"Has anything odd or unusual happened recently?" he asked.

"No, not until *she* showed up," I said as I looked past him toward the dining room. Before Detective Grant arrived, I'd been retrieving surveillance video, but I could hardly concentrate. The whole time I kept wondering who she was and what she wanted from me.

An officer poked his head in my office. "Medical examiner's here."

Detective Grant nodded. "I'll be out in a minute."

The thought of a dead body in my dining room gave me the chills. "She's...I mean, they're going to..."

"She'll be taken care of. In case you need it, there are companies you can call for clean-up and stain removal. Your insurance should cover it."

"I have to do that?" I asked.

Detective Grant didn't reply, but reached into his pants pocket, pulled a card from his wallet and handed it to his young partner. "Give this company a call. See if they can come over tonight and wait for them outside. And see if they can secure that broken window."

"Thank you." I shuddered. I hadn't thought about having to deal with the clean-up. My mind was preoccupied. What would I say to her family? Could I have helped her if I hadn't run away? It all happened so fast. And what was she trying to tell me?

Then there were the more practical concerns. Who was going to want to eat at a restaurant where a woman had been shot? Would business suffer? I couldn't afford to lose any revenue. I didn't have enough saved to cover payroll. All I needed was a few busy summer months to replenish my cash reserve, but now that was at risk. I sighed. I shouldn't have spent so much money on our lavish vacation. It was against everything my father had taught me, but I'd allowed myself to be irresponsible.

"We can call the clean-up company," the detective said, "but you'll have to sign the paperwork. Do you mind if I ask you a few more questions, since we have to wait for them anyway?"

"Okay," I replied as I exhaled. The last thing I'd been doing before all this happened was pouring myself a glass of wine. Now I really wanted a drink to calm my nerves.

"How about we get you some water?" he offered.

I shook my head. "How about we get some wine?" I stood and walked into the hall where Alex, my bar manager, had stored a few crates of the latest delivery. I grabbed a bottle of Josh Cabernet and took it back to my office. Fortunately, I had a corkscrew in my desk because there was no way I was going back into the dining room to retrieve one. I rummaged through my drawer and found a sleeve of plastic cups, ones we used for wine tastings with vendors. I poured myself a glass and offered one to the detective.

"Can't. I'm on duty," he said.

"Oh, of course." I had no idea what had possessed me, offering alcohol to an on-duty cop. Exhaustion and the stress of the last few months were clouding my mind.

He continued with his questions. "So, can you walk me through your day? When you arrived at ten, where did you park?"

"At the edge of the lot. I drive a Jetta."

"And you said the chef and her staff were already here?"

"Yes."

"You came in through the front door?"

I nodded.

"Was the door locked?"

"Yes. We keep it locked until we open."

"When you unlocked the door, was there anything unusual about the lock or how it worked?"

"No, nothing."

"Okay," he said, jotting something quickly on his notepad. "Then what'd you do?"

"I did some paperwork in the office, the usual stuff. I double-checked the evening menu against our supplies in the kitchen. My dad always insisted on that, even though our chef, Samantha, is always on top of things. Brunch ended at three and I went out for a smoothie before getting ready for the dinner crowd."

"And then?"

"Let's see. We went over the specials—it was a fixed-price menu for the holiday—and the staff started setting up. I took a few more reservations. We reopened at five, as usual. Between the reservations and walk-ins, it was a busy night, but everyone was in a good mood. Around ten, we all poked our heads outside to watch the fireworks at the pier. Our last customers left around eleven fifteen."

He nodded, jotting down a few more notes.

"What time do you normally close?"

"Around eleven, but we don't push anyone out. I have the servers start changing the linens on the empty tables, which usually gives the hint to the stragglers that it's time to leave."

"And then?"

"We cleaned up. The staff left. Usually Samantha, Alex and I leave together."

"The chef and bar manager?" he clarified.

"Yes, they're a couple. I had some paperwork to finish, so I told them to go ahead and start their day off. I was only fifteen minutes behind them."

"What time was that?"

"Probably around twelve forty-five."

"Do you remember locking up?"

"Yes," I replied. "I locked the front door behind them."

"Are you sure?" he asked.

"Positive. I even jiggled it to make sure it was secure."

"What did you do after they left?" He shifted in the chair as he spoke.

"I came back to my office to finish closing out the receipts. It had been a long day, so I decided to get a glass of wine at the bar. I was pouring my drink when I heard the woman's voice behind me saying that we needed to talk. At first, I thought it was Samantha. I turned around and saw this woman next to the hostess stand. I couldn't figure out how she'd gotten in. I told her we were closed and then she started cussing at me. Next thing I know, I hear a blast and glass shattering."

"And then?"

"She fell to the floor. I wasn't quite sure what had happened. I mean, I think I realized she'd been shot, but it felt surreal. I ran in here, locked the door, called 9-1-1 and got my pistol. I hid in my office until the operator assured me that police were at the front door."

His brows furrowed. "Where's your pistol now?"

"In the safe. The operator told me to put it away before I opened the door for the police."

Detective Grant's partner reappeared. "Room's clear and the clean-up crew is on the way."

"Thanks, Hall," he said. "Did someone canvass the neighboring businesses for cameras?"

"Already on it," the young detective replied. "There's a nail place, a pool supply shop and a few retail stores. Looks like one of the stores has a camera. I'll call the owner in the morning."

Detective Grant shook his head. "Do it now. If it's looping, we can't risk losing the last few hours."

The young detective nodded and disappeared again. I was starting to feel the effects of the wine, which was making me more tired. All I wanted to do was to go home and I wondered when I'd be allowed to leave.

"Do you happen to have any other clothes you can change into?" he asked.

I looked down at my white shirt, dotted with blood spatter, and suddenly felt nauseous. Good thing I had skipped dinner.

"I have gym clothes in my car."

"If you could get them, please, and come right back. I'll need your clothes for evidence. But first, I'll need to swab your hands for gunshot residue."

"What?" I stammered. "You think I shot her?"

"No," he replied. "I don't think you shot a woman in the back while standing in front of her." He pointed to the blood on my shirt and his voice softened, "But I'm responsible for figuring out who did and need to collect evidence."

I exhaled with relief.

"And I'll need to temporarily secure your firearm until we get everything handled with the autopsy. Don't read anything into it. Just following procedure."

My mouth fell open. He'd just said he didn't suspect me, but he was swabbing my hands and taking my gun. How was I supposed to protect myself?

The detective repositioned himself in the chair so he could reach into his pants pocket. "Here's my cell phone number." He handed me a business card with a hand-written number. I hesitated to take it, fearing I'd somehow be tampering with my hands before they were tested. He added, "Do me a favor and give me a call tomorrow, once you get up. I'll meet you wherever you like."

"Tomorrow like today, or do you mean tomorrow like Tuesday?"

"Tomorrow like today," he said. "Okay, so let's secure that gun and get you swabbed. Once you've changed clothes and the clean-up crew finishes, you're free to go home."

I started to get up to open the safe when the younger detective reappeared. "I have a few questions. Had you ever seen that woman before? What exactly did she say to you?"

Detective Grant stood abruptly. "Hall, a word?" The two men left my office and walked into the corridor. I could hear hushed whispers. I took another chug of wine and looked at the clock. It was just before 6:00 a.m.

Detective Grant returned to my office, alone. "Sorry about that. He means well, but he's a little eager. Let's pick this back up once you've had time to rest. Is there anyone I can call for you?"

Who could I call? There were Samantha and Alex. They were more than my chef and bar manager—they were like family—but they'd find out about the shooting soon enough. Better to give them a couple more hours of sleep. As far as other friends, I had acquaintances, but no one I could think of calling to a crime scene at 6:00 a.m. I'd been so married to this restaurant that I'd had little time for anything else. Then Michael came along and revealed a whole new world I'd been missing, complete with flying, fishing, long walks and great sex.

Now he was gone.

Jasper still lived with me, but he was celebrating the Fourth in Miami with friends. How pathetic that I truly had no one to call.

When I didn't reply, Detective Grant suggested that one of his officers give me a ride home.

"I'd prefer to drive myself, if that's okay. I don't live far."

He hesitated, then asked, "You mentioned a stepson?"

I nodded. "He's in Miami for the long weekend. I assure you, I'm fine to drive home."

After turning over my gun, getting my hands swabbed and retrieving my gym clothes from the car, I changed out of my blood-spattered shirt and jacket. The detective waited just outside the bathroom. Maybe this was all protocol but I felt like I was in a precarious situation. Did he believe me or was he trying to put me at ease so I'd slip up and say something wrong?

When I emerged from the bathroom, I asked, "Do you need my key to lock up?"

"No," he replied. "Not much else we can do here. You can lock up. The window should be secure enough for now. I'll have a patrol car follow you home."

All of the police officers and cleaning crew departed with me. Detective Grant walked with me to my car at the edge of the parking lot. As I sat in the driver's seat, he leaned over and asked, "By the way, how long has your husband been missing?"

"It'll be three months this Friday."

"I imagine it's been a long three months," he said softly.

His voice was full of compassion, something I hadn't heard for quite some time. Sure, people were supportive, at first, but they changed as time passed. Now, it seemed no one wanted to talk about Michael, as if he'd never existed, which was so strange and isolating. I hadn't expected to feel comfort from a stranger, especially on such a horrific night, but for a brief moment, the massive solitude I'd felt since Michael's plane disappeared lifted.

4. Grant | Monday, July 5

I waited outside the women's restroom for Julianna Sandoval to change her clothes. An elongated female silhouette marked the door. Maybe Brittany Jones had stowed away in there until everyone else had left. It was a possibility. That, or she came in through an unlocked back door or had a key. Those were the only other options I could come up with, unless my witness was mistaken about locking the front door.

Once I had Ms. Sandoval's clothes bagged and sealed and the cleaning crew had finished their work, we had her lock up. I escorted her outside while Hall paced like a madman at the parking lot entrance. He lifted the crime scene tape so she and Jenkins, who followed her, could pass under. Once they were clear, Hall made a beeline for me, obviously frustrated that I'd cooled his jets.

"Why wouldn't you let me ask her those questions? We need to know what the victim said."

I put my hand on his shoulder. "Look, Hall, she can't give you what you want yet. She hasn't processed it herself. It's best to let her get some rest. We're not done questioning her. You must have patience or..." I stopped.

"Or what?"

"Never mind."

Hall pressed on. "Do you think it's gang-related?"

I glanced at my watch. It was almost 6:30 a.m. and we'd been up all night. How was he not tired? In fact, he never seemed to get tired. I sighed. "I doubt it. People don't just walk up and kill other people for no reason ninety-nine percent of the time. There's a link here that we need to figure out."

"How?" he asked.

I already had my crude but time-tested approach. Start with who the victim was fucking, who she used to fuck and who was trying to fuck her. I cleaned it up for Hall's young ears. "We need to check out the men in her life."

"You think it's jealousy?" he asked.

"That, or she knew too much about something. And we'll look at the money trail. It's usually one of those things."

"You think?"

"Welcome to investigations," I said, not hiding my sarcasm.

Hall's eyes darted back and forth. I could see his brain churning. "I've gotta cancel my vacation. I can't leave now."

"Hold on," I counseled. "You need to put your family first. There'll be plenty of times in your career when you have to cancel your vacation. Don't let this be one of them."

Hall shook his head.

"Besides," I added. "This won't be over in a week. Go rest, recharge, spend time with your family. You'll come back fresh and I'm gonna need you, since this is my first murder investigation in Ormond Beach."

"What will Chief Jamison think?" he asked.

"That's not the woman you need to care about right now." I paused. "Trust me, if you put your wife second enough times, there'll come a point when putting her first won't matter. It'll be too late. You won't be able to repair the damage, no matter how hard you try. Now, listen to me: You have a ship to catch."

Hall finally relented. "I'll check in from the ship," he offered. "Every day."

"Okay. Now go."

I watched Hall trudge toward his Malibu. The sun was just beginning to rise, a bright orange ball over the calm ocean. The morning air was thick and my shirt was already sticking to my back. I unlocked my car, cranked the engine and blasted the air conditioning. I'd seen a Dunkin' Donuts on the ride up and headed that way. At the drive-through, I ordered an extra-large iced coffee, an egg wrap and a blueberry donut. The caffeine and sugar would keep me awake. Who was I kidding? My brain was already in overdrive.

As I headed to the station, a million questions flooded my mind. Who was Brittany Jones? How could she afford a condo on Myrtle Street? Did she have a rich daddy or a generous sugar daddy? And why did she need to talk to Julianna Sandoval?

I thought about the shooting as I chugged my coffee. It didn't feel random. It was targeted, almost like a hit, and completely impersonal—a shot to the back. A scorned lover would want to see her face. A current lover could have killed her at home. The shooter could have easily taken out Julianna Sandoval before she ran to her office, but he didn't. He'd let her escape.

What about Brittany's keys? One was presumably to her car and two others probably to her condo. What about the green key? Why did she have a recorder and a burner phone? I'd need to expedite that research. I could always call Sheila at FDLE. Maybe if I took the recorder there in person, she'd fast-track it. Then I grimaced, remembering our last interaction. Sheila and I had casually dated after my divorce. On our six-month anniversary, she threw me a real curve ball. If we weren't engaged by the one-year mark, she was breaking up with me. Somehow, I'd missed the part where a few casual dates had become a relationship. Needless to say, I didn't call her back. She was probably pissed, which meant I could forget about asking her for a favor.

I blinked my eyes, erasing the uncomfortable memory of Sheila, and focused on the road. It was a quiet morning, with only a few cars out. As I drove to the station, I thought about Julianna Sandoval. Now there was an impressive woman. She had the presence of mind to retreat, lock her office, call 9-1-1 and arm herself. She'd obviously been to the shooting range because she recognized the sound of a high-caliber gunshot. And in the middle of a stressful interview, she had the grace to offer me and Hall a cup of coffee.

Under different circumstances, I'd be tempted to ask her out. I'd always had a thing for cute blondes. Then I remembered the news reports of her husband's plane disappearing over the Atlantic. The last thing I needed was a widow on the rebound who also happened to be a witness in my murder case. Julianna Sandoval was strictly off limits.

I polished off my donut as I pulled into the police station. The white stucco building was one story, with long rectangular windows on all four sides. Unlike Daytona, where I had a cubicle, I had my own office here, a nice perk. I still had boxes to unpack and pictures to hang, but I hadn't gotten around to it yet. Chief Jamison had asked a few times when I was going to "settle in," likely concerned that my reluctance to unpack was a sign I was considering going back to Daytona. As usual, she was probably right. Still, the boxes remained stacked in the corner of my office.

I walked past the inquisitive gazes glued to me from the moment I entered the building. In my office, I shut the door, sat down at my desk and started my list of tasks to move this investigation forward. I needed to get everything on paper to organize my thoughts. Maybe it was old-school, but it was how I worked. My first priority was to log the evidence so that it could be delivered to FDLE. Instead of waiting for the evidence custodian, I'd take it there myself, to expedite the processing.

At 8:00 a.m. sharp, I called the medical examiner's office to find out when the autopsy would take place. It was scheduled for 1:00 p.m. That was one advantage of still being in Volusia County—the ME's office was the same one as I'd used in Daytona.

I fired up my computer and ran Brittany Noelle Jones's criminal history. The printout was a few pages long—she'd covered a lot of ground between ages eighteen and twenty-two. I was willing to bet she'd been in trouble as a juvenile, too. To know for sure, I'd have to call the jurisdictions where she'd lived. Unlike criminal histories of adults, juvenile offenses are not kept in a state or national database.

There were multiple counts of shoplifting. She'd been given probation. Next was possession of marijuana, less than an ounce. The drug charge was disposed of in Tampa with time served. There was a charge of criminal trespass in Orlando, also with time served. She appeared to be drifting around the state, getting caught for misdemeanors along the way. The time served indicated to me that she had no one to bond her out of jail and no money to pay a fine. So how'd she go from penniless in Orlando to a nice condo in Ormond Beach?

The most recent arrest on her criminal history was for credit card fraud and forgery just over a year ago. It was in Daytona Beach, which gave me an idea. I rang my buddy, Tom Butler, a detective down in Daytona.

He answered on the first ring. "That didn't take long. I bet you need me to come help with that murder I just heard about."

"Well, actually, I do need your help," I replied. "Can you look up a report for me?"

"Sure."

I gave him Brittany's name and the date of her arrest and asked him to pull up the incident report so he could give me the basics. Butler ran the search while I waited in silence.

"Let's see. Yeah, I found it," he said. There was more silence as he skimmed the file. "So, a dude was in town for a medical convention, staying at the Crowne Plaza. Reported that he paid for a girl's drink in the hotel bar. She didn't have any money and was making a scene, so he gave the bartender a twenty to cover her. When he goes to check out of the hotel two days later, he notices his credit card is missing. He called to cancel it and was told several thousand dollars of charges had been made."

"Anything else?" I asked.

"Hold on. There's a supplemental note from the officer who took the report. The victim was concerned that his wife would find out. When asked if he had spent time with the girl, he denied it. Officer reported that the victim had no explanation for how she got access to his credit card, given that he covered her bar bill with cash."

"Thanks, man. Very helpful."

"Sounds to me like she got in his pants in more ways than one," he joked. "I'll send you the report. Don't forget to shoot over a request."

"I will. I'll need an in-house records check, too," I said.

"Sure thing." He paused. "So seriously, once this is over, you gonna come back?"

"I don't know," I replied. "Kind of needed a fresh start."

The line was quiet for a moment. "Hey, you can tell me to shut the hell up, but who gives a shit if your ex is with that sleazebag lawyer? Your job is here."

I didn't reply. Butler and I were close enough friends for him to know part of the reason why I left. My ex, Debbie, starting shacking up with a local asshole ambulance-chaser right after we divorced. I never asked if she'd cheated. Didn't need to. Hell, I'd been unfaithful, too. My mistress was the police department. When she called, day or night, I was hers. When the job in Ormond Beach came up, I'd jumped on it. Turns out I couldn't get away from his obnoxious TV ads, which ran statewide. At least I was able to avoid the daily reminders of our past life. Ormond Beach was my new start or so I thought. I stared at the brown boxes in the corner of my office. So why wasn't I unpacked?

I hung up with Butler and continued my research. Brittany's offenses started at age eighteen and ran fairly consistently until age twenty-one, just over a year ago. Then they stopped. Some event had changed her life, gotten her off the streets and given her access to money. Maybe she'd targeted another man in a hotel, but instead of robbing him, turned herself into a kept woman. I checked her driver's license. Date of issue was just over a year ago, also coinciding with this life change.

I spent the next hour sending requests for all the police reports and in-house record checks for every law enforcement interaction involving Brittany Jones. It was tedious work, nothing they ever show on crime scene shows, but it's part of the job. Then I faxed a form to the Department of Labor asking for any employment records.

Through the interior glass window of my office, I watched a few more officers filing in to start another day. None of them dared disturb me. I half-expected Hall to come bounding into my office instead of going on his planned vacation, but he didn't. I guess I'd gotten through to him after all.

When I ran a background check on Brittany, it came back with two associated addresses. One was for her condo on Myrtle Street. The other was an address on Grandview Avenue in Daytona, from nine years earlier, but there were no people associated with the location. It was like she'd been a gypsy until a year ago, and I wasn't finding anything that would lead me to her next of kin.

I was just about to start my checks on the other names on my list when my mobile phone rang.

It was Julianna Sandoval.

She wanted to talk.

5. Julianna | Monday, July 5

I pulled into my garage a little before 7:00 a.m., completely spent. My body knew it hadn't slept, but it also knew that it was morning and time to wake up. The last time I'd stayed up all night was when Michael and I took a red-eye home from Napa Valley. It was a crazy, impromptu trip that started with a delayed wine shipment. One of my distributors had called to tell me that their delivery had been bumped. It wasn't the end of the world because we had inventory, but Michael had a better solution.

"Ever been to wine country?" he'd asked. He grinned in that devilish way that I knew our adventure was about to begin. We literally flew out that morning, landed at Napa County Airport, right in the valley, and grabbed an Uber to a nearby hotel. The next day, we picked up the cases ourselves and the vintner treated us to tastings, lunch and a tour of his estate. Then we fueled up, which cost more than the cases of wine, and headed home. Michael had told me that I could sleep on the flight, but I couldn't. He obviously had to stay awake to fly the plane, so I forced myself to stay up, too. I remember looking at his profile illuminated by the blue light of the instruments and thinking this truly must be a dream. The next day I felt like I had cotton stuck in my head from the lack of sleep, but I didn't care.

Then I realized I'd felt this way more recently—three months ago. In fact, the last time I'd stayed up all night wasn't the wine trip. It was after Michael's plane disappeared. How could that horrible night have slipped my mind?

I walked inside, stripped off my gym clothes and started the washing machine, adding extra detergent. As I stood naked in front of the washer, it occurred to me that Jasper could come home early. I hurried to my bathroom, turned the shower dial to hot, as hot as I could stand, and began scrubbing my body. As I showered, I pictured that woman standing at the entrance of my restaurant and replayed her words: "We need to talk," a phrase that was never the start of anything good. I'd initially dismissed her, but the more I thought about it, the more her words struck me as a warning. Who was she talking about? Who wasn't who I thought he was?

When my fingers started to look like prunes, I reluctantly turned off the water. I stepped out of the shower, wrapped myself in a thick bathrobe and pulled my wet hair into a bun. Facing the mirror, I had to admit I looked like someone who'd been up all night. My green eyes were bloodshot and my cheeks and lips were taut. The long shower, on top of the wine, had me completely dehydrated.

I glanced at the clock. It was 8:03 a.m., a bit early to call Jasper, but I didn't want him to hear the news from anyone else. He'd already been through so much. We both had. I scrolled through my Favorites, tapped his name and waited as the phone rang.

"Hello?" Jasper said. His voice was groggy.

"Jasper, it's Julianna."

"Yeah?"

"Look, I'm sorry to call so early, but I think you should come home."

"Come home?" he asked.

"Don't worry, I'm fine, and so is everyone else at the restaurant, but there was a shooting."

"What!" he exclaimed, becoming instantly more awake.

"A woman was shot at the restaurant last night. Well, I guess technically it was this morning. Anyway, I'm sure it'll be on the news. But I didn't want you to worry."

"Okay," he replied slowly, still sounding a bit dazed. "I'm on my way." He paused, then added, "You okay?"

"Yes, a little rattled to be honest, but I'm okay. The police want to interview everyone who works at the restaurant. I know you weren't here, but they'll probably want to talk to you, too."

There was silence.

"Well, I better go," I added. "I need to call Samantha and Alex. I'll see you soon."

"Okay, I'll be there as soon as I can. You need anything?"

"No, I'm alright." I thought about asking him to pick up breakfast. If he were closer, I would have. Then, a strange feeling of guilt came over me. I was alive. I could have breakfast. I could eat anything I wanted. The dead woman could not.

I hung up with Jasper and made my next call to Samantha, also waking her up. There was no greeting. Her first words were, "What's wrong?"

I started to tell her about what happened, that a woman had been shot at the restaurant, when Samantha interrupted.

"Is she dead?" I heard her frantically urging Alex to wake up. She put me on speaker so he could hear the rest of our conversation.

"We're coming over," Samantha insisted.

I appreciated her concern, but told her to stay put. There was nothing she could do. Samantha reluctantly agreed, but made me promise to call her later.

I went to the kitchen, still in my bathrobe, and opened the refrigerator. The contents were sparse. Michael had done most of the grocery shopping. When he was here, there were always eggs, slices of cheddar cheese, Canadian bacon and English muffins on hand for homemade breakfast sandwiches, his specialty. I had to make do with a fried egg over a piece of toast.

"Where are you?" I pleaded out loud to him. "I need you." I shut my eyes and imagined the comfort of resting my head against his chest with my body wrapped in his strong arms. As I daydreamed, the eerie quiet of my perfectly still home jarred me back into reality. The shades of silence morphed from subdued gray to harsh black, forcing me to face the truth. I might never feel his embrace again, and I could possibly live the rest of my life not knowing what happened.

I shook my head, unwilling to follow that train of thought. Looking for a distraction, I picked up the TV remote. Local reporters were camped outside my restaurant, broadcasting the details of the shooting. I gasped when the reporter pointed out the broken window. It had been covered with plywood and taped, but it wasn't exactly secure. I quickly called a repair company who could do same-day glass replacement.

The media didn't reveal the woman's name, but they seemed to have no problem sharing mine and my parents' names. I shoved my plate away, went back to the refrigerator and poured myself half a glass of orange juice. Then I took a bottle of Grey Goose vodka from the freezer and filled the glass. If there was ever a morning for a drink, this was it.

I switched off the TV and stretched out on the couch, propping my head on a pillow as I sipped my screwdriver. Michael and I had picked out this couch and loveseat when he and Jasper first moved in. I wanted the place to feel like *our* home instead of *my* home. We'd enjoyed shopping together—holding hands as we walked around the furniture store, testing every couch on display.

The image of shopping faded, replaced with that woman standing at the front of my restaurant. One minute she was so indignant and the next, she'd dropped helplessly to the floor. I wondered why the media hadn't shared her name and assumed it was because the police hadn't notified her next of kin. I started to speculate what her name might be, not that knowing would change anything. Unable to calm my mind, I retrieved the business card on my kitchen table and called Detective Grant's mobile phone.

He sounded surprised to hear from me, but I needed to know more details, and if he had more questions for me, I wanted to get them over with. He offered to come to my house in an hour.

I chugged my drink and walked to my bedroom closet to get dressed. Michael's clothes still hung on his side, neatly grouped by type. Jasper had taken most of the casual shirts; he and his dad were about the same size, although I think the gesture was a sentimental one. I also sensed he was trying to help me move forward by starting to clear out the house. But what if there was a miracle? What if Michael had somehow survived and was making his way home? I just couldn't discard his things. In my gut, I knew the odds of him returning grew worse with each passing day. Still, I wasn't ready to let go of my glimmer of hope.

I walked past the bathroom mirror and took a second look at myself. I found some Visine in the medicine cabinet and doused my eyes. Then I swigged some mouthwash. Back in the kitchen, I filled the French press with ground coffee beans and boiling water as I waited for Detective Grant to arrive.

When the doorbell rang, my stomach tightened. Even though I'd done nothing wrong, I dreaded being questioned again. I opened the front door and invited him in. He was in the same clothes as the night before which made me wonder if he'd ever gone home. Or maybe that's what he wore every day?

"You couldn't have gotten much rest," he said as he followed me to the kitchen.

I shook my head. "I tried, but I couldn't turn off my brain."

He nodded. "I understand. With cases like this, my mind goes into overdrive. Even if I could've gone home, I wouldn't have slept."

I had my answer.

"Would you like some coffee?" I offered.

"Sure. I'll take an IV of the strongest you've got."

I laughed, surprising myself. It had been such a long time. I reached for a coffee mug and stopped. That was Michael's mug—the one that matched mine. Instead, I took a different one and poured a heaping cup of coffee for Detective Grant. Normally, the French press was reserved for days off. Michael made pancakes and I made the gourmet coffee that we drank from our matching cups. So why had I chosen to use the French press today? Maybe, in some crazy way, I was searching for normalcy?

"Cream or sugar?" I asked before I realized I didn't have any fresh cream.

"Just black." He raised the cup to his nose, inhaled deeply and took a sip. "Wow. That's really good coffee. I mean *really* good."

I smiled. "My mom's recipe." A dash of nutmeg was her secret ingredient. We still served it that way at the restaurant.

He took another sip and shut his eyes as he savored the taste. Oddly, I found something endearing about him enjoying something so simple.

"Would you like to sit down?" I asked, pointing in the general area of the kitchen table and living room, not knowing which he preferred. He walked to the table and took a seat, careful to place the mug on a coaster. He was obviously "house trained" but wore no wedding band. I assumed he was divorced or maybe he was married but didn't wear a ring.

Detective Grant reached into his pocket and pulled out a small recording device. "Do you mind?" he asked. "It's easier to transcribe later. I don't write very fast."

I imagined he was just being polite, and I couldn't actually refuse to be recorded.

"Okay," I said reluctantly. I sat down at the table and my stomach started to do flips.

He began. "I know it's been a rough night. You haven't rested. I haven't, either. But I want to go back over what happened. It's not uncommon for people to remember new details after they've had time to process everything."

I nodded. "Before we get into that..." I paused. "I'm curious.

Can you tell me who she was? Do you know her name?"

He put his mug on the coaster, looked away briefly and then made eye contact with me. "It's not released to the media yet. Her name was Brittany Jones. She was twenty-two."

"Twenty-two," I repeated. "She was just a kid!"

In fact, she was barely older than Jasper. Could this girl have possibly known my stepson? Was *he* the person she was talking about? Was *he* not who I thought he was? No. It wasn't possible. I knew Jasper's friends and I'd never seen her.

Brittany Jones, I thought. Somehow, I hoped knowing her name would help me, but it didn't.

"That just gives me more questions," I admitted.

"Me, too," he replied. "I'm hoping you can help me with that."

We reviewed my entire day again, starting with the morning. I recounted everything, just as I had during our first meeting. I'd forgotten about leaving the restaurant to pick up my dry cleaning, which rattled me. It wasn't that my dry cleaning was an important detail, but that I'd so easily forgotten about it. It made me wonder what else I might have forgotten.

"Can you walk me through everything you remember about your chef and bar manager leaving?" he asked. His speech was slow and deliberate.

I sat back in my chair, tucked one foot under my knee and closed my eyes to better picture the scene. Alex was behind the bar, putting rubber bands around the receipts. Samantha was coming out of the restroom carrying her white chef's jacket. She was a slender woman, half-Caucasian and half-Korean. She was about my age, but her flawless skin made her look much younger. Her hair was pulled up into a high pony tail. I took the jacket from her to put in the laundry service bag. She offered to do it herself, but I didn't mind.

As I described the scene to the detective, I thought of something. "Oh, wow!" I exclaimed.

"You remembered something?" he asked.

"The restroom," I replied. "It's a single unit. There's a toilet and a sink next to it. And there's a little cabinet with tissues and extra toilet paper, but it's all one room. I thought maybe she'd hidden in there, but Samantha would've seen her." I paused and thought out loud. "So how'd she get in?"

"You have a men's room, too?" the detective asked. "Could she have hidden in there?"

"I guess," I replied. I hadn't thought of that option, although I didn't recall seeing the girl at all while we were open.

"You had Samantha's uniform," he continued. "What did you do with it?

"I put it in the laundry. It's still there. Do you want to check?"

"No," he said with a smile. "I believe you. This is really helpful. What happened next?"

"I walked with Samantha and Alex to the front door. They left and I locked it behind them. I jiggled it to be sure it was closed."

"How'd you lock the door? Dead-bolt? Key?"

"With a key."

"And what'd you do with your key?"

"It's on my key chain with my car keys. I put them back in my jacket pocket. When I leave at night, I like to have them handy so I'm not digging for them in my purse outside in the dark."

The detective nodded. "You're certain you locked the front door. What about the back?"

"It stays locked. We only open it if we have a delivery."

"Besides you, who else has keys to the restaurant?"

"Five of us: me, Samantha, Alex, Jasper...and my husband."

Out of habit, I clasped my engagement ring, rubbing the shiny diamond between my finger and thumb. The cut edges sparkled in the natural light. I'd protested to Michael that it was far too big, nearly a carat and a half. His response was that he was going to trade it in for a bigger one for our five-year anniversary. But we never made it to five years.

And where were his keys now? Probably in the Atlantic Ocean? I shuddered at the thought. It was impossible to accept. Michael was an experienced pilot. It had been a clear day with no thunderstorms or bad weather in sight. Besides that, before every flight, he always checked the weather report. He always reviewed the maintenance logs of the plane and conducted a meticulous preflight inspection. What could have possibly gone wrong?

I tried not to, but when my mind invariably drifted to the worst outcome, I prayed the end came quickly. I prayed he didn't have time to think about dying and he didn't suffer. Early on, I'd hoped the authorities would not find any signs of wreckage. That would mean he'd managed to land somewhere and just needed to be found. But as time passed and the search team found nothing, I began to hope for some kind of clue. Then the unthinkable came to pass: after only three days, the search abruptly ended. The plane was never found and Jasper and I were left without any answers at all.

I looked up at the detective, expecting to see that familiar expression of pity, the one that most people had when I brought up Michael. But he remained stoic. For once, it was nice not to feel the suffocation of another person's sympathy.

"And your stepson," he asked. "Have you talked to him?"

"Yes. I called him this morning. He's on his way home now."

"Okay. I'll need his contact information."

I tilted my head. "How can he be of any help? He wasn't even in town."

"I'm going to need to talk to all the people who have a key," he explained.

I supposed that made sense. There seemed to be so little to go on that he'd grab whatever leads he could, however small.

"After Samantha and Alex left, what'd you do?" he asked.

"I went to my office to label and file the receipts for the night. I decided to get a glass of wine so I walked to the bar and poured a glass of Cabernet that was already open. I started to take a sip when I heard her voice behind me."

"Can you remember what she said?"

"Yes. She said that we needed to talk. I remember that clearly."

"And then?"

"I told her we were closed and that she needed to leave. I thought I was alone, so her being there startled me. She said my name. She asked if I was Julianna. She came looking for me. But why?"

"You're doing fine. What'd you say to her?"

"I just kept telling her we were closed."

"And then?"

"She said something about *him* not being who I thought he was, which made no sense."

Detective Grant's back stiffened, but just as quickly as he had jerked upright, he relaxed again and repositioned himself in his chair.

I continued, "I pulled out my keys and started walking toward the door to show her out. When I was almost in front of her, she started cussing at me."

"What'd she say?"

"She called me a bitch. And then…"

I remembered the loud bang and the glass shattering. I could see her grabbing her chest and lunging forward, spitting blood as she fell. None of it felt real.

Detective Grant said my name, which made me flinch. Just seconds before, I had been in the dining room of my restaurant.

"Are you okay?" he asked.

I nodded slowly. "Could I—could I have helped her if I hadn't run away?"

"I doubt it," he told me firmly. "You ran to safety instead of being a second victim. I know this is hard, but you're doing a really good job of remembering details."

"It doesn't feel like it. I didn't see anyone."

"Let's talk about that. So when she first spoke, you were behind the bar?"

Before I could answer, I heard the front door of my house open. The alarm chirped three short beeps. I glanced at my mom's antique wall clock, which displayed 11:30 a.m.

"Jasper, is that you?" I called out.

"Yeah. I'm home," he said.

Jasper walked quickly into the living room but stopped short when he saw Detective Grant. He was wearing tan cargo shorts and a yellow polo shirt that hung loosely over his slender body. His brown hair jutted in all directions, the typical boy-band look. He carried a small backpack, which he dropped to the floor.

I introduced my stepson to Detective Grant, who stood and shook his hand. I sensed an awkwardness between the two men. At first, I attributed it to typical guy behavior, sizing each other up, but I got the sense there was more.

I stood to break the tension. "Would either of you like some coffee?"

"No thanks." Detective Grant was the only one to reply. He looked at his watch. "Actually, I've got another appointment to get to." Then he looked at me. "We can finish this another time."

He took a step toward Jasper, towering over him with both his height and girth. "I'm going to need to talk to everyone who works at the restaurant, but for now, best that you take care of your step-mom. She hasn't had much rest."

"I'm at the restaurant most days," Jasper replied.

"I'll be in touch," the detective added.

Both men stood their ground, not moving, not even blinking.

"Shall I walk you out?" I suggested.

Detective Grant reached over to the table where he had left his recorder, picked it up and followed me to the front door. He asked, "Would you be able to come down to the station tomorrow to finish this up? I'll need to get a written statement, too."

Although I couldn't fathom yet another round of questioning, in fairness, we'd been interrupted by Jasper. I wasn't sure what else I could tell him that I hadn't already shared.

"I suppose I could come over tomorrow morning, before we open," I replied. Thinking about the restaurant made me anxious. Normally, we'd open on Tuesday for lunch, but would the murder scare everyone off?

The detective walked out the front door, pulled his sunglasses from his pocket and turned toward me. His hazel eyes squinted in the bright sun. "I know you told Jasper what happened. Have you spoken with your chef and bar manager yet?"

"Yes," I replied. "I called them this morning."

"Do you remember what time?"

I pulled my phone from my jeans pocket and scrolled through the recent calls, showing the screen to him. I'd called Jasper at 8:03 a.m. and Samantha at 8:11 a.m.

"Why?" I asked.

"Do you think they'll be up? I was planning on giving them a call, to set up a time to meet."

"They should be," I confirmed. It was the middle of the day.

6. Grant | Monday, July 5

Lying little shit.

No way Jasper was in Miami at 8:03 a.m. that morning and back in Ormond Beach by 11:30 a.m. Even if he'd been in North Miami, it would've taken at least four hours to drive back. So why was he lying and where had he really been? And what was in that backpack he tossed so quickly when he saw me? That was a sure sign he was up to something. I had to leave for the ME's office, but I was going to run Jasper's criminal record as soon as I was done. I was willing to bet my alimony check that I'd find dirt on him.

I made a pitstop at the local Wendy's and ordered a hamburger and iced coffee to go. The Volusia County Coroner's office was a thirty-minute drive south and inland, so I ate my lunch in the car, my second office. The campus consisted of two side-by-side buildings, one for offices and the other for medical labs. Intentional or not, it kept the smells contained to the medical side. Seeing my badge, the receptionist buzzed me in and called one of the investigators to escort me to the medical building.

"Well look what the cat dragged in," a familiar voice said.

Don Anthony was the Deputy Chief Investigator, next in line to take the Chief Investigator job. Our paths had crossed many times when I was in Daytona. He added, "I thought you retired."

"I wish," I replied. "Just transferred north, to Ormond Beach."

"You back in patrol?"

I shook my head. "No, Chief Jamison brought me in to handle investigations."

Usually a transfer to another police force required starting at the ground floor, in patrol, but I'd been lucky. The chief needed an experienced investigator and made it clear at our first meeting that I'd start where I'd left off. I'm still not sure how she'd gotten my name, but obviously word had spread that I was ready for a move. I wasn't just looking for a fresh start, but also for something quieter. I expected Ormond Beach to fit the bill, though it wasn't starting out that way.

I followed Anthony to the medical building. He was a stocky guy with a pronounced swagger. As he pushed open the heavy metal door to the lab, I braced myself. As much as you prepare for the smell, you never get used to it. Today's odor wasn't rancid decomposing bodies. Instead, I inhaled a mixture of exposed organs and expressed bowels, combined with cleaning fluids and the iron-sweet smell of blood.

My goal was to get in, get my answers and get out.

Chief Medical Examiner, Dr. John Anglin, was dressed in blue scrubs shielded by a long-sleeved, plastic apron. He was a tall man with sandy hair parted on the side. His thick glasses made his brown eyes look oversized, almost cartoonish.

Brittany's body lay on the table, supine and nude. Even in death, I could tell she'd been a beautiful woman. A thin tan line ran across her hips to her well-groomed pubic hair. She wasn't the typical ratty, rotten-toothed meth head I was used to seeing. It had been twelve hours since her death and her body had turned pale, which made the tattoo on her neck more pronounced. Lividity was setting in, making the backside of her legs and arms appear bruised. Her hands, which had been bagged at the crime scene to preserve evidence, were now clean and resting palms up.

Seeing me, Dr. Anglin asked, "So, what's her story? Jealous boyfriend or husband?"

"Not sure yet, though I think the shooter knew her," I said.

Behind the autopsy table were two large stainless-steel sinks and a biohazard bin. Next to the table was an instrument cart with the medical tools necessary for the work at hand: a skull chisel, scalpels and a bone saw. Behind the instrument cart was a table with the victim's belongings, the items we'd collected at the crime scene—her bag, jewelry and shoes. They'd already photographed and catalogued them. I didn't see her navy dress and guessed it was in the drying cabinet.

Dr. Anglin motioned me over to an X-ray monitor mounted on a portable stand and pointed to a small circular mass on the image.

"There's the bullet," he said. He drew his finger across the image as he spoke. "It entered her back, traveled slightly downward and to the left, and penetrated and perforated the aorta. It continued through the left ventricle and came to rest in the left lung. It didn't exit the body, which caused significant internal bleeding."

I nodded, my suspicions from the crime scene confirmed.

Without speaking, he turned toward the body and reached for a scalpel on the instrument cart. Like most autopsies, he began by cutting her torso with a Y-shaped incision. Next, he used rib cutters, which looked like pruning shears, to separate her ribs in order to lift off her chest plate. With the body cavity exposed, he methodically removed her organs, weighed them and placed them on a stainless-steel table. Later, he'd use a long knife to cut each organ into slices for further examination.

When he got to the section of her lung where the bullet was lodged, he used metal forceps to retrieve the chunk of metal and dropped it into a bowl. It made a high-pitched *clink* as it landed. The tech took the bowl, washed the bullet and put it in a clear plastic vial. I'd have to wait for the doctor to initial the fragment, then have it bagged and logged into evidence before I could take it. I picked up the vial so I could study the bullet more closely. Given its size and shape, I guessed the gun was a .40 or .45 caliber. The bullet was a hollow point, the kind designed to expand inside the body for optimal damage. My next step would be to send the bullet to the ballistics lab to determine the type of firearm and exact caliber of the ammunition.

"It's a medium- to large-caliber," Anglin offered.

"How close was the shooter?" I asked.

"There wasn't any stippling on her skin and I didn't find gunshot powder or residue on her clothing. Given that, I'd say the muzzle-to-target distance was at least ten to fifteen feet."

"Did you find any glass particles on her dress?" I asked. "The round went through a window first."

"No," he replied. That fact also supported his estimate of the distance the round had traveled. At ten to fifteen feet, the glass projectiles from the window would have lost their velocity. Everything Anglin was saying matched what Julianna had described, which was good. I thought I had a credible witness, but you never knew until the facts were confirmed.

Next, he took a scalpel and cut from the bottom of her ear, around her earlobe and over the top of her head. With this type of incision, he was able to peel back the scalp and expose her skull. Once her facial tissue was rolled and tucked, it almost looked like her blonde hair was growing out of her chin. When he was done, he'd roll everything back in place and stitch the skin as if it had never been touched. Until you've seen it, you have no idea how flexible the face is.

"Any head trauma?" I asked.

"There doesn't appear to be any blunt force trauma to the head," he observed. "I'll look for abnormalities in the brain to see if there were any bleeds or aneurisms." As he spoke, he reached for the vibrating saw used to cut open the skull. "I'll do a toxicology screen for drugs and alcohol, but I'd say the cause of death was a single gunshot wound which perforated the aorta."

With this conclusion, there was no need for me to stick around for the brain examination or organ dissection.

"What about a rape kit?" I asked. I didn't think Brittany had been raped, not from Julianna's description of her demeanor, but it wouldn't hurt to have DNA from any sexual partners.

"Already did that, and we scraped and clipped her nails." As we talked, another body—a middle-aged white male—was wheeled into the adjacent station. "Anything else?" he asked.

"Just the bullet," I said, and paused. "One more thing. Quick or slow?"

"It was probably thirty seconds before she went into shock. Then her body shut down."

Brittany never saw it coming and, apparently, she didn't suffer for long. I waited for the tech to package the ballistics evidence and then headed back to my office. By the time I had the ocean in view, it was nearly 3:00 p.m. There was no point in going home, not until I could complete the research that had been nagging at me all afternoon. The lack of sleep was starting to make my brain feel like mush, but I pressed on. In my younger days, I'd pulled all-nighters with no problem, but with each passing year, recovering from them was getting harder. I'd be fifty-five this year, although I wasn't one to be bothered with birthdays.

When I pulled into the parking lot of the police station, my cell phone rang. It was the chief. "Got a second to brief me?" she asked.

"I'm pulling in now. Be right there."

Chief Jamison's office was a few doors down from mine, at the corner of the building. It was larger and let in more light, mostly because she kept the shades open. We had tinted windows so no one could see inside, but we could clearly see out. The chief's office had a large rectangular desk with a matching dark wood credenza behind it. The few folders she had out were neatly stacked and would be promptly filed away.

Two diplomas in fancy frames hung on the wall, one showing a Bachelor's degree in criminal justice from University of North Alabama and another for her Master's degree in Public Administration from Florida State. Four framed certificates hung next to the diplomas, from the International Association of Chiefs of Police, the Women's Leadership Institute, the Southern Police Institute Administrative Officers Course and the FBI National Academy. She probably had dozens more, but these were the ones I assumed she valued most.

A few plaques were displayed on the credenza behind her desk, one for dedication and service to Florida Cares, the other a public service award from the Tallahassee Business Association. The last award looked a lot older than the others. It was a red, white and blue ribbon with a small medallion that read "Hometown Hero" from Huntsville, Alabama.

Everything in her office had a place and everything was there for a reason.

She motioned for me to have a seat. "What do you have?" she asked, as she rolled her chair back from her keyboard.

I collected my thoughts so I could be brief yet thorough. "This wasn't random, so the victimology is going to be crucial. Our victim was twenty-two, living in a high-end condo with nice clothes and jewelry, but a year ago she was on the street getting locked up for petty crimes. I can't find any next of kin or any residential history other than an address in Daytona that I'm going to check out."

Her eyes narrowed. "No next of kin and nobody's contacted us, even with all the media coverage?"

"Exactly," I replied. "A year ago, she was arrested for fraud. One of my buddies read me the report. Looks like she rolled a guy to get his credit card. She had a few arrests prior to that, for shoplifting, marijuana and loitering. I've sent in requests for prior juvenile arrests and any reports from surrounding agencies."

Jamison nodded, appearing pleased with my work. She reached across her desk, grabbed a pen and jotted something on a Post-it note.

I continued. "I've interviewed the witness at the scene, the restaurant owner. We spoke twice, but I need to bring her in for a formal interview, along with the restaurant employees. Hall did a cursory review of the surveillance video while we were on scene, but it didn't capture the shooter. I'll look at it again."

As I spoke, I could tell her mind was elsewhere. She was staring through me. I dipped my head to see if I could regain eye contact.

"I don't like the stepson," I added. "He came home when I was interviewing the witness this morning. Almost shit a brick when he saw me. Claims he was in Miami, but turned up too soon to have driven back, given the time she'd called him this morning. Something is off about him. I don't know what it is yet, but I'll find out. Next on my list is to check all the histories, do the formal interviews and go by the victim's condo. I was just coming back from the ME's office when you called. Shooter used medium- to large-caliber ammo. The bullet entered through her back and penetrated and perforated the aorta. It was a kill shot."

The chief leaned back in her chair, but she didn't speak. When she interviewed me for this job, she'd asked me to describe my best and worst bosses. I'd described my worst boss as a guy who riddled me with questions before I had a chance to explain anything. He had no patience and would start spitting out suggestions before hearing all the facts. It drove me nuts. Either her style was to be pensive or she'd taken my feedback to heart, but I couldn't remember the last time I'd debriefed a superior with so few interruptions.

"I've dropped off the evidence at FDLE and asked if they could expedite it. Everything this girl had was high-end, except a burner phone and a digital recorder. I really want to hear what's on that recorder."

Jamison crossed her legs and smoothed her hands over the sharp crease of her pants. "A digital recorder?" she repeated. "Sounds like this girl needed to cover herself." She peeled off the Post-it note and handed it to me. "This is a friend of mine, the head of Florida Cares. Are you familiar with them?"

"They fight sex trafficking?"

"Yes. They're the state's leading non-profit agency serving domestic minor sex trafficking victims. You should call Emily Pickett," she said, gesturing to the note. "Tell her we work together. I'd like to know if this girl was on their radar at any point."

I took the note and tucked it into my pants pocket. The thought had crossed my mind about Brittany turning tricks, but I hadn't specifically thought about her being trafficked as a minor. It could explain why no one appeared to be looking for her now.

"Any idea why our victim was trying to talk to Ms. Sandoval?" the chief asked.

"No, but there's a connection. I just haven't figured it out yet."

"Are you familiar with the missing person's case involving Ms. Sandoval's husband, the pilot?"

"She mentioned him, and I remember hearing about it on the news. Going to look into that, too."

"There's a lot of drug activity where he disappeared. I wonder if he crossed the wrong people. Last thing, Gage Holloman has been calling."

"The kid reporter?"

She nodded. "He contacted me for an interview about the case. Unless you want it, I'll handle the media for now."

Gage Holloman was barely out of college. He worked for OBN, the Ormond Beach News, which was a hyper-local print and online paper that kept the community updated on local events. He did a decent job with dog shows and bake sales, but I couldn't imagine why she'd grant him an audience, unless it was to keep him off my back. With Hall on vacation, I was already short-staffed and pressed for time. I rattled off my canned response when dealing with the media, "The incident is currently under active investigation. No additional details will be released at this time."

She smiled. "Exactly."

With the chief updated, I tackled the final thing standing between me and a hot shower. Back at my desk, I logged onto NCIC, the National Crime Information Center, and started my research on Jasper Sinise. To my surprise, he didn't have a record on file. No way was he squeaky clean. More likely, he just hadn't been caught. I ran an in-house records check, which would provide information on any type of contact he'd had with our agency, whether he was a victim, a witness or a suspect. There was only one entry, an accident report, where he was one of the passengers in the vehicle.

Next, I ran an Accurint check, which revealed two addresses associated with him: one in Las Vegas, and his current address at Julianna Sandoval's house. I typed up a request for all in-house records for Jasper's name in Vegas. With Hall out, this glamourous part of the job was left to me. Truth be told, I didn't mind. It gave me something concrete to do.

One curious tidbit surfaced when I ran Jasper's name through the Volusia County court docket records: a name change a few years ago from Jasper Kiely to Jasper Sinise.

Jasper had avoided being arrested, but he couldn't hide his identity. I immediately re-ran all my record checks with his former name and found a few more reports, including possession of alcohol as a minor and vandalism. It amazed me that criminals thought that, by simply changing their name, they could erase their past, giving them an instant clean slate. Not true. Now a couple petty crimes didn't make Jasper a criminal mastermind, but a name change outside of a marriage or divorce was a red flag.

Next, I ran criminal histories on Julianna Sandoval, Michael Sinise and the list of restaurant employees. Julianna had no criminal history, Michael had a DUI—kind of alarming for a pilot—and the rest of the employees were pretty vanilla...except for one, Alex Walker. He had a few DUI's, less alarming for a bartender, but he also had an arrest with probation for credit card fraud. The arrest was from eight years ago. According to the report, Alex was working as a waiter at a local pub. His boss, the restaurant manager, had pressed charges. Alex was apparently pocketing cash in a scheme I'd seen before. Two unrelated customers would receive their checks. If one paid with a credit card and the other with cash, the waiter would run the credit card twice to pay both bills. Then he'd pocket the cash. The only way he'd get caught would be if the credit card owner noticed a double billing. Apparently someone did and confronted the restaurant management, and Alex's theft was uncovered. Further investigation showed that he'd been running this scam over the course of several months. Alex was promptly fired, prosecuted, found guilty and placed on probation with restitution.

Julianna Sandoval struck me as a savvy business owner who operated a classy restaurant. I would've expected her to run histories on all of her employees before hiring them. Why would she take the risk of hiring someone with this kind of background? I made a mental note to ask her about Alex during her formal interview.

With all my checks done, I packed up for the day and drove home. The sky was growing dark from a fast-approaching storm. The thunderclouds rumbled, followed by a crack of lightning. Rain started to drizzle against my windshield and then turned into heavy drops. I cursed under my breath at my outside parking spot as I made a dash to the front door of my apartment. Once inside, I made a fold-over peanut butter sandwich and set my coffee maker so it would be ready for the morning.

The steam of a hot shower washed off the day. In bed, I turned on the news but barely remember my head hitting the pillow. At 3:00 a.m. I jolted awake to the sound of a high-pitched alarm—the testing of the Emergency Broadcast System on TV. It was louder than the damn smoke detector and ten times more obnoxious. There was no use trying to go back to sleep. My brain had kicked into gear, and I was ready to hit the ground running.

7. Julianna | Tuesday, July 6

The amusement park ride looked enticing yet daunting. It was a water rapids ride in a small yellow boat. A man-made river gushed behind the loading station, with white caps forming as they peaked and crashed. Maybe it was better left for another day? But the young man attending the ride encouraged the girl to give it a try. It would only last a few minutes, and what a rush!

The girl cautiously stepped forward to board the little boat, her heart racing, but then she was stopped. All personal belongings, especially items that could get lost or damaged, must be put in a locker for safe-keeping. She reluctantly emptied her pockets into a wire basket and watched the attendant put her possessions in a locker and slam the door.

Now allowed to board, she carefully stepped into the boat, fastened the seatbelt and braced for the ride. It wasn't until she was being swept away that she realized the ride didn't go in a circle. Instead, she was being whisked downstream, increasingly separated from the security of the dock. She began to scream hysterically, but her high-pitched voice was muffled by the crashing water.

No one would hear her.

No one would save her.

I awoke in a panic, feeling the desperate need to rescue the little girl, but I couldn't. She was already gone.

This wasn't the first time I'd dreamt about her and the fateful boat ride. It was always the same: she was unaware of the danger until it was too late and was being swept away against her will. I didn't know the girl, yet I felt a strong bond with her. I could only imagine my subconscious was conjuring up what might have happened to Lily.

I never knew my older sister. I'd only seen pictures of her. As teens, we looked a lot alike—we both had our mother's straight blonde hair and our father's green eyes, and we both tanned easily in the Florida sun. I often wondered if my looking like her was a comfort to my parents, but I never asked.

Lily had disappeared at fifteen, before I was born. Up to that point, she'd been their only child. They were young parents, in their late teens. I don't think they would've tried for a second child if they hadn't lost her. Having me helped them heal, a little, but they never fully recovered. Every week, they took leftover food from the restaurant to the local women's shelter. They said they were "giving back," but I knew what they were really doing. They were still searching for Lily, hoping she'd miraculously turn up. They'd spent forty-five years silently searching for her, right up until their deaths.

Samantha continued the tradition of the weekly food donations, which I appreciated. If there was one comfort in my parents' passing, it was knowing they finally had answers to Lily's disappearance. In Heaven, they would learn everything, maybe even see her again if she was already there. Maybe they'd already met Michael?

I'd watched my parents live with the heartache of no closure. Before, I never fully appreciated their pain. Now, ironically, I was living with the same torture. I'd always imagined holding on to the slight chance Lily would come home would be a comfort. Now I knew better. Unanswered hope was worse than death.

So much worse.

They had endured years of the unknown, yet I was only at the beginning of the journey. I couldn't fathom living with this dull ache the rest of my life, but like them, what choice did I have?

I showered and put on a sundress. Normally, I wore pants to the restaurant, but today I was going to the police station to continue my interview. I peered into Jasper's room. He was still asleep. I'd wake him in another thirty minutes if he wasn't up, as he needed to go to the restaurant to help with lunch. We had to continue like normal, for the sake of our business.

Jasper didn't have a specific job at Café Lily. He was kind of a "catch-all," depending on the day. If we needed another bartender or more waitstaff, he would step in, but he mostly helped out in the kitchen. I jokingly called him my "chief taster," because the kid was a bottomless pit. He liked the perks of working in the kitchen, but I think he most preferred the days when he got to hang out with Alex at the bar. Alex was about ten years older than him, but when they paired up, it was like watching two frat boys. They'd invent new drinks, juggle jiggers or make up silly contests to entertain the crowd. In reality, they were entertaining themselves more than anyone else.

I made a slice of toast and slathered it with peanut butter and a drizzle of honey—not a breakfast of champions, but good enough.

After a few bites, I pushed away the plate. A knot grew in my stomach as I thought about the upcoming interview, where I'd have to rehash what had happened. A few minutes later, Jasper trudged into the kitchen, still in boxers and a T-shirt, his hair flopping in his face.

"Good morning. How are you?" I asked.

"Okay," he mumbled as he poured some coffee.

I had gone to bed early the night before, worn out from the lack of sleep. When I woke up around midnight, I noticed Jasper wasn't home yet.

"You were out late last night?"

He raised an eyebrow but didn't answer. I wasn't spying on him—I just happened to notice his empty bed when I refilled my water glass.

"Yeah. I couldn't sleep, with everything that's happened."

I didn't pry further. After Michael and I had gotten engaged, having them both move in was an easy decision. This big house had been so lonely without my folks, so the more the merrier. Sometimes it felt strange that it was just the two of us now, but I think we silently comforted each other. We both missed Michael. I supposed Jasper would want to move out at some point, but as far as I was concerned, he could stay as long as he liked.

"You think anyone is going to show up at the restaurant today?" he asked.

I inhaled then let out a deep breath. "I don't know." I'd been wondering that myself. Our regulars would probably stay loyal, but I was fearful the tourists would shy away.

"Jasper, I have to go over to the police station so I won't be there when we open. Can you text me and let me know how it's going?"

He banged his coffee mug on the marble countertop with enough force that I thought he'd break it. If Michael were here, he would've said something, but it wasn't my place to correct Jasper. I reminded myself that I could get new mugs. I couldn't get a new stepson.

"I thought you already talked to the police," he commented.

"We didn't finish."

Jasper turned and opened the refrigerator, staring into it blankly. I could hear my mother's voice, imploring me to shut the door or I'd cool the entire house.

He finally closed the door without taking anything and turned toward me. "Maybe…"

He stopped.

"Maybe what?" I asked.

"Never mind."

"What?" I insisted.

"I just wonder what dad would do."

It was the first time he'd said "dad" in a while. I knew he was silently suffering, but he didn't talk much about his father. What would Michael have done under these circumstances? Knowing him, he would've suggested something over the top, like changing the name of the restaurant, to steer away the bad press. That's how he was—I mean, how he *is*: full of big ideas and grandeur. I felt that familiar pang in my chest, a heavy ache that had become a permanent resident.

"I wonder, too," I replied. "Hey, aren't you supposed to talk to Detective Grant?"

"Yeah, I've got to call him back."

"Don't wait to call him, okay? You don't want to piss him off."

I was a rule follower. If the police called, you answered on the first ring, but my stepson was the type to blow off a call from the detective. He'd do what he pleased and didn't worry about consequences. He got that carefree gene from his dad.

Jasper and I left the house at the same time, me to the police station and him to the restaurant. I'd grown up in Ormond Beach, but I'd never been to the police headquarters. Once I arrived in front of the single-story white building, I parked my Jetta in a visitor spot. At the front reception, a woman took my identification and called Detective Grant. He entered through a side door, smiled and politely asked me to follow him. He was wearing the same black shirt and tan pants, obviously his uniform. We walked into a large room with cubicles in the center and offices lining the walls. As we passed a break room, he offered me a drink.

"Would you like some water?" he asked. "Or coffee, although it doesn't taste anything like yours."

"No, thanks," I replied.

He led me into a small interview room, just down from the break room. It had a table, two chairs, pale blue walls and patterned carpet.

"Apologies for the space, but we won't get interrupted here."

He motioned for me to sit and he took the chair across from mine.

"Thanks for coming down today," he began. "I know it must feel like I keep asking you the same questions, but you may know more than you think."

A large mirror covered most of the wall behind him. It had to be a two-way, like the kind you see in police interrogation rooms on TV. That's why he'd chosen this room. It wasn't for privacy. Instinctively, I stiffened. Did he think I was somehow involved? Is that why he wanted to meet again at the police station? Should I ask for my lawyer?

I recalled the news stories where the witnesses became suspects—the broken-hearted parents of a missing child who suddenly became the accused; the grief-stricken husband of a missing wife who overnight became the prime suspect. Why hadn't I thought of that? My heart began to pound. I needed to call Ed.

"I'm not asking you to repeat what happened because I think you're lying," he said. "Remember yesterday when you said that you didn't know how you'd help me? This is how you'll help me. By talking to me. And every detail counts. As we continue to talk, you may remember more."

My heartbeat gradually slowed. He wasn't accusing me—at least it didn't appear that way. Had he seen my panic? Had my face given me away? Something must have signaled him to not begin the interview by peppering me with questions.

"Can you start at the beginning of your day on the fourth of July and walk me through it just one more time?" He spoke softly.

As my fear dissipated, my annoyance grew. I'd already told him everything I knew. Somehow he thought I could give him more, but I couldn't. I didn't know the girl and I didn't see who shot her.

I walked through my entire day again. Oddly, today's description felt clearer, maybe because I was rested. Detective Grant took notes but didn't ask many questions. Unlike at my house, he didn't use a recorder. I wondered if one was hidden in the room but was pretty sure he'd have to ask my permission. Maybe not. He let me talk, up to the point where the girl arrived.

"At first, I thought it was Samantha," I said, "that she'd forgotten something. But when I turned around, I saw that it wasn't. The girl said we needed to talk, that *he* wasn't who I thought he was. When I tried to get her to leave, her whole demeanor changed. She called me a stupid bitch. I remember thinking, 'I don't know you. Why are you being so hateful?'"

"What did she say again, about him not being who you thought he was?" Detective Grant asked.

"Just that," I replied. "She said that he's not who I think."

"Who do you think she might have been talking about?"

"I'm not sure." In fact, I had a hunch. Based on their ages, I thought she may have known Jasper. But I wasn't going to sic Detective Grant on my stepson based on a feeling, not before I could figure out more on my own.

He continued. "At this point, she was still standing next to the hostess stand?"

"Yes."

"Do you remember any movement—around her, behind her, in the parking lot outside?"

"No. Nothing. And I never heard the door open. I still don't know how she got in."

"Was she carrying anything? Anything in her hands?"

I pictured her in my mind. "She had a purse in her right hand. Nothing in her left. Once she turned ugly, I remember thinking that I needed to get her out of my restaurant."

"And then?"

"Just as I was walking toward her, I heard the gunshot." The whole thing felt surreal, like I was describing a movie I'd seen, not a real event I'd witnessed. Finally, I said, "I want to know why she came looking for me."

"That's what we have to figure out." He shifted in his chair, leaning forward. "I believe there's a connection between the two of you. Maybe your paths have crossed somewhere, but you didn't notice her. Can you tell me about the places you frequent? Where you grocery shop? Get your hair done? Do you belong to a gym or have any hobbies?"

His question about hobbies made me picture Michael at the helm of his speed boat, sunglasses on and smiling like a kid at Christmas. Boats, planes, motorcycles—anything that spelled adventure had his name on it. His zest for life was part of what had attracted me to him. We were so different. I was a workaholic. I'd always believed that the time for living large would come later, once I'd saved enough money and the restaurant was thriving. But I could always save more money and the restaurant was a twenty-four seven job, like any small business. Then Michael showed up and changed me more than I thought was possible. He taught me that the time for living was now.

I looked up. The detective was waiting patiently for my answer.

"Michael and I used to go boating most Mondays, when the restaurant was closed. We'd go out in the morning and have lunch along the Intercoastal."

"Could she have worked at a restaurant you frequented?"

"No," I said. "I would've noticed her. I always pay attention to the servers, on the lookout for anyone I might want to hire."

"Do you go anywhere else on a regular basis?" he asked.

I shook my head.

"How'd you meet Michael?"

I questioned how that was relevant and if I should answer. Finally, I replied, "We met at Café Lily."

"When was that?"

Michael had come into my restaurant in early December, two and a half years ago. He sat alone at the bar, but I noticed him. In fact, all the female servers noticed him. He was a good-looking man. After a few visits, with him always sitting alone, we struck up a conversation. I had just gone through my first Thanksgiving without my parents, the worst time of my life, and he had managed to make me laugh. For New Year's Eve, he'd reserved a table just for himself. Right before midnight, he ordered a bottle of champagne with two flutes and convinced me to take a break to have a quick toast. "To a brighter year ahead," he'd said, as if he knew what a difficult year I'd just endured.

I blinked and Detective Grant came into focus. "We met two and a half years ago. But how does that matter?"

"And how long have you been married?"

"Just over two years." I squinted. He was doing the math, judging me. Yes, Michael and I had met in December and had gotten married the following April, but we hadn't intended to marry so quickly. Right after Valentine's, we'd flown to Vegas. Jasper wanted to visit his friends and Michael wanted to show me the city since

I'd never been there. We joked about having a quickie wedding at one of those chapels. But then the talk of marriage started to sound good to us. I certainly wasn't going to defend my short courtship to Detective Grant. Besides, for any of the naysayers, it had lasted.

"And you said he's a pilot?"

I nodded. "He was a commercial pilot but retired. Then he started working at a charter company."

"How old is Michael?"

I crossed my arms. Why so many questions about my husband? There was no way he was involved with this girl. And it wasn't fair. He wasn't here to defend himself.

"Fifty-three."

Detective Grant tilted his head. "And already retired?"

"Well, he retired from the airline but was still working until he was old enough to collect his pension."

A thought hit me. I'd never asked about his airline pension. Not long after Michael's disappearance, my lawyer called. Actually, Ed Harrigan was my parents' lawyer. When they died, he'd been a life-saver, guiding me through all the necessary steps to execute their will and transfer assets. I'd basically inherited Ed from my folks, which was a huge benefit. I knew he was honest, loyal, and cared deeply about my family. He'd called to check on me, but also to explain the complicated steps ahead of us. Assuming my husband wasn't found, I'd have to petition the court to declare Michael dead. That was the only way to get a death certificate and begin the process of collecting his life insurance, but I refused to discuss it. It was all too overwhelming, and we'd never even talked about his airline pension.

I rubbed my throat, which was starting to feel dry and scratchy, like the beginnings of a cold.

"I think I'd like a glass of water," I said, my voice turning raspy.

"Sure. I'll be right back." The detective got up and left the room. I looked at the mirror and wondered who was watching me. I could feel my eyes starting to water and gritted my teeth. I was not going to break down, not here.

He returned with a bottle of water. I took a sip and cleared my throat. "Why are you asking about my husband? What does he have to do with the girl? Is there something you're not telling me?"

"No," he said. "If I knew something, I'd tell you. What I do know is that Brittany Jones sought you out and we don't know why." He continued, "I need to figure out how this woman knows you or how she's connected to you. You have a small circle—the restaurant and your family, Michael and Jasper. I know this must feel uncomfortable and invasive, but Brittany suggested she had information that involves you. How many men in your life could she be talking about?"

I shook my head. What if she was mistaken or mixed up? Just because she said it didn't make it true. It even could've been some kind of scam.

I paused.

What if there really was something unsavory going on? Had she gotten herself killed trying to tell me about it?

I blurted, "Do you think I'm in danger?"

He considered my question but didn't respond.

"Well? Do you?" I insisted.

Finally, he spoke. "No, I don't think so."

"Why not?"

"Because the shooter could have gotten off a second shot before you ran for cover, but he didn't."

I gulped in a short breath. Was he saying that I could've been killed if the shooter had wanted me dead? Unable to stifle my emotions any longer, I burst into tears.

Detective Grant slipped out of the room and returned with a Kleenex box. I thought he might leave the room again, but he sat quietly while I sobbed. I felt embarrassed. Rarely did I cry in front of anyone else. My breakdowns were saved for the shower, my sanctuary. I willed myself to regain some composure; I could have a good cry later when I was alone.

The detective spoke softly, "I know all of this must be overwhelming, and I appreciate you speaking with me, going over all of these questions. Look, you probably want to get out of here and I understand. Could I ask you about Jasper before you go?"

I dabbed my eyes with a tissue. Did he already suspect Jasper was linked to this girl?

"Do you get along with your stepson?" he asked.

"I do," I sniffed. "He seemed genuinely happy that Michael and I were together."

"You didn't think he would be?"

"Well, some kids don't want to share their parents with a new spouse. But with Jasper, I got the feeling that he was pleased someone was looking after his dad. Like it was a relief for him."

"He lives with you?"

I nodded as I crumpled the tissue in my hand.

"And he works at the restaurant?"

"Yes."

"Does a good job?" he asked.

"He needs a push sometimes," I admitted.

Detective Grant didn't speak, waiting for me to elaborate.

"You know kids these days. He wants instant success without putting in the work, but I have to say, he's stepped up since…"

He leaned forward. "Did Jasper ever go by any other name that you know of?"

I shook my head. "It's a bit unusual, but Jasper is his real name."

"I meant his last name."

"No, why?"

He hesitated.

"What is it?" I asked.

"It's protocol to run backgrounds on everyone surrounding a case. Two last names have come up for Jasper—Sinise and Kiely, both with the same birthday and social security number."

"I don't understand."

"Court records show a petition for a name change a couple of years back. I'm trying to figure out why."

I hadn't known Jasper by anything other than his father's name— Sinise—but there had to be a logical explanation. Then I realized what they'd done.

"Michael was very honest with me," I explained. "He and Jasper's mom weren't married. She was a flight attendant and they had a short fling. When she told him she was pregnant, he didn't believe the child was his, at least not at first. Years later, she got terminal cancer and gave Michael one last chance to take Jasper, or he was going to live with her parents. So Michael took him in. I guess Kiely could have been her name?"

Detective Grant rubbed his jaw line, considering my explanation. "Was Michael sure that Jasper was his son?"

I'd never given it a second thought, until now. "He did the right thing. He took in a boy who was about to lose his mother. After that, I don't think he questioned it again. I mean, I don't think he ever did a paternity test."

The detective leaned back in his chair. I thought about pulling out my phone to show him pictures of Michael and Jasper. If he saw them together, he wouldn't be asking these questions. They had the same lanky build, the same brown hair, the same shaped face.

"I need to ask," he said. "Did Michael have any life insurance?"

"He did."

"Who is the beneficiary?"

"Me."

"It was a new policy?"

"I don't think so."

"So he had the policy before you were married?"

"I believe so. Jasper had been the beneficiary, but Michael changed it to me."

The silence between us went on a heartbeat too long, and my own heart began to race in response. I didn't want Detective Grant getting the wrong idea about Jasper.

"I don't think he even knew about it," I added. "But it didn't matter. Michael knew I would take care of his son if anything happened to him, and it was actually better this way."

"How's that?"

I was starting to feel like I was divulging more about my family than was necessary or appropriate. "Jasper grew up in Vegas, without a lot of supervision. He liked to gamble. Michael said it would be better if I were in charge of the money, if something ever happened."

He glanced at his watch. "Look, I know I've kept you here for a long time and I appreciate it. I think that's all for now."

"Will you need to talk to me again?" I asked.

"I might. You don't have plans to leave the country, do you?" he joked, but I didn't laugh.

With all of the questions about Michael and Jasper, it seemed like Detective Grant was trying to create an angle that didn't exist. He was being judged on how quickly he solved the case, and with so few leads, he was going after *my* family.

He stood and offered to walk me out. As we exited the small

room, he turned and asked, "By the way, who does the hiring for the restaurant?"

"I do," I replied. "Why?"

"Do you run background checks?"

"Of course."

"I'll be running background checks on your staff," he commented, "but I imagine I won't find anything, if you've already done them."

"I highly doubt it," I confirmed. "Samantha's been with us for years. She brought in Alex. As far as the waitstaff and cooks go, they've all been checked. The records are in my files if you'd like to see them?"

He said that wouldn't be necessary. At the front reception, he shook my hand, gently cupping his warm palm over mine. The gesture no longer felt sincere, a fake attempt to put me at ease in the midst of this horrible ordeal. I considered his invasive questions about my family and wondered why he'd stopped the interview so abruptly.

8. Grant | Tuesday, July 6

As soon as Julianna Sandoval left, I put the finishing touches on my search warrant for Brittany's condo and had it ready for the judge when he came off the bench for lunch. With the warrant signed, I headed south, driving through a Chick-fil-A for lunch. I ordered the grilled chicken wrap meal with fries and a Coke. My ex used to pack my lunches. Back then, I complained about the carrot sticks and apple wedges. She used to draw little smiley faces on the paper bag. I should've realized our marriage was in trouble when those sketches stopped.

Brittany's condo on Myrtle Street was walking distance to the beach. Unlike the high-rises along the coast, these units were only three stories and set back from the main road. Sprinklers were running out front, the mist evaporating before it could properly soak the grass.

I parked in a visitor space and entered the front office, carrying my kit to conduct the inspection and search warrant. The room had a vaulted ceiling and thick carpet. A few lit candles filled the space with an overpowering, sweet smell. Large windows at the far side showed off a nice view of the pool. Everything about this room was designed to lure new tenants into the luxurious community.

A young girl sat at the front desk, smacking gum as she squinted at her computer monitor. Her brunette hair was pulled in a ponytail sitting high on her head. When I approached, she looked up, seemingly pleased to have a distraction.

"Hello. I'm Detective Grant," I said, flashing my badge. "I'm handling the homicide case of one of your tenants."

She popped up from her chair and quickly circled the desk. "Oh-em-gee, isn't it horrible? Did you catch who did it?"

"I'm looking for evidence to help us figure that out." I handed her the search warrant. "Could you get me the key to Ms. Jones's unit?"

The girl looked at the warrant, puzzled. "Am I allowed to do that?"

"You are," I assured her. "Or I could kick open the door if that's easier."

She looked confused. This was why I didn't date younger women. They didn't get my jokes.

"Okay," she replied. "I'll get the key. I don't think you should kick down the door."

"Good idea," I agreed. "Oh, and while you're at it, could you get the leasing documents? I'm trying to find her next of kin. I'm hoping she put a name and phone number on the emergency contact."

The girl nodded.

"Did you know Brittany Jones?" I asked.

She shook her head. "Not really. I just started working here. I saw her a few times at the pool, but we didn't really speak."

The girl disappeared into a back room, where I presumed they kept the tenant files. I walked to the window facing the empty pool and pictured Brittany sunning in one of the lounge chairs.

"Can I help you, officer?" a woman's voice said.

I turned around to see a middle-aged woman approaching with a ring of keys in her hand. She wore a conservative blue suit with a gold name badge that read *Judy Fobbs*.

"I'm Detective Grant. I'm investigating the Brittany Jones case."

"I'm the property manager," she replied. "We've already had police officers here."

"Yes, I know. I'm here to conduct a more detailed inspection. The young lady was just getting me the key." I pointed to the empty chair where the girl had been sitting. Just then, she returned with the key and a file folder.

"May I see your paperwork?" Ms. Fobbs asked.

I handed her the search warrant and she reviewed it thoroughly. "Well, I'm sorry to meet under these circumstances," she said, looking at me while taking the key and file from the girl. "I can send up maintenance to let you into the condo. It's unit number 206, on the second floor."

"And the next of kin?" I pointed to the file.

"I'm sorry, but I cannot provide you with a resident's file without a subpoena."

I smiled politely but silently stewed. She was right. I should've brought a subpoena in addition to the search warrant, but I didn't expect to be blocked on a technicality.

"I'll just go to the unit and wait for maintenance," I told her and walked out.

As I climbed the stairs to the second floor, I called an on-duty patrol officer for back-up. Odds were that the place was still deserted, just as it had been when they first checked it, but we had procedure for a reason.

The maintenance man and my back-up unit showed up about the same time. Once the patrol officer cleared the condo, he watched the front door while I began my search. I started by pulling gloves from my kit and sliding them on.

The front door opened into a living room, with a kitchen and bedroom off to the side. It wasn't a large space, but it was impeccably decorated. The furniture was white and littered with furry white pillows. There was a big-screen TV hanging on the wall and a remote control on the floor in front of it. Either Brittany didn't have a lot of stuff, or someone had already cleared the place out before we got here.

I checked out the kitchen. The refrigerator had a six-pack of wine coolers and several loose cans of beer. A Styrofoam take-out container had leftover hot wings and fries. A bottle of ketchup and a bottle of lemon juice were the only items on the side shelves. Next to the Styrofoam container was a large plastic bag of assorted candy bars.

I opened the dishwasher and saw two dirty plates, two glasses and a few cereal bowls with food caked on. One cabinet had a few dishes and cups, and one was stacked with plastic take-out containers, slightly warped from their trips through the dishwasher. The other upper cabinets were empty. Under the sink were dishwasher packs, stacks of various sized napkins, plastic bags and an empty garbage bin.

The bedroom had a low bedframe and mattress with a satin comforter and pillows. A yoga mat and a few free weights lay next to the bed. Glass nightstands held two lamps with a few gossip magazine on one side.

The bathroom had one sink, a shower and a toilet. Makeup was scattered across the counter. Under the sink were a few bath towels, beach towels, toilet paper and tampons. One drawer had a hair dryer and dozens of hair clips. Another had an assortment of toiletries, mostly hotel soaps and shampoos. The last drawer was empty. I didn't see any toothbrushes or toothpaste. I also didn't see a garbage can. On the floor next to the toilet were several newspapers. I didn't figure Brittany the type to sit on the john reading the paper. A guy must have been here at some point.

The closet was filled with women's clothes, mostly skimpy dresses and high heels, typical party attire. I sifted through a chest of drawers but found nothing out of the ordinary: bathing suits, workout clothes, socks, and lacy panties and bras. Next, I dumped the hamper on the floor. Most of the dirty clothes were women's workout pants and tops, but I found a single white polo shirt with a shark emblem on the chest. It was a man's large, probably not Brittany's. I photographed the shirt and put it in an evidence bag.

With nothing else to see in the bedroom, I walked back into the living room and looked around. In the corner, a phone charger was plugged into the wall, but there was no phone. A glass coffee table sat on a furry white rug. On the bottom shelf were several high-fashion magazines with an assortment of pens—felt and ball-point, blue and black.

When I picked up a magazine and flipped through the pages, several sheets of paper fell out and landed on the rug. The first sheet was a photocopy of Julianna Sandoval's driver's license. Several of the other sheets had row after row of Julianna's signature. Why was someone, presumably Brittany, trying to forge Julianna's signature? I photographed each sheet and placed them in an evidence bag. Later, I'd process the pages with Ninhydrin to look for fingerprints. I expected to find Brittany's, but maybe we'd get lucky and find someone else's.

Whoever had tried to sanitize this place, taking the garbage and toothbrushes, had missed a few things: the polo shirt, the newspapers on the bathroom floor and the pages of Julianna's signature. I now had a concrete link between the two women.

I glanced at my watch, eager to get back to the station to give the chief an update. As I exited the condo, both the back-up officer and the maintenance man were waiting outside. I let the officer go and told the maintenance man he could lock up. As he bolted the door, he mumbled to himself. "Hell of a thing. Pretty young girl, getting shot like that."

"Did you know her? Ever talk to her?" I asked.

He faced me, his slight shoulders hunched forward with age. "She wasn't the kind of girl who'd have a conversation with the guy who fixed the toilet. I'd see her coming and going, or out at the pool, but to her, I was invisible."

I nodded and started to leave, when he added, "But even if I was nothin' to her, it didn't mean I didn't notice things."

"Things?" I asked.

"I saw that fellow she was with. They tried to keep it real hush-hush, but I saw him a time or two. And let me tell you, he was old enough to be her papa, but I don't think he was, if you know what I mean."

"You know his name?" I asked.

"Nah, but I think it's his place."

"Thank you," I said and shook the man's hand. I gave him my card in case he thought of anything else, but he'd already confirmed my suspicion about a man spending time in the condo.

Back at the office, I typed up the subpoena requesting all tenant rental and lease records. I was annoyed that I hadn't asked for them at the same time as the search warrant. As I was finishing the subpoena, my cell phone rang.

"Grant, it's Hall," he said.

"Where are you?" I asked.

"On the ship."

"How much is this call costing you?"

"Costing me?" he repeated. "Nothing. I'm calling over the internet. What have you found out?"

"You're on vacation," I said. "Be on vacation. I'm not going to solve this case before you get back."

"Did you talk to the stepson yet? What'd he say?"

"Not yet. Next on my list." I didn't want Hall to feel like he needed to check in, although his phone call was a good reminder. I'd reached out to Jasper several times to set up his interview but kept getting his voicemail. "Look, Hall. Get back to your family. I'll see you soon. I'll get word to you if anything major comes up."

I hung up before he could say more.

Flipping through my notes, I dialed Jasper Sinise's cell phone. After a few rings, it went to voicemail. I left him another message, this time more stern. Then I called Samantha Cobb to set up her interview. She offered to come in with Alex the next morning, before work. Before she hung up, I asked if Jasper happened to be at the restaurant.

"Yes. He's at the bar with Alex. Do you need to talk to him?"

"I do," I said. "Would you mind taking your phone to him? No need to mention who's calling."

I heard footsteps and her voice in the background say, "Jasper, it's for you."

This time, Jasper had no escape and no excuse. The little prick was forced to agree to a morning interview.

9. Julianna | Tuesday, July 6

I drove straight to the restaurant after my interview with Detective Grant. Jasper hadn't texted me, which made me anxious to know how things were going. When I pulled into the parking lot, I immediately noticed the absence of cars. A young black reporter stood in front of the newly replaced window. As I approached, he met me at the front door. "Ms. Sandoval, I understand you were a witness to the shooting that took place on July Fourth?"

I took a step back. If I said *no comment*, I'd look callous, but I couldn't think of anything to say. I finally managed to utter a brief sentence, "We're fully cooperating with the investigation." and scurried inside.

There were a few regulars, but the lunch crowd was small. I sidestepped over the spot where the girl had died and greeted Myra and Gene Cohen, a sweet old couple who'd eaten lunch at the restaurant every Tuesday for as long as I could remember.

"Thank you for coming in," I said.

"Of course, dear," Myra replied. "Why wouldn't we?"

I sighed. The only people coming to the restaurant were the ones who didn't watch the news. Myra reached over and took me by the arm.

"How are you holding up, dear?"

I was wrong. They did know about the shooting but showed up anyway. I surveyed all of the empty seats and shook my head.

"I know how you feel," she said. "Gene, remember when we lost Dixie? I couldn't sleep for days."

I looked at her puzzled. Who was Dixie?

"Dixie was our little Dachshund," she explained. "She was so precious. Well, one day she just up and disappeared, like your Michael. I kept her fenced in the backyard, but she must have dug her way out. I posted signs all over the neighborhood with her picture, but we never found her. So, you see, I understand how you feel with your missing husband."

Anger flashed inside me. I wanted to grab that old lady by the shoulders and shake her. Losing a dog was not the same, not even close. And how dare she speak to me about my missing husband when hers was sitting across the table! She knew nothing of my despair, wondering if I should give up hope. It took all of my self-control to nod at her and walk away. I couldn't afford to alienate the few customers we had left.

I stopped by the kitchen on the way to my office. Samantha was making minestrone and Jasper was cutting vegetables. The rest of the cooking staff were at their stations: rolling out pasta, mixing sauces and kneading dough.

"You didn't text me," I chided Jasper, letting the anger from my last conversation land on him.

"Sorry." Jasper looked away sheepishly. I couldn't bring myself to scold him more. I wasn't prepared to add strain to our relationship over a forgotten text.

I continued down the hall to my office, feeling on the verge of a meltdown. Myra Cohen's insensitive comments had caused my tears for the second time that day. I thought about all of the things going wrong in my life: Michael was missing, a woman had been murdered in my restaurant and the only patrons we had left were the ones who hadn't heard the news.

My mother had always preached about gratitude. *Be thankful for what you have,* she used to say. *Comparisons are odious. There will always be people who have more than you and people who have less.* But I didn't have the strength to be grateful, not when I was concerned about the future of my restaurant and everyone's safety until the shooter was caught.

Before the shooting, I'd kept my gun locked up, but now I wanted it close by, just in case. During my panicked 9-1-1 call, I could hardly remember the code to the safe, even though it was the date of my parents' wedding anniversary. I'd watched them celebrate February sixteenth my entire life, but the shock of seeing that girl being shot had made my mind go blank. It was only after I opened the safe that I remembered Detective Grant had taken my Walther pistol. I wanted it back. I felt defenseless without it.

I heard a tentative knock at my door. It was Samantha, holding a tray with two bowls of soup, some freshly baked rolls and home-made butter. She waited for my nod to enter and stepped forward, setting the tray on the corner of my desk.

"Have you eaten today?" she asked softly as she tilted her head toward the steaming bowls. Although she'd been born in the United States, Samantha had the mannerisms of her Korean mother. With her striking beauty and demure manner, there wasn't a person who didn't love her.

I knew the implied message. Samantha didn't want me back in the emergency room, dehydrated and malnourished, which had happened after Michael's plane disappeared. But this was different. While I felt bad for the murdered girl, I didn't know her. Michael's disappearance had hit me on a completely different level. I thought back to that dreadful day three months ago. Michael's boss, Chet Huff, had called me in the late afternoon, asking if I'd spoken to my husband. I thought it was odd, but it didn't set off any alarm bells. Not long after, Chet called a second time to tell me they'd lost contact with Michael's plane. The way he'd worded it made me think there was a problem with the radio, nothing major. Even when he said the plane hadn't landed as planned, the gravity of the situation just hadn't registered.

So I waited for Michael's call. He always called or texted when he landed, but my phone never rang. I waited up all night but never heard from him. The next morning, I drove to Flagler Airport, spoke to the officials and continued to call his cell phone. By the end of the day, I began to realize something could be very wrong. I tried to sleep but couldn't rest. Samantha brought me food, but I had no appetite. Then the investigators arrived and started asking all kinds of ridiculous questions. Was Michael depressed, taking any medications, drinking excessively, had we gotten into a fight, were there money issues?

They just didn't understand.

Michael didn't take drugs or medications. We didn't fight; we were practically newlyweds. And we didn't have money problems. After losing my parents, I sold my condo and moved back into their house—I couldn't bear to sell the family home with all its memories. The income from my condo and the restaurant covered our expenses, and with Michael's charter income and pension, we were financially set.

Eventually, after days of no sleep, I started having trouble speaking. I knew what I wanted to say, but I couldn't articulate my thoughts. Samantha tried to comfort me, but she couldn't. Jasper retreated, staying with friends more often than he was home. My world was imploding, yet just about everyone else kept going on with their lives as if nothing was wrong. I resented them, which isolated me even further.

Finally, I collapsed. My body forced me to rest.

The one advantage of medically-induced sleep was that I was able to see Michael again in my dreams. We'd be on the boat or enjoying dinner or making love. In the morning, during those few waking moments, he was still with me. Then reality would sink in, reminding me that this nightmare was my new normal.

Samantha sat down in the chair next to my desk, forcing me out of my daydream. She took a bowl of soup for herself, placing it on the corner of my desk, and nudged the other bowl closer to me. Steam curled above the minestrone, which had large chunks of potatoes, white beans, wilted greens and orecchiette, topped with gremolata, a café specialty.

"*Jalmukesumneda*," she said, Korean for "eat well." Samantha was why people came to our restaurant—for her delicious recipes and hospitality. The dish reminded me of the wonderful Italian wedding soup she'd made for my wedding reception. Even though I'd been a first-time bride, I was far too old to indulge in frills. All I'd wanted was a ceremony on the beach with close friends, delicious food and an open bar. I already had the most important part, my handsome groom. I'd chosen a simple, off the rack, white tea-length dress. Michael wore white pants and a linen shirt. Our witnesses were Samantha and Jasper, and Alex had gotten himself ordained to perform the ceremony. He flubbed a few parts, but we all just laughed.

It was the best day ever.

Some couples fight when it comes to weddings. I'd witnessed it first-hand more than once, as we'd hosted many receptions at the restaurant. My mom's old adage was true—relationship troubles were usually driven by religion, children or money, but Michael made sure our wedding was drama-free. Right after he proposed, he came home with legal documents, a prenuptial agreement. I hadn't even thought that far ahead, but he suggested we sign the papers because I had more assets than he did, with the house and restaurant. I'd never been worried, but I also appreciated the gesture.

In retrospect, the only hint of discord came when I said I wasn't changing my name. Sandoval had been my last name my whole life and I wasn't ready to give it up. Besides, people knew me by it. When I told Michael I didn't plan to change my name, the sparkle in his eyes dimmed and he became very quiet. We didn't have a fight, but I did feel like I'd hurt his feelings. Now, more than anything, I wished I'd taken his name.

Samantha buttered a piece of bread and placed it on the plate next to my soup bowl. She was being a sweet mother hen.

"How was your interview this morning?" she asked.

I let my spoon rest in the bowl. "Okay, I guess. I think he believes me, but he asks a lot of questions."

Her eyes widened. Samantha wouldn't make a good poker player. I could see the worry all over her face.

"What's wrong?" I asked.

"We have to go in tomorrow." Her voice was a whisper, although there was no one around to hear our conversation. "Why does he have to talk to us?"

"He's talking to everyone," I assured her. "It's just his protocol."

She nodded her head, but the small crease in her brow remained. "But we weren't even here. We don't know anything."

"He's going to talk to everyone who works at the restaurant, even Jasper, and he was in Miami."

The mention of Jasper made me recall Detective Grant's comment, about Jasper having two last names. Was it a simple switch from his mother's to his father's surname, and why hadn't Michael ever told me about the name change?

"You should eat," Samantha encouraged, "because I'm hungry."

I chuckled. Over time, I'd learned several Korean customs from Samantha. One was that it was impolite to eat faster than anyone else at the table. So if I didn't eat, she wouldn't.

"Don't blame me," she added. "Blame my Korean mother."

A thought occurred to me. "You did ancestry testing, didn't you?"

"I did. Why?"

"How'd it work?"

"It was simple. You spit into a tube and send it off, and then they return your ancestry profile. No surprise I'm half Korean, but my dad's side was from all over Europe. Are you thinking of doing it?"

I shook my head. Ancestry was different from paternity, and having Michael spit into a tube wasn't a possibility.

"I need you to keep this in confidence," I told her. I knew she would. I could trust Samantha with my life. "When I first met Michael, he said there was a chance that Jasper's mother had tried to trap him, and that Jasper wasn't his son."

She stared at me, intrigued. "Jasper may not be Michael's son? No way. They look too much alike. They even sound alike."

"Right?" I replied. "The detective just made me think about it earlier."

"Would that change things for you?" she asked. "If they weren't related?"

I considered her question. When I married Michael, Jasper became my stepson. That hadn't changed.

We ate in silence. I knew I could trust Samantha but felt like I'd carelessly opened a can of worms. If she slipped and told Alex, he might say something to Jasper. They were close.

"They have paternity tests at the drug store," she offered. "I'm not sure how they work, but I think you can do them with samples from a hairbrush."

"Please don't say anything," I begged.

"I promise," she vowed and we continued eating in silence.

The dinner crowd was even smaller than lunch, so we closed the restaurant early. I drove home with an ache in the pit of my stomach. How long would it be before the bad news subsided and people returned? As I passed by a CVS, I impulsively swerved into the parking lot. Once inside, I found the medical tests in the far corner. As Samantha had indicated, they had paternity tests done using a cheek swab. It was an impractical idea, especially since I didn't have Michael's saliva sample, but I purchased the test anyway and drove home.

10. Grant | Wednesday, July 7

I waited in my car outside the condo leasing office. A little before 8:00 a.m., Judy Fobbs pulled into her assigned parking spot. As she exited her car I approached, subpoena in hand. She seemed startled to see me, then slightly annoyed. I was probably disrupting her morning routine. She looked like the type to show up to work early, get her cup of coffee and organize her day.

"Hello, detective," she said, looking at the paper in my hand. She unlocked the front door and I helped her push it open. Rather than appreciating the gesture, she glanced at me sharply. Open the door, you're a chauvinist. Don't open the door, you're a pig. It was a no-win situation.

I stood back to give her a moment, but she got right to business, outstretching her arm to read the subpoena. I had written it to be broad, asking for any and all information regarding the owner of Brittany's condo.

"Do you want to look through the file?" she asked. "Or will you need copies?"

"I'll look through the file for starters."

Without saying anything more, she disappeared into a back office. Soon after, she returned with a manila folder labeled with the apartment number and handed it to me.

"Thank you," I said. "May I?" I pointed to the couch and coffee table in the greeting area.

She nodded, sat at her desk and continued with her morning routine.

I paged through the papers in the file and learned that the condo was owned by Hamilton Property Group. I knew the name. They owned several properties in the area. The condo was leased by a Joseph Ricci. Brittany Jones was also listed as an authorized occupant. Mr. Ricci's contact information was a P.O. box in Morristown, New Jersey, not too far from my parents' place. A copy of his driver's license showed his home address and basic stats: 5'10, 190 pounds, brown hair, green eyes. Given his date of birth, I calculated him to be fifty-six years old. From the maintenance man's description of an older man, I'd speculated that Brittany's roommate could've been

Michael Sinise, but this information led me to believe I was looking at someone else.

Additional papers showed a credit check done for the initial lease, which was dated over a year ago. The lease had been renewed five months ago for another year. The only car listed was a white Mini Cooper, Brittany's car, and the only emergency contact was Brittany Jones. The rest of the file had insignificant documents like maintenance records and the pest control schedule. I took the lease agreement, which also included Joseph Ricci's phone number, to Ms. Fobbs and asked if she'd make a copy. She managed a half-hearted smile, more likely because this was a sign I'd soon be on my way.

As I waited for the copy, I considered the possibilities. The most obvious one: this guy was married, probably had a family and was keeping Brittany on the side. Had she threatened to expose him to his wife? Then I thought about Brittany's final action, appearing at the restaurant. Was there a connection between Joseph Ricci and Julianna Sandoval?

I glanced at my watch. Jasper Sinise was due for his interview at 9:00 a.m. so I headed back to the station. There, I ran a background check on Joe Ricci. He had lived at the same home for over twenty years, had no criminal history and made his living amassing car dealerships in New Jersey. As I suspected, there was a Mrs. Ricci and three kids. Patti Ricci's Facebook page, which was public, revealed a big-haired socialite and proud mom. She and her husband spent their summers at backyard barbeques and watching their kids' baseball games. There were photos posted from a Fourth of July party, including a video of dad and the kids lighting sparklers. Mom shrieked as they chased her around the yard. In the footage, I witnessed a middle-aged family man, pot-bellied and balding, living a typical, upper-middle-class American life. His wife, who frankly looked out of his league, was certainly unaware that her husband was stepping out on her. This guy, who seemed to have a good thing, was about to screw it up.

I stopped and checked myself. I'd gone pretty far into the affair theory, but short of Brittany being a long-lost daughter or something strange like that, I was pretty sure I was seeing it right. I checked my watch—9:15 a.m. Jasper was late. I grabbed another cup of coffee as I researched Joseph Ricci's dealerships, which appeared to be doing well. When I'd exhausted as much as I could find through a cursory check, I called the number listed on the lease agreement. After a few rings, the voicemail kicked in, with a computerized voice stating the number and to leave a message. I hung up.

Another ten minutes passed, then twenty. I was going to have to track down that little asshole, Jasper. Just then, my office phone rang. It was the front desk clerk letting me know that my appointment had arrived. Nice of him to bother showing up—over half an hour late.

I walked to the front and opened the door to allow Jasper through. Immediately, I noticed his polo shirt. It was light blue with a shark emblem on the chest, the same style and brand as I'd found in Brittany's laundry basket. Sure, a lot of people wore Greg Norman golf shirts, but this seemed like more than a coincidence.

I held the door open as he eased past me. His hands were shoved deep into his pockets, forcing his shoulders to hunch forward awkwardly.

"I thought you weren't going to make it," I remarked casually.

"Sorry, man," he said. "I lost track of time."

As he passed, I observed his damp, shaggy hair and smelled fresh shampoo. He lost track of time all right—in his sleep.

After taking a few steps into the corridor, he stopped and looked back. "Where am I going?"

"Straight ahead," I replied, pointing forward. We passed the break room. I could have offered him water or coffee but didn't. Instead, I showed him to the same interview room that Julianna and I had used the day before. I pointed to the chair and said, "Have a seat."

Jasper sat down, leaned back and interlaced his fingers behind his head. "Wow, this is just like that TV show, *The First 48.*"

I'd seen this façade before—playing it cool, acting as if being in an interview room didn't faze him. I already knew he'd lied about being in Miami. Soon, I'd catch him in that lie. And now there was the similar shirt. Something was up with Jasper Sinise. I didn't know what it was yet, but there was definitely something.

For now, I needed to try to build rapport. As smug as this little shit was, and as much as I wanted to rattle him, I needed to break down that defensive guard he was pretending he didn't have.

"I won't keep you long," I said. "How have things been at the restaurant?"

He shrugged, as if the murder was no concern of his, then said,

"Well, the shooting is all people are talking about."

"I'm sure Julianna is glad to have you to lean on."

"Yeah, I stayed with her through closing last night. She was kind of jumpy."

Of course she was jumpy. What did this little prick expect?

"I'll probably end up having to close every night," he added, as if he were being a hero. Julianna was putting a roof over his head and giving him a stable job, and he acted like he was doing her a favor. I suppressed my urge to smack him.

"Hey, I appreciate you coming in," I began. "I know you weren't in town the night of the shooting, but I have to talk to everyone who's associated with the restaurant. It's just standard procedure. So what has Julianna told you about that night?"

He shrugged again. "She said she was closing up when some girl came in and got shot."

"Did she tell you anything else?"

"Naw, just that she didn't know how it happened because there was nobody else around."

"What did the girl want?" I asked.

"I don't know. I didn't know her."

I followed up, maintaining my poker face. "How did she know Julianna?"

"Who knows? Maybe she didn't. Maybe she was looking for money or something. There's a lot of people strung out on meth these days."

"True," I agreed. "Have you heard any of the other employees at the restaurant talking about what happened?"

"Sure. Why?"

He was playing "cooperative" without really being cooperative, but he'd already slipped twice without realizing it. For now, my goal was to keep him talking.

I continued, "I was just curious what the others were saying."

He furrowed his brows as if he was thinking deeply about my question. "Well, everybody's talking about it. Samantha keeps going on and on about how she and Alex shouldn't have left Julianna alone."

"Having additional witnesses would've been helpful," I said. "As you know, Julianna's our only witness. Obviously, I've interviewed her, but maybe she said something to you that she's forgotten. Could you walk me through what she told you when she called you Monday morning?"

"We didn't talk long. She said somebody was killed at the restaurant and to come home."

"What time did she call you?"

"I'm not sure. It was early. I was still asleep. We'd been out late the night before."

"You were down in Miami?" I asked.

"Yeah."

"Why were you down there?"

"It was the Fourth of July," he replied sarcastically, as if I'd never partied as a kid.

"Where'd you go?" I asked.

"Just around, mostly South Beach with my friends."

"You can give me the names and numbers of those friends?"

He flinched but agreed.

I slid a piece of paper and pen to him so he could write down that information, and then I continued the interview. "So Julianna called, told you what had happened and asked you to come back."

"Yeah. She was pretty upset so I got up, got my bag and hit the road."

"Hit the road," I repeated.

"Yeah, got an Uber."

And here we were, the implausible timeline. "You Ubered back from Miami?"

"No," he smirked. "I Ubered to the airport and got a flight. I rode down with my friends so I didn't have a way back since I was leaving before them."

Well, fuck. It was entirely feasible to fly back in less than four hours. The impossible timeline now might work, and my gut told me his story about flying would check out.

"That must've been expensive," I commented.

"Not really. The flight was half empty. The airport was dead." He chuckled. "I guess I shouldn't use the word, *dead*."

I suppressed my frustration. My trap had just evaporated. I handed him my card and asked him to forward copies of his flight and Uber receipts, which I was fairly certain he'd have.

Time to switch gears.

"Do you know of anyone who's had issues with Julianna?"

"Nope." He leaned back in his chair making the front legs come off the floor. Then he looked around the small room as if I were boring him.

"I know your family has been through a lot this year and I hate to mention it, but could anyone have been upset with your father?"

Jasper eased the chair forward, bringing the front legs to the floor. He sat upright and crossed his arms. "Look, some random slut getting shot has nothing to do with my dad."

"Yeah," I agreed. "I didn't mean any disrespect."

"Are we done here?" he asked, clearly agitated.

"Yes, I think so. Just need your travel receipts if you don't mind. Thanks for coming in."

He got up to leave.

"One last thing," I added. "On the flight you took back. What name will be on your flight record, Sinise or Kiely?"

"Sinise," he sneered. His glare could have bored a hole through me.

I escorted Jasper to the front reception and thanked him for coming in. Back at my desk, I called the Miami airport police and gave them Jasper's name and birthdate. They confirmed he was on an American Airlines morning flight that departed Miami at 9:01 a.m. and landed in Orlando at 10:08 a.m. Taking an Uber back to Ormond Beach easily would have put Jasper home by 11:30 a.m.

"Damn!" I said aloud.

Though the flight checked out, I was more convinced than ever that Jasper was somehow involved. During the interview, I'd asked what he thought Brittany wanted. He replied that he didn't know the girl. I never asked if he *knew* her—that was his deflection. Then he tried to steer me toward the shooting being a random crime by a girl who needed money for drugs, when I already knew Brittany Jones wasn't hurting for money. He'd called her a slut. If she were a stranger, he'd have no reason to disparage her. And finally, he'd flared up when I asked about his father. A normal reaction would have been one of sadness at the loss, but that wasn't how Jasper behaved. He'd immediately gotten defensive.

"What have you been up to, Jasper Sinise?" I asked the empty room. "Just what have you been up to?"

11. Julianna | Wednesday, July 7

My cell phone rang, waking me from a deep sleep. Although it was difficult to fall asleep at night, my best slumber always came during the morning hours. I sat up quickly, which made my head spin. I'd been sprawled diagonally across the king-sized bed, so I had to lunge to reach my phone on the nightstand.

When I was single, I used to toss about the bed in search of a cooler spot. For the last few years with Michael, I'd learned to keep to "my side." Now, for the first time since his disappearance, I'd reverted to my single-girl habit of taking over the entire bed. I didn't like it. As insignificant as it seemed, it was a small sign I was accepting that Michael was gone.

The call was from Ed Harrigan. I must have sounded groggy because he apologized for calling so early, although it was after 9:00 a.m. He spoke in that gravelly tone that comes with old age, asking me several times how I was doing. I could tell he didn't believe me when I said I was fine.

"I heard on the news about the girl who was shot at your restaurant."

There was no reproach in his tone, although it occurred to me that I should've called him, as a courtesy if nothing else. Ed had set up the LLC for the restaurant when my parents first opened it, and he'd advised us on everything from taxes to employee benefits.

"I'm sorry," I said. "I should have called you."

"What happened?"

"I don't know much at this point. The girl came in late, after closing, and was shot in the back while I was trying to get her to leave. The police have interviewed me a few times, but I didn't see anyone. I don't think they have many leads."

"Oh my," he replied. "If they ask to speak to you again, I want you to call me first."

"I don't think they will, but I appreciate it." I was about to thank him and say goodbye, but he continued.

"I have some news. Is this a good time?"

"Okay," I replied. He sounded quite serious.

"Julianna, I spoke with the court…about having Michael declared dead."

I took a deep breath, bracing myself for what would come next. Everything since Michael's disappearance had been like a slow-motion nightmare. First there was the search, a roller coaster of hope and despair. Then, after only a few days, the Coast Guard suspended the operation. I couldn't believe they were giving up so soon. I'd called Ed in a panic, asking for guidance. In the kindest way he could say it, he counseled that I couldn't afford to hire my own search team. It would bankrupt me.

I'd never felt so helpless.

Several months had passed with no news. Then Ed had asked if he could come to the house to speak with me and Jasper. As we sat in the living room, he'd advised on the process of having Michael declared dead. It had seemed too soon, but at the same time, I felt as if Michael had been gone for ages.

My concern was also for Jasper. Was he ready to have his father declared dead? What if he didn't agree? In fairness, he had just as much say in this decision as I did. But to my surprise, he'd agreed, even seemed relieved. I suppose Jasper had come to grips with reality sooner than I had. At the end of the meeting, I'd agreed to let Ed contact the court, though I wasn't sure I'd take any action.

Ed cleared his throat. "In order to petition the court to issue a death certificate, and without concrete proof, we'll need corroborating evidence."

"Concrete proof?" I asked.

"I don't mean to be indelicate, Julianna, but we don't have a body. Therefore, we'll have to submit corroborating evidence, like the records of the search. That would be a good start. Are you able to access that information from the charter company?"

I had no idea if Michael's employer had those records.

He continued, "From there, it will depend largely on the judge, who may grant the certificate immediately or we may have to wait."

"Why would we have to wait?" I asked.

"In cases of missing persons, they want to be sure the person is really…" He stopped himself.

I finished his sentence: "Dead." It was the first time I'd said it out loud.

"Yes, I'm afraid so. The court would not want the embarrassment of issuing a death certificate only to later find Michael alive. I don't mean to alarm you, but there are instances where the family has waited years before the court would take action. Granted, those typically have had suspicious circumstances." He cleared his throat again and continued. "I also wanted to tell you about my call with the insurance company, as that could be problematic."

"Problematic?" I stood from the bed, cell phone still to my ear, and walked into the bathroom. In front of the mirror, I looked at my reflection. My hair was a disheveled mess and my mascara left dark smudges under my eyes. I was wearing one of Michael's T-shirts—his smell lingered slightly on the fabric.

"As I said, I spoke with the insurance company," Ed continued. "Assuming the court issues the death certificate, they will likely do their own investigation, especially for a $2 million policy. They have a special investigations unit, SIU, that they use for cases like this. I wanted you to be informed because it could be years before they agree to pay out the policy, and they could contest it altogether."

"I see," I said and quickly walked back to my nightstand. I needed to find a pen and paper to write all of these details down. I'd never counted on Michael's life insurance. As long as the restaurant ran smoothly, we'd be okay.

Ed added, "I want you to be prepared for them to pry into every aspect of Michael's disappearance. They'll look at video footage at the airport, review the search protocols, interview the Coast Guard, you name it. You'll need to be ready for a very intrusive investigation. However, if there is a bright side, it may augment the search that you couldn't do on your own."

"I had no idea about all this," I said. "So what do I need to do?"

"Well, let's start at the beginning. Can you get documentation from Michael's company—his employment record, maintenance of the airplane, anything like that? We have some time, but the longer we wait, the more likely those kinds of documents will get deleted or lost. So I'd go ahead and collect them now if you can."

I was dumbfounded by the potential legal complications ahead of me. I thanked Ed, grateful that I had someone so meticulous on my side.

"It's my pleasure, Julianna. Your dad was a good man and a dear friend. Anything I can do to help you, I will. I promise you that."

Dad was gone, but with friends like Ed around, he was still helping me.

I washed away my tears in the shower, then dressed and drove
north to Flagler Airport. Island Connections, the charter company
where Michael worked was located in a small building positioned at
the edge of the taxiway. The planes were secured next to the building behind a locked fence. When I opened the door, a burst of cold
air greeted me from a window air conditioner blowing at full speed.
It was loud but effective, making the small reception room ice-cold.

Chet Huff was sitting behind the counter. Average height and
very skinny, he perpetually had a cigarette dangling from his lips. His
skin was tan and weathered and his dark eyes were set close together.
When he saw me, his expression changed from surprise to concern.

"Julianna," he said. "Wow. What brings you by? If I'd known you
were coming…I have to leave soon."

I glanced at the whiteboard behind the counter that showed the
flight schedule. There was one flight out late that afternoon and
nothing else. He saw me scan the board and his face turned red. I
wasn't a pilot, but I knew how to read the schedule, plus Michael
had taught me a lot about flying. I'd never been in the Caravan,
his work plane, but he'd often rented smaller ones like a Piper or
Beechcraft for us to take on trips. On Mondays, our day off, if we
weren't boating, we'd fly somewhere for lunch. Michael called it the
$100 hamburger because the trip cost more than the meal, but it was
always an adventure.

"It's okay," I said. "I won't take up much of your time. I just
spoke with my lawyer. He needs me to collect some paperwork…
for Michael's life insurance."

I paused, realizing I'd driven to Flagler on autopilot. I probably
should've called ahead instead of catching Chet off guard. I'd been
given a task by Ed and had set out to accomplish it, without really
thinking it through.

"What kind of paperwork do you need?" he asked.

I shrugged. "Anything you have for the insurance company, like
Michael's employment file and the maintenance records for the plane."

Chet removed the cigarette from his mouth and crushed it
repeatedly in a glass ashtray. "I'm not sure it's what you'll need, but I
have files for the plane. I spent weeks collecting paperwork for our

insurance. Every time I gave them what they asked for, they'd ask for something else. It's a stall tactic."

He retreated to his office and returned carrying a banker's box, which he heaved onto the counter. "You can borrow this to make copies, but I'll need it back. Do you want me to carry it to your car?"

"Thanks. I'd appreciate that." I didn't expect this trip to be so efficient. Of course, it made sense that Chet would have compiled the needed documents for his insurance. He was down a plane. I had no idea what a Caravan was worth, but it had to be millions.

I turned to leave, but he wasn't following me. Had he changed his mind? Was he afraid I'd lose the files?

"Look," he said. "Are you sure you're ready for this?"

"Ready?"

He patted the lid of the box. "There's video footage of Michael's preflight. Everything's normal, but it's the last footage of him alive."

I didn't know that footage existed. When I didn't reply, he pointed to a corner of the ceiling. "We have cameras on the roof taking security video of the planes. It also captured Michael before takeoff."

I pictured Michael walking around the plane, doing the preflight inspection we'd done dozens of times together. I didn't think it would be disturbing. If anything, it might be comforting to watch. I'd already played and replayed our videos. Every day, I'd scroll through our photos on my phone. I'd listened to his voicemail over and over. This couldn't be any worse.

"I'll be okay," I assured him.

With some hesitation, Chet carried the box to my car and loaded it into the back seat. I was due at the restaurant soon but called Samantha to let her know I'd be late. Instead of going there, I drove home, took the box inside and hoisted it on the kitchen table. On the top of the stack of papers, I found a CD labeled "Preflight." I sat down, turned on my laptop and inserted the disk.

The footage, taken from the vantage point of the roof, showed the fenced-in lot full of planes. It looked like a still shot until I noticed a flag billowing in the background. Then I saw Michael approaching the Caravan carrying his gear bag. He walked with his typical confident yet casual swagger.

I lifted my hand and brushed my fingertips against the monitor. If only I could go back to that morning. If only he hadn't taken that fare. I felt a tug in my heart because I knew I could've prevented it. I could have kept him safe.

Michael opened the pilot-side door, pulled down the collapsible ladder and climbed inside. I couldn't see what he was doing, but assumed he was checking the gauges, the battery, and the fuel and oil levels. He jumped out of the plane and felt along the fuselage to the right wing. I could see him inspecting the wing, ensuring that the bolts and nuts were tight, and that the flaps were functioning. He knelt down by the landing gear and examined the tire tread and brake pads. Next he proceeded to the empennage, testing the movement of the rudder, the elevator and the stabilizers. Everything looked normal; he conducted the inspection exactly how he'd taught me.

Suddenly, to my surprise, Jasper appeared in the frame, walking toward the plane. Jasper had driven Michael to the airport so he could keep the car, not having one himself. I watched as Michael opened the cowling to inspect the engine. Next, he ran his fingers over each of the propeller blades, looking for any rough edges or cracks. At the same time, Jasper conducted the preflight on the passenger side of the plane.

As Michael took fuel samples from the tanks, testing for impurities, Jasper climbed up on the passenger side wing to check the fuel level. My stepson unscrewed the fuel cap, looked inside the tank and seemed to fumble with the cap before replacing it. Michael checked the fuel on the pilot-side and then climbed down from the wing. They talked briefly before Michael climbed into the cockpit. Jasper stepped back from the plane as Michael started the engine.

I spoke out load to Michael, "Wait. Aren't you going to check the fuel on the passenger side?"

It didn't matter if someone else inspected the fuel levels, Michael always checked the tanks and caps on both sides himself. Early on, he'd explained this precaution to me by showing how the fuel cap could be seated improperly. It could appear to be tight, but if the tab was flipped in the wrong direction, it could leak, which would siphon gas from the tank. That's why he always examined the fuel levels and caps himself.

Always.

I watched him taxi away and out of range of the camera. Jasper was also out of range, presumably headed back to the car.

"Wait, Michael!" I shouted at my computer. "Check the fuel cap!" The video stopped.

I sat, frozen. Was it possible that Jasper had improperly seated the fuel cap? He knew the basics of conducting a preflight. Michael had taught him, but Jasper wasn't nearly as meticulous as his father. If the cap had been loose, Michael could've lost half of his fuel. The Cessna Caravan was a high-wing plane, which meant Michael might not have seen the fuel leaking out of the top of the wing.

But if that *had* happened, Michael would've seen the fuel levels drop on the gauges. He would've had time to react, or to at least place a distress call. The evidence from the search indicated that he'd never made any calls. It was as if he'd instantly vanished.

I looked at the clock. I wanted to watch the video again, but I was already late. Lunch would be in full swing soon, and it wasn't fair to ask Samantha to juggle both the kitchen and the dining room. I closed my laptop, grabbed my purse and headed for my car. During the drive, I couldn't erase the image of Jasper fooling with the fuel cap.

When I arrived at the restaurant, my guilt for leaving the crew alone was replaced with anxiety. Only a quarter of the tables were full. Wednesday lunch was normally busy but not today. This was the second day in a row the restaurant felt almost deserted. I took a deep breath, wondering how long this dry spell would last.

Jasper and Alex were joking behind the bar, apparently mixing up a new concoction. I didn't forbid them to drink on the job, but I expected them to remain professional. Now they were on the verge of getting rowdy, which was not the image I wanted for Café Lily. I walked toward them. Alex immediately recognized my disapproval and quickly put the liquor bottles back on the shelf. Without a play-mate, Jasper settled down as well. I motioned for him to come to the side of the bar, out of earshot of everyone else.

"I have a question about the day Michael disappeared," I said.

Jasper's face sobered instantly.

"You drove him to the airport, right?"

"Yeah," he said.

"Did you notice anything unusual?"

"Like what?" he asked.

"I don't know. Maybe the way he did the preflight?"

As a pilot, Michael preached about following his checklists. He was dogmatic about verifying the fuel levels himself. Anyone who flew with him, including Jasper, knew that.

Jasper's reply sent me into utter shock.

"I didn't see the preflight," he said. "I just dropped him off and came home."

I stared at him, trying to contain my astonishment, knowing this was a blatant lie. Jasper walked back to the bar and tried to entice Alex to continue their games. I should've confronted him, but his reply had left me speechless. Instead, I retreated to my office to collect my thoughts. Why would Jasper lie about the preflight? Obviously, he didn't know I'd seen the video. Then it hit me: Maybe he realized what he'd done. Had it occurred to him, after the fact, that he could've misplaced the fuel cap? Did he understand the gravity of that mistake? Was he silently carrying enormous guilt, something he'd never be able to confirm or refute? Jasper had always seemed more ready to accept that Michael was gone. Could this be the reason?

From out of nowhere, Brittany Jones's warning played in my head. *He's not who you think he is.*

A second thought occurred to me. Could Jasper have misplaced the cap deliberately or dropped something explosive into the fuel tank? Had he actually sabotaged the plane? But why? Why would he do something like that to his father?

Not who you think he is. Did she mean Jasper wasn't Michael's son? Did Jasper know that truth already?

I reached in my purse and pulled out the paternity test. Without hesitating, I called the 800-number. A woman in customer service came on the line.

"I have a question about your paternity test," I said. "If the potential father is unavailable, but I have his toothbrush and hairbrush, would either of those work?"

"The toothbrush might work," she replied. "We'd have to do a viability test first to see if the sample is usable. If it is, we can proceed with the paternity test."

"And how long would that take?"

"A few days. We need you to wrap the toothbrush in paper and send it to our lab. Don't use plastic, as mold can grow in a sealed plastic bag. The viability test will cost an additional $150, non-re-fundable."

"And how would I get the results?"

"I can email you a form to submit the samples with all of the details. You'll create a private account with a user ID and password. Once the test is complete, we'll send you an email to log-in and check the results."

"And that will tell me the likelihood of a father-son paternity match?"

"Yes. It will either be 0% or 99%."

"It's that black or white?" I asked.

"Correct. If the sample is viable, the results will be quite clear."

I gave the woman my email address and intentionally left the restaurant before Jasper that evening, so I could go home and col-lect his and Michael's toothbrushes. I carefully wrapped Michael's toothbrush in tissue paper, labeled it and placed it in an envelope. As crazy as it sounded, I'd miss seeing that toothbrush sitting in its holder every morning. It had been a part of our life together, but I'd have to sacrifice it to solve the bigger mystery.

Then I crept into Jasper's bedroom, careful not to disturb any-thing. I doubted he would notice a new toothbrush, but I replaced his with one in the same color and style, just to be safe. An email from the company was already in my inbox with the instructions on packaging and shipping the samples.

I wrapped Jasper's toothbrush and packed it with Michael's. With the envelope ready, I drove to the FedEx store. If the test was done as quickly as the woman indicated, assuming the samples were viable, I'd have the results within a week.

When I returned home, Jasper wasn't there. He often stayed at a friend's place, and for the first time, I preferred he was gone.

Before going to bed, I locked my bedroom door and jammed a chair under the knob. I reached inside my nightstand and put my can of pepper spray within easy reach. It was absurd, barricading myself in my own bedroom. I'd promised Michael I would take care of Jasper if anything ever happened to him. At the time, it had been an easy promise because I'd never expected it to come true. I'd expected us to grow old together. What would he think of me now, suspicious of his own son—if Jasper actually was his son?

12. Grant | Wednesday, July 7

Samantha Cobb and Alex Walker were due in for their interviews that morning. As I waited for them to arrive, I pulled the restaurant surveillance video from my case file. Watching video was worse than watching paint dry, but it had to be done. The chief popped her head in my door, and I gave her a quick update. She didn't ask any questions, but said, "Keep at it. Let me know if you get any breaks." She started to walk away, but then poked her head back in my office and said, "Grant, I'm glad you decided to come on board."

I thought she'd eyed my stack of boxes, but maybe not. No time for that right now. I put the surveillance CD in my computer and backed it up to 12:30 a.m., thirty minutes before the 9-1-1 call. The view of the parking lot was the same until 12:43 a.m., when two people left the restaurant, presumably Samantha and Alex. They walked to a dark sedan parked on the far side of the lot and drove away. Referring to my notes, their departure aligned with the timeline Julianna had given me.

Another fourteen minutes passed before the video showed anything new. Then, a white Mini Cooper pulled into the lot and parked by the front door. Someone got out of the car on the driver's side. From the angle of the camera on the restaurant roof, I could only see the top of the person's head. The long blonde hair and type of car led me to believe it was Brittany, and that she hadn't stowed away inside the restaurant. She walked out of the camera's field of view before she reached the front door. Unfortunately, the camera was pointed to capture the parking lot, but not the restaurant's entrance.

About a minute later, I glimpsed a shadow at the top of the screen. I couldn't see an image, just a slight change in the light shining down from the streetlamp. I backed up the video and watched it again. There was definitely a shadow—likely my killer following Brittany to the restaurant. Either he was lucky and avoided the camera or he knew the range and how to evade it. I guessed the latter, which meant the killer was familiar with the restaurant. I reminded myself not to get tunnel vision, because the list of people who knew the restaurant's surveillance system was small.

The video was still again for another eleven minutes, until it showed blue police lights flashing in the parking lot. The first responders had arrived on scene, but I didn't see anyone on the video yet, which meant the officers were waiting for backup. A few minutes later, two officers approached the door. I could only see the tops of their heads until just before they entered the restaurant. I presumed it was Phelps and Jenkins.

What was curious was what I *didn't* see in those preceding eleven minutes: the shooter leaving the scene.

I backed up the video to 12:15 a.m., before Samantha and Alex left, and scanned a fifteen-minute interval. Nothing on the screen changed. Then I backed it up to midnight and watched another fifteen minutes. It wasn't until around 11:30 p.m. that I saw a few employees leave, probably the last of the kitchen and waitstaff. Between 11:15 and 11:30 p.m., a few customers departed. I jotted notes on each fifteen-minute interval as I compared them to witness accounts, which seemed to line up.

The night of the shooting, Hall had canvassed the neighborhood for any other surveillance. There was only one camera nearby, at a high-end boutique in the lot next to Café Lily. Hall had called the store owner and requested their surveillance video, but we didn't have anything back yet. He'd put the owner's contact information in the case file, so I called her myself. The woman's cheerful hello turned serious as soon as she realized I was a detective inquiring about video footage. She assured me that she'd called her alarm company and was still waiting. I took their contact information and was about to call them when my intercom buzzed from the front reception. Samantha Cobb and Alex Walker had arrived.

I put away my file, walked to the front lobby and thanked them for coming in.

"Samantha," I said. "I'll start with you, if you'll please follow me."

She froze and looked at Alex.

He chimed in, "We were together the whole time. Can't we both meet with you?"

"Sorry. Afraid not. Hang tight. It won't be long."

I left Alex in the front lobby, although it took Samantha a few seconds before she stopped looking in his direction. Like with Julianna, I took Samantha to the small interview room next to the break room. On the way, I offered her water or coffee. At first she declined, but then asked for water so I doubled back and grabbed a cold plastic bottle from the refrigerator.

As we sat down, she unscrewed the bottle cap and took several swigs of water. She replaced the cap and started crinkling the thin, plastic bottle. She looked around the room and swallowed hard a few times. Something about this interview was making her very nervous.

The background check I'd done on Samantha Cobb indicated that she was forty-nine years old. Sitting across from her, I wouldn't have put her a day over thirty-five. She had smooth skin and her black hair was pulled into a ponytail that made her look young.

She sat at the front edge of her chair, her back as straight as a rod. Maybe having Alex here would have put her at ease, but I couldn't interview witnesses together. It'd be too easy for them to build on each other's stories instead of telling their own distinct version of events.

"How are things going at the restaurant?" I asked.

Her forehead creased. Looking past me, she said, "It's slow."

I dug deeper. "How's Julianna doing?"

Her eyes finally met mine. She stopped fidgeting with the water bottle, put her hand in her lap and said, "She's putting on a good front, like she always does."

"How so?"

Samantha took a deep breath. "I've known Julianna a long time. She's a strong person and she's been through a lot. She just buckles down and gets through it."

"How long have you known her?"

"I came to work for Norman and Frances, her parents, a year after they opened the restaurant. Julianna was fresh out of college and had come home to learn the business, so we started working at Café Lily at about the same time."

"What'd she study in college?"

Samantha reached up and pulled out a round clasp from her ponytail. She stroked her hair and refastened it. "Julianna studied business and something to do with hospitality." She paused and looked up and to the right. "Hospitality management, that's it."

"She always planned to take over the family business?"

Samantha nodded.

"So you weren't the original chef at Café Lily when it opened?"

She shook her head. "No. When they opened the restaurant, a family friend was the head chef, but it didn't work out. So Norm took over and taught me."

"What happened with the family friend?"

"I'm not quite sure."

Her reply was hesitant. I waited.

"At first, I thought it was a conflict about the restaurant," she explained. "I assumed he and Norm disagreed on how to run the business. I'm not like that. I stick to the kitchen, which is why Julianna and I work so well together. She handles the business and I take care of the food."

She reached for the water bottle and started crinkling it again. Just when Samantha seemed to be relaxing, something had set her off. Maybe she was lying about her amicable relationship with Julianna. Or was there more to the story about this family friend?

I remained quiet. The second hand on the wall clock ticked loudly. I counted the clicks and waited.

She broke the silence. "But then, when I was going to take some vacation, I suggested he fill in for me. It made sense because he knew the place. Norm wouldn't hear of it. He didn't want the guy anywhere near Frances or Julianna. It always made me wonder if there was something off about him, or maybe there was some connection to Lily. I don't really know. It was just a feeling."

And there it was. I knew she'd say more if I stayed quiet. What I didn't expect was this turn in the conversation about the family friend...and who was Lily?

"Who's Lily?" I asked.

"Oh, right. You wouldn't know about her. Norm and Frances had a daughter before Julianna. She went missing when she was fifteen. I never knew her, but they kept her memory alive in little ways. They named the restaurant for her, and Frances created her own version of Bananas Foster called 'The Yellow Lily'. Every Sunday, we'd take the buffet leftovers to the local women's shelter. I think they started doing it in the hopes they might find her, but now it's done more in her memory."

"Any idea what happened to her?"

"No," she sighed. "No one knows. That was the hardest part for them. People speculated that she ran away. No disrespect, but that's what the police thought. I don't think anyone really looked for her, except Frances and Norman. They'd been having some problems with her, you know, typical teenage rebellion stuff, but they were sure she hadn't run away."

"Do you remember the chef's name?"

"Keith, or maybe it was Kevin. It started with a 'K'."

"Last name?"

She shook her head. "Sorry, I don't remember."

"How old was he?"

"Oh, he was around their age. He'd be in his late seventies now."

"You think there was a connection between this family friend and their daughter's disappearance?"

"Maybe," she shrugged.

"What were Frances and Norman like?"

Her face brightened for the first time since she'd sat down. "Oh, they were the kindest, warmest people. Julianna likes to tell the story of her first date when she was fifteen years old. It wasn't with a boy—it was with Norman. He asked her out. They both got dressed up. He brought her to a nice restaurant, opened the car door, pulled out her chair for her and even ordered for her. At the end of the meal, he took her hand, kissed it and declared that she'd been on her first date. Norman explained that he wanted her to know how she should expect to be treated by a man."

All the while Samantha was talking, she looked up and to the right, as if she were watching the date in her mind. Throughout my career in investigations, I'd learned that when witnesses were remembering and telling the truth, they usually did that.

She continued, "What Norman did was sweet, but it might explain why Julianna stayed single for so long. What man could compare to her dad? And he was…"

Samantha stopped herself.

"Was what?" I asked.

Her eyes darted from one end of the table to the other. She must have felt she was divulging too much, not that it would affect my case.

"Let me guess," I said. "He was overprotective?"

She looked at me. "Yes, but he meant well. I guess after losing Lily, he wasn't going to let Julianna out of his sight. She's a grown woman, but in some ways, she's still like a little girl."

"Her parents never met Michael?" I asked.

She shook her head. "No. It's too bad. They would've liked him. Finally, she found someone who treated her as well as her father had." Then the brightness in Samantha's face dimmed. "But he's gone now, too."

"What was he like?"

"Well, if her dad set expectations for a first date, Michael sure exceeded them. He was a pilot, you know, so on their first date he flew her to Savannah for lunch."

"Quite a first date," I commented.

"That was Michael, always up for an adventure. Julianna can be so serious. He made her more carefree. And it was good that she finally had 'her person.' It's just not fair."

Something buzzed. It was Samantha's phone, which was in her bag. It vibrated a few more times before she could stop it. She glanced at the screen and then tucked it away. My guess was it was Alex, checking in. She reached for the water and, with one last swig, finished the bottle.

"Would you like another one?" I asked.

"No thanks. Will we be much longer?"

"No, I shouldn't need much more of your time," I told her. "I know we spoke briefly on the phone, but the reason I asked you here in person is that you may know something that could help us solve this case." Realizing that her connection with Julianna was genuine, I added, "I'm sure it would bring Julianna peace of mind, too. Can you walk me through your day on July fourth, even before you went to work?"

Samantha sat up straight again, and described her day with some prompting from me. I learned that she got up around 8:00 a.m. and was at the restaurant by 9:00 a.m. for the usual Sunday brunch. With a standard buffet, the cooks didn't need much supervision. When I asked her if there had been any problems that day, the only thing she could think of was an unhappy customer who thought the prime rib was overcooked. Dinner had been busy but ran smoothly because there was a limited, fixed menu.

When Samantha was describing the earlier part of her day, she seemed calm and unconcerned. Her descriptions weren't overly detailed but provided enough information to summarize her activities. When she got to the part about leaving the restaurant that night, her demeanor changed. She became overly detailed in her descriptions and she fidgeted with her ponytail so much that I thought she was going to pull out half of her hair.

"All of the servers left, so it was just me, Alex and Julianna. Julianna wanted to stay behind and finish up some paperwork. Normally, we'd stay with her and all leave together, but she insisted we go home. We left and she locked up behind us. Alex said we needed to get gas, but I said we could do that later because I was tired. So we went straight home. I parked in the garage and went inside. I took a shower and then Alex took one. I started a load of laundry. Then we got into bed and watched an episode of Colbert on the DVR. Lady Gaga was the guest. I wanted a cup of tea, so Alex went downstairs and made it for me. He drank a beer and then we went to sleep."

Samantha leaned back in her chair, spent from the timeline she'd just rattled off in nearly one breath. All the while she'd been looking at the floor. Something was definitely up.

"So you drove home?" I asked.

She nodded. I waited.

"Alex doesn't have a car. Well, he has one he's repairing, but it's kind of in pieces in the garage."

"How long have you and Alex been together?" I asked.

Her eyes widened.

I asked again, "You and Alex, how long have you been dating?"

"Uhm, seven years."

"You seem unsure."

Her head tilted down.

"Samantha," I said with a stern but quiet tone, "why don't you go ahead and tell me what you don't want me to know. Because I might already know it."

She became a statue. Back in Daytona, we used to call this "possum pose." If you don't move or speak, maybe I'll forget that you're sitting right in front of me.

I added, "You know, part of a murder investigation involves running criminal background checks on everyone—you, Julianna, the servers, Alex…"

Her dark, almond-shaped eyes widened. "You know about Alex?"

"What do you know about Alex?" I asked.

"He got in a little trouble a while back." She spoke so quietly I could hardly hear her.

"Committing fraud at his prior job, which also happened to be a restaurant, is not 'a little trouble.' Does Julianna know?"

This time her response was almost unintelligible. "Would you please let us tell her?"

"I suggest you do it sooner rather than later, because I'll be talking to Julianna about my interviews."

Samantha's phone buzzed again.

"Tell Alex to sit tight," I said, not hiding my annoyance.

With that, she silenced the phone.

"Look," I said. "I know you and Julianna are practically family to each other. I know you care about her. This could have turned out much worse for her. If you know anything else, I need you to just tell me."

"I don't know anything else. I swear! And Alex hasn't done anything like that since he's been at Café Lily. He'd never betray Julianna. She's been so good to him."

I'd exhausted what Samantha had to tell me, so I walked her back to the front lobby. Alex shot to his feet the instant I opened the door. He rushed to her. "Are you okay?" he asked.

"I'm fine," she told him.

I watched the unspoken communication that occurs between lovers. Then I looked expectantly at Alex, who pushed past Samantha and said, "Let's get this over with."

I held the lobby door open and watched him march determinedly down the corridor. He wore flip flops, cargo shorts and a loose-fitting T-shirt, easily passing for a street bum or spring breaker. Eventually he stopped when he realized he didn't know where he was going. I caught up with him by the breakroom and offered him something to drink. He declined so we went into the interview room.

He took a chair and sat down, so I decided to mess with him a little.

"I need you to sit in this chair," I said, pulling out the other chair. The camera covered the entire room, so it didn't matter where he sat, but I enjoyed making him move. We were way past the point of trying to build rapport.

Alex huffed, got up and switched chairs. He sat at the edge of the seat with his feet planted apart. His palms were on his knees and he leaned forward like he was ready to make a tackle. Unlike Samantha, who *looked* young for her age, this guy *acted* young for his age.

"You said this wasn't going to take long," Alex complained.

"We had a lot to talk about."

"We need to get back to the restaurant."

"Samantha's free to go," I replied.

He ignored my offer for her to leave. Instead, he inched the chair forward, leaned back and crossed his ankle over his knee, nearly putting his exposed foot on the table. He laced his fingers in his lap and smirked.

Alex would need a different approach than the one I used with Samantha.

"Tell me about what happened at Kelly's Pub," I said.

His face flashed with confusion, followed quickly by anger. "What does that have to do with anything?"

"I'm getting background information for a homicide investigation," I replied. "I'm looking into everybody and everything."

I studied his face. His first thought was probably to deny any wrongdoing, but he knew that wouldn't fly. I already had the arrest record and he'd just acknowledged it by asking why it mattered. His next step would likely be to downplay the arrest, which was just what he tried to do.

"Look, man, that was years ago. The other servers were doing it, too, but I'm the one they blamed. And I paid every one of those people back. Every dime. I didn't have to, but I did. Did they bother to mention that?"

I was intrigued by his sudden turnabout, from being angry and defensive to openly discussing his past transgressions. He'd opened a chink in his armor.

"Samantha said things are pretty slow at the restaurant. How are the female staff holding up after the shooting?"

"They're scared. Me and one of the guys walked all the girls to their cars last night. I'll be staying with Samantha and Julianna every night from here on out."

"Last night was pretty uneventful?" I asked.

"Yeah, it was slow, but what do you expect?"

"I know Julianna has been through a lot, with Michael missing and now this."

He didn't comment.

"Did you know Michael well?" I asked.

"Not really. His attention was always on Julianna."

"What about Jasper?"

"Jasper's cool. We hang out sometimes."

It made sense that Alex and Jasper would get along. They were closer in age and maturity level, which made me question why he was with Samantha, or rather why she was with him.

I asked Alex to walk me through his day, which he did. He'd dropped Samantha off at the restaurant, gone to the gym, showered and changed there, and then headed back to the restaurant. Sunday brunch was his easy day because they mostly served mimosas and Bloody Mary cocktails, so he had fewer types of drinks to mix. After brunch, he'd taken the leftovers to the homeless shelter alone because Samantha was busy getting ready for dinner. He'd gone to a friend's house and watched some baseball, then returned to the restaurant to prepare for dinner. I took the friend's name and contact information, although I expected it to check out.

Unlike Samantha, who had easy tells, Alex looked directly at me the entire time he spoke. He didn't vary his pace and didn't move.

"How'd the rest of the night go?" I asked.

He shrugged. "It was packed. Good night for tips. We were selling a lot of bottles and the bar seating was full."

"Any issues?"

"Nah, everyone was in a good mood."

"What time did you close?"

"We took our last customer around ten. I still had a few strays at the bar at eleven, but when I started wiping the counter, they got the hint."

"What time did you actually lock up?"

"A little after eleven, I think."

"When did you leave?"

"Samantha and I left around 12:45. We went straight home, even though we needed to get gas."

"Did you do anything else that night?"

"We both took showers. She did some laundry and then we watched an episode of *Late Night* I'd recorded."

While their descriptions of events should have matched, the details were too identical and too detailed. Next, I was pretty sure he was going to tell me he had a beer and she had tea.

Not revealing that I wasn't buying it, I said, "I like Colbert. Also a fan of Kimmel. You ever watch him?"

"Sometimes, but Samantha likes Colbert better."

"Did you watch anything else that night?"

"No. I had a beer and I made Samantha some tea and then we went to sleep."

And there it was, the rehearsed detail I'd expected. I asked, "Who was on Colbert?"

"Lady Gaga."

"She did an interview or just sang?"

Up to now, his answers had been at the tip of his tongue, with a definitive cadence. With my last question, he paused and his mouth gaped open. Finally, he found an answer. "I don't know. I must have fallen asleep before she came on."

He was lying. I just needed to figure out why. What were Alex and Samantha hiding?

There was no point sitting through more of his bullshit. This interview was over. I politely thanked Alex, shook his hand and walked him to the lobby. Samantha's eyes zeroed in on her boyfriend as soon as we entered the room. With him in front of me, I couldn't see if he made a gesture or mouthed something, but her expression changed from questioning to relieved. Another silent exchange passed between them.

What they didn't realize is that they had not aced their interviews. Instead of dispelling suspicion, they were forcing me to follow a new trail. I'd start by tracking their cell phones the night of the murder.

13. Julianna | Thursday, July 8

I watched as the little girl was swept away from the loading area in the small yellow boat. Once she realized she was being whisked downstream, she began to scream hysterically, but her high-pitched voice was muffled by the crashing water.

She screamed until my throat was raw. It was me screaming, me in the boat. I gripped the sides and frantically searched for help. I was surrounded by ocean with no land in sight. Salty mist sprayed into my face and huge waves swelled and crashed around me. At any minute, my tiny craft would capsize and I'd be thrown into the water.

What if there were sharks?

I scanned under the surface when I saw a large object in the dark blue depths. At first I thought it was a whale, but it was perfectly still. It had an oblong body and symmetrical fins.

Not fins.

Wings.

Airplane wings.

I leaned over the side of the boat so I could get a better look, nearly plunging headfirst into the turbulent water. Inside the cockpit, a dark silhouette of a man's head and shoulders leaned against the broken glass window. He wasn't moving. He wasn't breathing. I strained to see his face, but I already knew.

I jolted awake, gasping for air and my heart pounding. I shut my eyes and tried to replay the dream, but the more I strained to recall it, the more the fragments disappeared. One image, however, did not fade—Michael's lifeless body, trapped in the cockpit of the plane at the bottom of the ocean.

He'd made a mistake, not checking the fuel tanks himself. What I didn't know was the extent of Jasper's involvement. I could understand an accident, even forgive it, but Jasper had lied about the preflight. Was he hiding his mistake, or was there foul play?

I slowly got out of bed and put my ear to the bedroom door, listening for sounds of anyone else in the house. All was quiet so I removed the make-shift barricade and crept down the hall to Jasper's bedroom. His door was open and the bed was still made. Apparently, he'd spent the night away again. I wanted to talk to Michael, to share what I'd learned and ask for his advice, but obviously I couldn't.

Impulsively, I called the only person I thought would understand. I didn't explain why I wanted him to come over and he didn't ask.

About twenty minutes later, Detective Grant stood at my front door. He quickly scanned me from head to toe like he was looking for something askew. I invited him in. He took a single step inside my house and stopped, surveying the room as if looking for someone. Maybe my cryptic request had made him think I was in danger. In hindsight, I probably should've explained more over the phone.

I offered him a cup of coffee, which he gladly accepted. We sat at my kitchen table. My laptop was open with the CD from the pre-flight inserted and ready to play.

"What's on your mind?" he asked.

I relayed the details of my attorney's call and how I'd collected evidence from Michael's employer, including the preflight video. As I played the video for him, I explained the process, including the part where Jasper checked the fuel tanks. At that point, I paused the video and described how the fuel caps had to be seated just right or they could pop open. Then I shared how Jasper denied being there altogether.

"You're saying Jasper claimed he wasn't at the airport?"

I shook my head. "No. He said he dropped Michael off. He doesn't know I have this video."

"Could you have misunderstood him?"

"No. I specifically asked about the preflight."

He leaned back and rubbed his chin. "Wouldn't the Coast Guard have questioned Jasper?"

"They did," I confirmed. "But I don't know what he told them. All I know is that he lied to me."

He took another sip of coffee and carefully placed the mug back on the coaster. Finally, he asked, "You think this is connected to Brittany's murder?"

"Well, I don't know, but he lied," I replied. "If he lied about this, maybe he's lying about other things."

The detective leaned forward. "I know you want answers. I do, too, but Jasper's alibi during the shooting checks out. He was in Miami."

Without hesitating, I made my case, something I'd been thinking about since Jasper's lie. "He could've shot her at one in the morning, then driven to Miami in time to catch an early flight back."

"True," he said, without skipping a beat. "But his cell phone pinged from Miami at the time of the shooting and two of his friends confirmed he was with them."

His response surprised me. I had no idea he was checking alibis so thoroughly, but of course, he would. I must have looked like a paranoid idiot. Obviously, Detective Grant was doing a thorough investigation. If he suspected Jasper was the shooter, he would've told me. He wouldn't let me continue living with someone he deemed dangerous.

Feeling self-conscious, I searched for a task, anything to move on from this awkward conversation. I stood, walked over to the coffee pot and refilled the detective's cup. When I sat back down at the table, I could feel his eyes on me.

"Can I ask you something?" he said. His hands were clasped together and resting on the table.

"I suppose."

"We've talked a few times and you've never mentioned any suspicion of Jasper, until now."

I waited for the question, but he didn't say anything further. "That was stupid of me," I replied. "You've obviously checked everyone's alibis."

He shook his head. "How you feel is never stupid. I was just wondering what's changed."

I looked at a framed photo on the fireplace mantel. It was of me, Michael and Jasper, taken by Samantha at the restaurant. I tried to pinpoint what exactly had changed. Jasper had become distant the last few months, spending more nights out than at home. But he was twenty-one. He had every right to do as he pleased. There was the name change, which came as a total surprise, and left me feeling slightly betrayed that neither of them had told me. And lastly, the one thing I couldn't get out of my mind, was the blatant lie about the preflight. All those things were starting to make me concerned. But now that Detective Grant had exonerated Jasper, what did I have to worry about?

"I guess I'm just uneasy. There's a shooter on the loose and we don't know who or why," I finally replied.

We sat in silence. I glanced at his coffee cup that was still full. Now that I'd shown Detective Grant the video and it had no relevance to his case, there wasn't much else to discuss. I thought he would be anxious to get back to work, but he didn't leave. I didn't mind. Sitting with him was comforting.

At last he spoke. "Do you feel unsafe with Jasper living here?"

I blinked. His question was so blunt. Truth be told, he was incredibly perceptive.

"I had some concerns," I replied.

"You could always ask him to leave."

I shook my head. "He's not here that often and I couldn't do that to Michael."

He pointed to the fireplace, just beyond the couch and love seat. The house had an open floor plan so you could see the family room from the kitchen table.

"Do you know how to use that?" He was pointing to my father's 12-gauge shotgun, which was mounted above the fireplace.

"It's been awhile since I've been to the range," I admitted.

My dad used to shoot skeet. Mom and I would sometimes watch his matches. When I was young, he'd taught me how to fire a pistol. When I got older and a bit stronger, he let me try one of his shotguns.

After my parents died, I stopped going to the range. It wasn't a conscious choice, but the thought of going there without them made me feel lonely. Then Michael came along and our days off were spent boating or flying, not shooting.

"I could probably use a refresher," I said. "Could you teach me?"

Detective Grant unclasped his hands and pressed them against the table. "Probably not a good idea. You're a witness in an ongoing investigation."

I felt foolish for the second time today. My cheeks blushed, which I'm sure he noticed. It wasn't like I was asking him on a date. I was asking for training, but I guess that was improper.

"There're some good instructors at Everglades Gun and Hunt Club. I'm sure any of them would work with you."

I forced a smile as if that was a great idea.

"I'll see if I can expedite the return of your pistol." He added, "Do you keep any other guns in the house?"

"No. I've got some pepper spray. My dad gave it to me a while back."

"How long ago was that?"

"Gosh, years," I replied. "Why?"

"You might think about getting a new one. Sabre Red, the kind we use at the department, has a shelf life of four years, which is double most other brands, but they all expire eventually. The cans tend to lose pressure over time."

"Oh," I said. "I didn't realize that. Have you ever used yours?"

He nodded. "And had it used on me."

"Really?"

"Part of training. They say it's sixty-seven times hotter than hot sauce, and I believe it." He rubbed his nose, as if just talking about it brought the burn back. "Can I ask you another question, about the restaurant?"

"Go ahead."

"How do you pay your employees? Do you write checks?"

"No," I replied. "They're on direct deposit."

"And your vendors?"

"Yes, for some of them I write checks. Once a month."

"Where do you keep the checkbook?"

"In my office. Locked in the desk."

"Who has a key to your desk?"

"Just me."

"Can you check that you still have it?"

I tensed my brows. Why so many questions about my checkbook and why did he think I'd lost my desk key? I got up and walked over to my purse on the kitchen counter. I kept my keys in the side pocket so they were easy to find. On the chain were five keys: one to my car, the house, the restaurant, my desk and a storage shed outside. I held up the keys and confirmed to Detective Grant that I still had my desk key.

His eyes focused like a laser on the chain. Without speaking, he quickly stood and approached me, taking the key chain. He singled out the green key, holding it up.

"This is the restaurant key?" he asked.

"Yes."

"It's green," he said, stating the obvious.

"Right," I confirmed. "I made the restaurant keys easy to recognize."

"You said that you have one, and Michael and Jasper, right?"

"And Alex and Samantha," I added.

"Theirs are green, too?"

"Yes. Why?"

Without explaining anything further, Detective Grant wanted to know the next time when all of us would be at the restaurant together. I told him that I expected everyone around 10:30 a.m. and that Samantha and Alex would probably be there earlier.

"What's up with the keys?" I asked.

"I just have to follow up on a detail."

"Did *she* have one of our green keys?" I guessed. That would explain how she'd gotten in, something I'd never figured out.

He abruptly looked at his watch and said, "I've gotta head out. I'll see you later, okay?"

With that he was gone, before I could ask any more questions.

14. Grant | Thursday, July 8

I had a few hours to kill before everyone would be at the restaurant so I returned to my office and tried the number for Joseph Ricci again. He answered on the first ring.

"Brittany, is that you?" he asked, in a hushed whisper.

"It's not Brittany," I replied. "But I'm calling on her behalf."

"Look," he said, his voice raised. "I've extended the lease and left the bank account open. I can't do anything more. I won't."

He obviously thought I was someone else. "Mr. Ricci, this is Detective Grant with the Ormond Beach Police Department. I'm calling about a property you lease on Myrtle Street with Brittany Jones."

He got quiet.

I continued, "You're familiar with this property?"

His tone was indignant. "I don't have anything to do with that place. If they trashed it, it's on them."

"Them?" I asked.

"Brittany and that low-life she's with."

"What's his name?" I asked.

"I don't know. So what's this about anyway? What happened?"

"I'm sorry to be the one to tell you this, but Ms. Jones is dead."

"What?" He sounded surprised. "What happened?"

"Mr. Ricci," I said. "I need you to talk to me and I need you to be honest. I know you have a lot to protect. I know you have a wife and kids. Believe me, I have no interest in whatever your arrangement was with Brittany, but we need to talk about her."

He got quiet again. He finally spoke just above a whisper. "Look, I'm in my office right now. Can I get somewhere else and call you back?"

"How long?"

"I just need to get to my car. Ten minutes."

"Okay," I allowed. As I waited for the return call, I mulled over what I'd learned. First, he didn't appear to have known Brittany was dead. Second, Brittany was hanging out with another guy, who Ricci called a low-life. And third, his initial reaction was that I was hitting him up for money—more money, to be exact.

As promised, he called back in ten minutes. I could hear the distinctive echo of a car's Bluetooth. Before I could speak, he bombarded me with questions. "What happened to her? When did this happen?"

I deliberately didn't provide details of her death, not yet anyway. I began, "Mr. Ricci, I've been unable to locate any of Brittany's family. Since you shared a lease with her, for all intents and purposes, you are her next of kin."

I heard stammering, but no legible words.

I continued, "Does Brittany have any family? I haven't been able to do a death notification."

"Uh, no. Nobody that I ever knew about. I think she's been on her own since she was a kid."

"And your relationship with her? That's been going on for how long?"

He sighed. He knew he'd been caught. "I met her at a bar when I was in town on business. You have to believe me, it was just supposed to be one night. But it turned into something else."

He confessed so freely. Although I said I was a detective, I could've been a private investigator for his wife. He'd just incriminated himself without ever verifying who I was. He clearly was not a calculating killer. Someone more cunning wouldn't give up that kind of information. I softened my tone. "I understand how that happens."

"Yeah…right, man. Don't get me wrong, I love my wife, but things change. And Brittany was so beautiful and she just couldn't get enough of me."

"When was the last time you spoke to her?"

"It's been months."

"Why's that?"

"It was starting to fizzle out. The last time I was down there, she'd changed. It was more like she was tolerating me, but didn't really want me there. I could tell. I left and we didn't talk for a while. Then she called, all sweet and nice, and I thought I had my old Brittany back. But what she really wanted was for me to renew the lease for another year. I told her I'd think about it, but I'd already made up my mind to end things. I'd never done anything like this before and I was afraid my wife would find out."

"How'd that go over, when you didn't agree to renew the lease?"

He exhaled loudly. "Her true colors came out. She threatened to come up to Jersey and show up at my house. I told her I was cutting off her credit cards. It was a real blow-up."

I heard the sound of a blinker. Apparently, he was aimlessly driving around as we talked, using his car as his cone of privacy.

He continued, "I was going to figure out a way to come down there, to sort it out, but the next day, I get a phone call from some dude. He listed everything he knew about me—my address, my wife's name, our kids' names, like he was reading a file on me. He said if I cut off Brittany's money and didn't renew the lease, he'd tell my wife. Said he had photos that would end my marriage."

"What'd you do?"

"What could I do? I'd been played. He was probably with her all along. I mean, why would a pretty young girl like her want to be with me? It was always about the money."

"So you renewed the lease and kept paying her credit cards?"

"Yeah. I don't want a divorce. And Patti, she wouldn't forgive something like this."

"When was the last time you were at the condo?"

"I never went back after that. I handled everything from here."

"Did you talk to Brittany?"

"No, not since that guy called. I've been trying to figure a way out of this. Did he hurt her?"

"Did you ever meet the man who called you?"

"No, we just talked on the phone. I thought that's who you were when you called."

"What can you tell me about him?" I asked.

"I didn't know anything about him, until that call. He said he was a friend of Brittany's, but he never said his name or how he knew her."

"What number did he call from?"

"From Brittany's phone. That's why I answered it," he said.

"Could you estimate his race or age?"

"Not really. He wasn't an old man, but he wasn't a kid, either."

"Did he have an accent?"

"You mean like a foreign accent?"

"No, a regional accent," I clarified. "Did he sound like he was from the south, the north?"

"Well, I know he wasn't from Jersey. It was kind of neutral, like one of those TV reporters."

I looked at my notepad. I hadn't jotted down much. He wasn't giving me anything concrete to go on.

"What else can you tell me about Brittany? Her childhood, upbringing? Had she always lived in Florida?"

"It wasn't like we had conversations." I could hear the sarcasm in his voice. "She didn't talk about herself or where she came from. I got the feeling she didn't have much growing up, though. I think she was poor because boy, did she love to eat out and shop. She saw what other people had and wanted it for herself, and she loved that I could give her those things."

"What else are you paying for?" I asked.

"I have an account set up down there. I transfer money from my business so she can pay the rent and her bills."

"The car is yours?"

"I gave it to her. Got it as a trade. I don't even sell Mini Coopers, but she wanted one, so I got it for her."

He went quiet for a while and then he spoke, "Did she wreck the car? Is that how she died?"

"No, Mr. Ricci. I'm investigating a homicide."

"What? How?" He sounded shocked.

"I was hoping you could help me with that information," I explained.

"How could I possibly help you?" His voice rose an octave and then cracked as he spoke. "You don't think I had anything to do with this, do you? I loved Brittany. It turned bad, but I wouldn't want her dead. Who was the guy? After I talked to him, I never heard from her again. I even tried to call her."

"I thought you said you hadn't spoken to her."

"I hadn't. I tried to reach her but she never answered. And there was no voicemail on her phone. You believe me, don't you?" He was panicking now.

"Mr. Ricci, you had a lot to lose. You had a girlfriend on the side who was threatening to expose you. That's a pretty strong motive."

He spoke in a rush. "Do you need me to come down there? I will. Do you need me to take a lie detector test? I'll do it. You have to believe that I didn't hurt her. I wouldn't. What do you need me to do?"

"Hold on," I replied. "I don't need you to jump on a plane today. As soon as you can reasonably get down here, let me know."

"I will. I promise," he vowed.

"You have this number?"

"Yes, yes. I've got it."

"And if you remember anything else, any little detail after you've had time to process all of this, I want you to give me a call."

"I will, I promise," he said again. After a brief silence, he spoke. "You never told me how she died."

"She was shot."

"Shot!" he repeated. "Where?"

"I can give you more details when we meet."

"Yeah, yeah. I'll come down. I promise. When's the funeral?"

"We don't have any immediate plans because we haven't found next of kin."

"She won't be buried?"

"That's up to the next of kin," I repeated.

More silence.

I ended the call, reminding him to let me know when he was coming to town. In reality, I didn't think there was much more information he could give me, although I wanted to see if he'd actually show up.

I leaned back in my chair and considered the evidence I'd collected against Joseph Ricci. From the July Fourth party at his house, it was clear he wasn't in town when Brittany was shot. She was a nuisance for him, but it appeared he was waiting and hoping the situation wouldn't bite him in the ass. My guess is he would've kept paying her bills indefinitely. And even though I thought she was targeted, I didn't see him hiring a hit man. He wasn't that savvy or calculated. Nothing about him felt like he had what it took to hire someone to end another person's life just to solve his problem. He clearly was still fond of Brittany, up to the point where he asked about her funeral. Poor chump. I decided to give him a few days to see if he followed through.

My phone rang. It was Hall, with another internet call. "How's it going?" he asked.

"I'll catch you up on Monday," I replied. "You have four days of vacation left. Go enjoy them."

"But—," he started to protest, but I cut him off.

"Go enjoy your vacation, Hall," I ordered. "And one more thing. Don't ever cheat on your wife."

Before I could hang up, an incoming call flashed across my phone. It was Julianna.

"I've gotta go," I said, ending the call with him and taking the new one.

Julianna told me that Alex had just asked for the day off. Since the restaurant was slow and Jasper was willing to cover the bar, he was going to get some personal things done. She added that he was only taking one day and would be back on Friday if I still needed to see everyone together.

My mind immediately went to the most sinister scenario. She'd already asked everyone about their keys. Alex didn't have his, so she gave him her master to copy and stalled me for a day. That was Alex's errand, making a new key. Sometimes I hated that my instincts were to expect the worst in people, but enough time in this job did that to you.

Would Julianna do something that deceptive? I didn't think so, but I also hadn't thought my wife would ask for a divorce out of the blue.

Short of insisting that Julianna deny Alex his time off, there wasn't much I could do. If she'd already warned him about the key, he'd have the new one made before I got there. I told her not to worry about it and hung up. Either way, I still needed to go over to FDLE and pick up Brittany's green key from evidence.

I also called Emily Pickett at Florida Cares. Didn't need the chief asking if I'd reached out to her yet and I hadn't. She agreed to meet the next afternoon, but it would have to be at her office in Orlando. I didn't mind. Driving there would give me time to think.

15. Julianna | Friday, July 9

As the staff prepared for Friday lunch, I sat in my office to review the books for the last week. Typically, July and August were our busiest months with the summer tourists. Once the vacationers headed back for school, the snowbirds would take their place, which sustained us through the winter, along with a few special events. The past week had been the slowest one I could remember. I scanned the bookings for the coming months. We had four receptions in September, one every weekend. Luckily no one had cancelled, at least not yet. If I had to, I could go without a paycheck for a few months. If things became more dire, the only option I could think of was to sell Michael's boat.

I heard a slight tap on my door. Without looking up, I knew it was Samantha. The guys just barged in, especially if my door was open, but Samantha always knocked politely.

"Yes?" I said.

"Is this a good time?" she asked, not entering my office until I gave her permission.

"Sure." Samantha slipped into the chair by my desk. She was wearing her white apron and chef's hat. Small wisps of her silky black hair peaked out from under the brim. She carefully tucked them back as she sat down.

"Have you heard anything from the detective?" she asked.

"You mean have they caught anyone?" I clarified. "No."

Without speaking, she stood and gently shut my office door.

"I'm worried," she confided.

"Me, too." I was worried on multiple fronts. The shooter hadn't been caught, I no longer had my pistol, Jasper had lied to me and we hadn't made enough money to pay the staff this week.

"Julianna, I did something I shouldn't have done. At the time, it seemed like the right thing to do. But now, I'm afraid I'll get caught."

"What is it?" I asked. Knowing her, she'd probably done something innocuous, like throwing away a parking ticket, and was overreacting.

She whispered, "I need you to promise you won't say anything."

How could I guarantee my silence until I knew what she'd done?

But I promised anyway, convincing myself that her big concern would be trivial.

"I lied to the detective."

"What!" I was shocked and concerned. "Why?"

Samantha glanced nervously at the closed door. No one could hear us. The kitchen was way down the hall and besides, it was noisy in there. Her eyes darted nervously from me to the floor. She started to speak, but looked away.

"What'd you lie about?" I asked.

"You said you wouldn't tell, right?"

Now I was regretting that promise. A lot depended on what she said next.

"I covered for Alex, the night of the shooting."

I shook my head, not registering what she was saying. I'd seen them leave together.

Samantha continued, "After we left here that night, I drove us home, but he went back out. He said he needed to get some cigarettes. He was only gone ten minutes."

I sat there speechless.

"When you called the next day and told us about the murder, I didn't even think about it. But then the detective said he needed to interview us. We figured it would be better if we just said we were both at home. I mean, Alex didn't shoot her, but he could've become a suspect, which wouldn't be right."

"Why lie?"

She pressed her hands against her face, covering her eyes and cheeks. All I could see was her petite nose and a sliver of her lips. I reached forward, tugging at her wrist so I could make eye contact.

"Why lie?" I asked again.

"I don't know," she sighed. "Alex said it would just make things simpler, but they checked his criminal record. He's going to be in trouble anyway."

"What?" I shouted.

"It was a long time ago," she explained. "He did some stupid things with some credit cards. Julianna, he's a good man. He just made a mistake."

My mind was reeling. How did I not know that Alex had a troubled past? Of course, I'd never done a background check on him.

Early on, he filled in for one of our bartenders as a favor. He did a great job, and because he was Samantha's boyfriend, I hired him on the spot. No checking required. How could I have been so naive?

"Tell me what he did," I insisted.

Her eyes begged me not to make her reveal more, but I didn't let my expression soften.

"It wasn't here, Julianna. I promise. He swore he'd never do anything to betray your kindness because you gave him a job when he needed one."

"What did he do!"

She exhaled. "It was where he worked before he came here. He pocketed some of the cash payments and double-charged the credit cards."

"Seriously?" I couldn't hide my disbelief.

"He knows it was stupid. He repaid everything, but then he couldn't get a job. You saved him by letting him work here, and he knows I would kick him out if he ever stole from you."

I shook my head. Jasper, Alex and Samantha were all lying. Who could I trust?

"Samantha," I said. "You need to tell Detective Grant the truth. Right away."

"It would just make things worse," she protested. "Alex didn't shoot that girl. You know that. He's not capable of doing such a thing and he was home five minutes later."

"I thought you said ten," I snapped.

She jerked back in the chair, shocked by my correction, which implied much more.

"You know what I mean. He didn't have time to come back here, so it was just simpler to say he was with me." She paused. "Detective Grant knows about the stuff with the credit cards. I was afraid he'd tell you, but I wanted you to hear it from us."

"From us?" I said sarcastically. "I don't see Alex in here confessing."

Tears started to well up in her eyes. Samantha was a fragile soul, and though she was going about it the wrong way, I could tell she was trying to do the right thing.

"Please don't say anything," she cried.

"How could you let Alex convince you to lie to the detective? That's not like you, Samantha."

"I know. It was wrong, and I've been worried sick."

"Of course you have, because you know right from wrong."

"Julianna, haven't you ever ignored your better judgment because you trusted the person you love?"

"No, I haven't."

Before the words left my mouth, my mind flashed back to an evening walk on the beach with Michael. It was late January, and we were strolling hand in hand along the shoreline. The air was chilly, but not cold enough for a heavy coat. My phone buzzed in my pocket. When I looked at the caller ID, the screen displayed that the call was from Michael's mobile, but he was standing right next to me, not on his phone.

"That's strange," I'd said. "It's from you."

He was visibly surprised. "Don't answer it," he'd instructed and then tried to take my phone from me.

I pulled away and pressed the phone to my ear.

"Hello? Who's there?" I'd asked.

The line was quiet, then dead.

After a moment, he explained that Jasper had taken his phone and was probably trying to reach him through me. When I suggested we call his son back, in case he needed something, Michael reluctantly agreed. He borrowed my phone and made the call. I couldn't say for sure, but it didn't sound like Jasper on the other end. It almost sounded like he was talking to a woman.

His behavior had struck me as very odd at the time, but it never happened again. I had no idea why I was thinking about that strange call now.

My office door burst open. Samantha and I both jumped in our seats. It was Jasper.

"That cop's here," he said, with a touch of disdain. "Wants to see all of us."

16. Grant | Friday, July 9

I drove to Café Lily before they opened. Without being seen, I took the green key that I'd checked out from evidence and tried it in the front door. As I expected, it fit. I was pissed at myself for not testing all of Brittany's keys on the lock the night of her murder. Sometimes the most obvious things are the ones you miss. I couldn't blame Hall, although a seasoned partner wouldn't have let this detail slip. I tucked the key in my pants pocket and knocked on the door. A female employee who was putting fresh linens on the tables approached, unlocked the door and let me in. The smell of fresh baked bread permeated the air.

Jasper and Alex were behind the bar, drying glasses and restocking the shelves. They both froze when they saw me. I approached the bar and asked if they, along with Julianna and Samantha, could join me at the front of the restaurant. Alex eyed me warily. Without a word, Jasper walked through the back archway to find the women.

In the dining room, the group formed a small circle just next to the hostess stand. The employee who'd let me in continued to set the tables, but periodically glanced our way. Who wouldn't be curious by an impromptu meeting led by a detective?

Julianna asked, "Do you need us to go somewhere more private?"

I shook my head, retrieved Brittany's green key and held it up. They watched, motionless, as I walked to the front door and fit the key into the lock. I didn't look at the key. Instead, I studied their faces. Samantha, Alex and Jasper looked puzzled. Only Julianna, who knew what I was doing, looked concerned.

"I need each of you to show me your key to the restaurant," I said. No one moved, so I prompted, "Now, if you don't mind."

Julianna held up her key chain and Samantha retreated to the back of the restaurant, presumably to retrieve hers. Jasper drew his key from his jeans pocket. Alex didn't move. They reformed the circle, with Julianna, Samantha and Jasper holding up their green keys. Alex's hands remained in his pockets.

"Where's yours?" I asked Alex.

"I lost it, a while back," he replied. "Samantha and I always come in together, so I don't need it." Instead of looking contrite, he was defiant.

Julianna spoke, her voice raised. "Why didn't you tell me, Alex? I would've changed the locks!"

She had a right to be pissed. Assuming he was telling the truth, anyone could have found his key. If they figured out it was to Café Lily, he'd put her business in jeopardy. Alex claimed to have lost the key, but I wasn't convinced. He denied knowing Brittany Jones, but this key provided a possible link.

I tried to hand him the key. "This it?"

Alex kept his hands entrenched in his pockets and barely glanced at the key. Obviously, he'd figured out where I'd gotten it, and wasn't going to touch it.

"Could be," he replied. "They're all the same." He paused, and then added, "Or it could be Michael's."

"How dare you!" exclaimed Julianna. "Get your things and get out! You're fired."

Samantha cried out, "Julianna, please!"

Without bothering to collect any of his personal belongings, Alex stormed out the front door, slamming it behind him. Samantha ran after him, leaving me standing there with Julianna and Jasper. I understood why she was angry and didn't blame her for firing him, especially after his jab about Michael. He was implying a connection between Brittany and Julianna's lost husband.

Julianna rushed outside. She stopped just past the restaurant entrance and looked in both directions. Not seeing Samantha or Alex, she turned and slowly walked back in. Instead of returning to me and Jasper, she motioned for me to join her in the front corner of the restaurant.

"Look," she said, tugging on my forearm to move me even further away. "I need to talk you, but I need Samantha with me. Can you wait for her to come back?"

I glanced at my watch. Either I'd have to leave soon or reschedule my visit with Emily Pickett in Orlando. The chief wouldn't be pleased if I missed this meeting.

"I can come back later this afternoon," I offered. I doubted Samantha would be back any time soon and there was no point chasing down Alex. A missing key wasn't enough evidence to bring him in for further questioning. "If you're worried about Alex, I can have an officer come by until I return. I don't figure he'll be back, but to be on the safe side, it might be a good idea."

"No, it's not that," she said. She wiped the back of her hand across her forehead.

Jasper was standing across the restaurant, trying to appear inconspicuous, but also craning his neck to hear us. I got a glimpse of his face before he turned away. If I had to guess, he looked amused. His stepmom was stressed and his friend had just been fired. How was this entertaining?

"I've got to go to Orlando," I said. "Could be a lead on Brittany."

She surveyed the restaurant. The staff who were watching us scurried back to work.

"Can I come with you?" she asked. "I need to get out of here for a while."

Normally my answer would've been a definitive no. I was not taking a witness on a fact-finding trip, but she seemed so frazzled. The hour drive to Orlando would give her a reprieve and it wasn't like I was taking her on a stake-out.

"Come on," I said.

17. Julianna | Friday, July 9

I entered the passenger side of Detective Grant's car and remarked at how mundane my life was that I'd never been inside a cop car. The seats were gray factory-grade cloth. A large radio took up most of the dashboard and a heavy-duty flashlight was plugged into the cigarette lighter. Paperwork was tucked under his visor and a stainless steel coffee tumbler rested in the holder between us. He turned on the air conditioner, which immediately started blowing on high.

"It's too much?" he asked as he reached for the knob to change the fan speed.

"It's fine," I said, yet tilted the blades toward him as we pulled out of the restaurant parking lot. He made a call asking for an officer to keep an eye on the restaurant. It wasn't a bad idea. The last thing we needed was Alex returning and causing trouble. Maybe I'd been too hasty firing him, but I couldn't deal with Alex—lying, stealing and making accusations.

"So what's in Orlando?" I asked.

"An organization called Florida Cares. Just following up on a potential lead."

"I know them."

"You do?" His voice rose, but he kept his eyes steadfast on the road ahead.

"They have posters up at the women's shelter where we take food." I paused. "I even called them once."

He glanced at me. I could see the surprise on his face.

"It wasn't for me," I clarified. "I called to see if they had any information on my sister, but they weren't even established when she went missing."

"You know what they do?" he asked.

I nodded.

"You think your sister was trafficked?"

"I don't know. After my parents died, I tried to find her. They never wanted me digging into her disappearance. I think it opened old wounds for them, but once they were gone, I felt this yearning to try to find the only family I had left."

I looked out the window. He took the entrance ramp on I-95

and drove south. Thick cypress and pine trees lined the highway for as far as I could see.

"You didn't have any luck?" he asked.

I shook my head. "I didn't have much to go on. My sister was fifteen when she disappeared. I was able to get her school records. She was an honor student in middle school, but her grades dropped when she entered high school. I've read that can be a sign of trouble. With a little digging, I found a few of her former classmates, all grandmothers now. They remembered Lily's disappearance because they'd all been afraid of getting snatched, too. But other than recalling the hysteria that some boogieman was on the loose, they didn't have much to tell me."

I reached in my wallet and pulled out Lily's freshman photo. She was in a maroon cheerleader uniform. Her blonde hair was styled in a flipped bob, a trend of the late sixties. You could tell we were sisters. In fact, if you put our school pictures side by side, we almost looked like the same girl. Only her clothing, hairstyle and the worn photo gave away the decade and a half between us.

"No one thought Lily ran away," I added. "They were all certain of that."

"Samantha thought your parents' friend, a chef, might have had something to do with it."

My eyes widened. How'd he know that? Moreover, Samantha had never mentioned anything nefarious about Keith to me.

"You think Keith McQueen was involved?" I asked. I pictured my stocky Uncle Keith with his shaggy beard sitting in his prize possession—a flashy red corvette. There was no blood relation, but I'd called him *uncle* my entire childhood.

"Samantha couldn't remember his name. It's Keith, is it?"

My mind spun. Uncle Keith and my dad had been friends for years. They both were cooks and bartenders and often helped the other find a job. I was still in college when Uncle Keith starting working for my parents. They'd finally made their dream come true, running their own restaurant instead of supporting someone else's. By the time I'd graduated, Samantha had taken over as lead chef. I didn't think much about it. I certainly never connected him to Lily's disappearance. He was so much older than her.

"Why would she think that?" I asked.

"A hunch maybe. I don't think she had anything concrete."

"Why wouldn't she have told me?" Before the words left my mouth, I understood why Samantha had stayed quiet. My parents didn't condone anyone talking about Lily's disappearance. Some things were allowed, like donating food to the women's shelter and naming the restaurant in her honor, but we couldn't speculate about what happened to her.

"Do you know where he is?"

I shook my head. "After he stopped working at the restaurant, he never came by again. I assumed he and my dad had some kind of falling out. I thought about calling him when my parents died, but I never did. I'm not even sure I could find him now."

"Do you have his social security number?"

"I'm sure I could find it in our employment records. Do you think he might know what happened to my sister?"

"Give me his social. I'll see what I can find out," he offered.

I couldn't understand why Detective Grant would help me, other than he was a genuinely nice guy. He wasn't full of pizazz like my Michael, but he was calm and steady. Actually, he was a lot like my father.

"Are you from Ormond Beach?" I asked.

He laughed. "I'm from Jersey City. Can't you tell?"

"No, not really. What brought you to Florida?"

"It's not a bad place to live."

"Wow," I said. "You don't like talking about yourself, do you?"

He shrugged.

"You just answered my question without answering my question."

He glanced at me and then looked back at the road. "Hazard of the job."

"How long have you been a detective?" I asked.

"Now *that* I can answer," he said. "Too long."

I smiled. "Well, you're good at it. The night Brittany was shot, you were the only person who seemed to understand what I was going through."

"I've talked to a lot of witnesses."

"Still, I didn't thank you back then. I guess I was in shock. And thanks for letting me ride with you. I needed to get away from there."

"Trust me, you're better company than Hall." He chuckled.

"Your partner?"

"More like my trainee. He means well. Just needs to learn some patience."

"And how do you teach patience?" I asked.

He spoke with a heaviness in his voice. "Unfortunately, patience doesn't come until you see the consequences of losing it."

"Sounds like there's a story there."

He winced slightly. A second more and I wouldn't have seen it.

"Well, you know my story," I said. "What's yours?"

He didn't reply.

"We have an hour drive," I added.

Detective Grant reached up and adjusted his rear-view mirror. At first, I thought he was going to ignore my comment, but he began to speak.

"I worked narcotics investigations for a long time in Daytona Beach. I had a CI, confidential informant, who was a young female. She was a crackhead. Her teeth were rotten and she couldn't have weighed a hundred pounds—all skin and bones. She lived in a yard shed in a poor section of town. There was no running water or electricity, just a small lamp powered by an extension cord hooked up to a power line.

"We were trying to clean up the neighborhood so instead of busting her, I let her walk. In exchange, she agreed to lead me to her sources. The operation was a year in the making. With CIs, you have to go slow and low, to gain their trust but more importantly, so their identity is protected. It was working. We were slowing getting warrants and making arrests.

"One day, I was in court, so I passed her off to a rookie officer. He was eager to make a name for himself. Without checking with me, he had her do back-to-back deals, three in a row, and then arrested all three of the dealers. Everyone in town knew who the snitch was. He might as well have strapped her to the front of his police car and driven around."

"What happened to her?" I asked.

"She was killed." He gripped the steering wheel tighter. "I couldn't protect her. I tried to get her into treatment, but couldn't force her. She wanted to be back on the streets, even with a target on her back. The drug use had impaired her ability to think straight and to see the danger."

"What else could you have done?" I asked.

"I could've seen her as a human being instead of a means to an end. If I had helped her instead of using her…all she needed was one person to give a damn."

"I'm really sorry," I said. "It's a terrible feeling—to carry around guilt."

He looked at me. "What do you know about that?"

I took a deep breath. "Michael and I talked about him joining the restaurant full-time. He worked at Café Lily part-time, but the business couldn't support two management staff. If I'd just agreed, even if financially it didn't make sense, he would've stopped the charter flights, and he'd still be here today."

"That's not your fault," he said.

"No more than her death is yours?"

He reached forward and turned on the radio. "How about some music?"

I sensed he was the type of man who didn't typically talk about his regrets, and we'd reached the threshold of what he was willing to share. Still, I detected a friendship forming, even under these unconventional circumstances, and very much appreciated his willingness to try to find Keith McQueen.

A wave of fatigue suddenly swept over my body. Inside the police car with Detective Grant, I felt safe, for the first time in days. I tilted my head against the window pane, closed my eyes and let the music on the radio lull me to sleep.

🛞 18. Grant | Friday, July 9

Julianna's eyes were closed, her shoulder was propped against the door panel and her head tilted against the window pane. The hour car ride to Orlando was probably the most rest she'd had in a while. I didn't want to wake her, but I couldn't leave her in the vehicle, not with my rifle strapped above her head.

I leaned over. "We're here."

She arched her back and turned her head toward me, but her eyes remained shut. "Michael?"

"No, it's Paul Grant."

She jerked up and blinked a few times.

"Sorry to wake you," I said. "We're here. Do you mind waiting in the lobby? I saw a Starbucks a few blocks back if you'd rather go there."

She wanted to come inside so we walked to the office of Florida Cares together. Their headquarters was in a nondescript strip mall between a health food store and a bargain shoe store. When I opened the door, a bell jingled. A young woman in her early thirties appeared at the counter.

"Detective Grant?" she asked.

I nodded. "Okay if my friend waits in the lobby?"

"Of course. There's coffee or tea if you like." Ms. Pickett pointed to a drink cart at the front of the lobby. She opened the door next to the counter and escorted me to her small but organized office. Emily Pickett was much younger than I'd expected for the CEO of the organization. Barely five feet tall, with wavy blonde hair that reached her waist. She had an innocence to her face that I didn't expect of someone who regularly dealt with commercial sex trafficking.

On her desk were several framed pictures, the largest one of her holding a newborn baby. Another was a group photo, probably of her staff, since they were wearing similar purple shirts.

"Thanks for making time, Ms. Pickett," I said. "Chief Jamison was eager for me to meet with you."

"Call me Emily," she offered. "And I'd do anything for Michele. She's one of my favorite board members. I've never met anyone who's so perceptive. I'm very tactical, but Michele…well, she thinks on a whole different stratosphere."

I didn't know the chief was on the board of this non-profit. She never mentioned it at work and it wasn't part of her online bio.

"How can I help you?" she asked.

"It's a long shot," I said. "But have you ever run across this girl?"

I pulled an enlarged copy of Brittany's driver's license photo from my case file and placed it on her desk. She shook her head. "I saw her picture on the news, but I'm afraid I've never seen her before."

Great. I'd just driven an hour for nothing, but that was how it was with investigations. You throw a hundred darts before you hit a bullseye. Surely the chief had spoken to Emily Pickett and knew she'd never seen Brittany. So why ask me to meet with her? Did she have a hunch I'd find something else?

I knew a little about Florida Cares, although our sex crimes unit in Daytona interacted with them more than I did. I figured I might as well educate myself to avoid making the trip a total waste.

"How long have you been the CEO here?" I asked.

Without changing the expression on her cherubic face, she said, "Take a guess, double it, and you'll be wrong."

I hesitated. She could only have a few years in the job, so if I were to guess, I'd say eight years, but I knew better than to speculate. Instead, I replied, "That's worse than asking me to guess your age."

She laughed. "Michele said you were clever, and the answer is fourteen years."

I nodded with respect. It was rare for my first impression to be wrong. I imagined she was often underestimated and used it to her advantage. Smart lady.

"Can you tell me more about your organization?"

"Absolutely. Florida Cares is a statewide agency serving children who have been victimized by sex trafficking and exploitation. We have a twenty-four seven hotline and counselors who create individualized plans for our survivors. You see, even if two people have experienced the exact same trauma, they may process it differently. We create programs that cater specifically to each person's needs and goals."

"How many counselors do you have?"

"Well, I wish we could afford more. We rely on grants for most of our funding. Right now, I have eight care coordinators, each with a caseload of twenty survivors, and then we have staff for the hotline. On average, we receive one hundred and thirty calls a month from individuals seeking support and services. And then we have our wonderful volunteers, many of whom come from the school system or law enforcement."

I quickly did the math. With eight coordinators, they could handle one hundred sixty victims at a time.

"Last year, we served seven hundred eighty-nine victims, which was up from five hundred ninety-six the year before, and four hundred sixty-nine the year before that. I'm afraid the problem is only getting worse. In the last ten years, we've received over twenty-seven hundred referrals of youth suspected to be victims of sexual exploitation or trafficking."

"Where are these girls coming from?"

"Good question," she said. "And mind you, it's not just girls. About eight percent of victims are male, though that figure likely represents under-reporting. There are so many myths that we need to debunk. The worst misconception is that sex trafficking is about strangers in some third-world country, but it's not. Children right here in our country are being sold for sex by criminals who are experts at manipulating them. Some of these kids are fleeing an abusive home, others are enticed by promises of a glamorous lifestyle, and many are coerced by threats against them or a loved one. We just had a girl come in yesterday; her mom is schizophrenic, there's no dad in the picture, and she ran away at fourteen with her baby boy."

"Fourteen?" I repeated.

"Yes. That's typical. The average age of our domestic minor sex trafficking, or DMST, adolescents is fifteen years old. About seventy percent of our survivors reported running away frequently. The trafficker who found this particular girl pulled the usual tactics. He fed her, bought her new clothes and put her and the baby up in a hotel. After a few days of relief, he brought in her first customer. She refused at first, so he took her baby and threatened to kill him if she didn't comply. What could she do? She felt trapped."

"How'd she get out?" I asked.

"Believe it or not, the hotel maid called the police. The girl never asked for help, but you don't need words to see fear on a young girl's face."

"And once your organization stepped in, what happened?"

"We have a process for intake and screening, which happens quite quickly. We also found her and her baby a safe place to stay and coordinated their medical services. Next, she'll go to one of our case managers for a customized care and service plan, like I mentioned before. And then we'll monitor her as she begins on her road to recovery."

"Was her pimp arrested?"

Emily winced. "One of our goals is to change the language." She spoke delicately, carefully selecting each word. "We want people to see domestic minor sex trafficking for what it is. Think of the word *pimp*. You think of the cool dude, the guy with the jewelry and the nice car. We even use the expression 'pimp your ride' to mean it's all decked out. In our training, we encourage people to call him what he is, a child sex trafficker. And we don't call the act 'turning tricks.' Rather, we describe what's really happening: the rape of a child."

I got her point and she was right. Words mattered.

"I'm sure you're busy, especially with this case, but you have an open invitation to take our training course. It's three hours and we spend time on things like language, statistics and how to notice the warning signs."

I was interested. Since our Ormond Beach department didn't have its own sex crimes unit, it could be useful. Maybe that's why the chief had suggested I meet with her.

"Count me in," I said. "How big a problem is this nationally?"

"That's tough to answer. Different agencies collect different data, and I'd bet that all of our numbers are under-reported. That said, Shared Hope International reports that 100,000 to 300,000 children are at risk of being victimized in the United States every year. The National Center for Missing and Exploited Children reports that one in six runaways are believed to be victims as well. The good news is that with the different agencies, we all have a means for people to get help. We have our state hotline, and the NCMEC have a national phone number for any missing child: 1–800–THE-LOST."

I pointed to a poster on her wall titled "DMST Warning Signs."

"I'll get that in class?" I asked.

"You certainly will."

DMST Warning Signs

The youth...

- Has a significantly older boyfriend.
- Shows signs of physical trauma, such as unexplained bruises, black eye, cuts or other marks.
- Shows signs of emotional trauma, including increased fear, anxiety, depression, tension and/or nervousness.
- Frequently travels with an older male or person who is not a guardian.
- Is labeled as a chronic runaway or has multiple delinquency charges.
- Has or is currently experiencing homelessness.
- Is abusing substances on a regular basis.
- Has started accumulating new clothes, shoes, jewelry or cell phone that she/he can't account for.
- Has an increase in income without explanation.
- Is very secretive about her/his whereabouts.
- Is chatting online with people her/his parents or friends have never met.
- Has possession of prepaid cards and/or hotel keys or receipts.
- Has suddenly changed her/his appearance, such as dressing more provocatively.
- Has special marked tattoos or branding on her/his body (that she/he might be unwilling to explain).
- Has been charged or has a previous record of prostitution.
- Has an explicitly sexual online profile found on internet community sites, internet classified ads and/or social media sites.
- Has no identification or is not in control of her/his identification documents.
- Gives conflicting personal information or stories to law enforcement.
- Has multiple or frequent Sexually Transmitted Diseases/Infections.
- Has family history in the commercial sex industry.

Before I could finish reading the poster, Julianna knocked on the door.

"I'm sorry to interrupt." She spoke quickly, clearly agitated. "I was looking at the photos in the lobby. There's a girl in one of them. Her tattoo. It's the same as Brittany's."

She motioned for me to follow her. Both Emily and I trailed Julianna as she hurried to the lobby and pointed to one of the framed pictures. The young Hispanic girl in the photo had a dagger and flower vine tattoo on her neck just under her earlobe. It was easy to see as her hair was pulled back in a ponytail.

"That's the same tattoo!" exclaimed Julianna.

She was right. In Brittany's license photo, the one we'd shown on the news, the tattoo wasn't obvious because her hair covered most of it. But of course, Julianna had seen the marking up close.

"Do you know this girl?" I asked Emily.

She nodded eagerly. "Angelle. She's one of our biggest success stories."

Julianna interjected, "Why does she have the same tattoo as Brittany?"

"Tattooing the girls has been on the rise," replied Emily. "It's not enough that these monsters own every aspect of their lives, but they've starting branding them, too."

"Are you still in contact with her?" I asked, hoping that I might find someone besides Joe Ricci who knew Brittany.

Emily nodded.

"What happened to her?" asked Julianna.

"About a year ago, Angelle was arrested in a raid. Instead of prosecuting her, the police brought her to us. She was no longer being sold for sex, but was manning the door, collecting the money. I'm not sure if she'd aged out or if her STD made her unusable. She had a terrible case of gonorrhea, which had spread to her eyes and throat.

"We put her up in one of our safe houses, got her medically treated and assigned her a counselor. I have to say, Angelle flew through the program. All she needed was a break. She just started college and is getting her degree in social work. Normally I wouldn't divulge her private story, but she shares it as part of our new counselor training."

"Do you think I could talk to her?" I asked.

"I'm sure she'd be willing to meet you, but let me ask her first. Part of what we teach our survivors is that it's their right to say no."

This was a huge break—finding someone who may have known Brittany. I was tempted to press Emily about how soon she'd reach out, but stopped myself. Instead, I handed her my card, thanked her and thought about Hall. This would have been a good lesson in patience.

On the drive back to Ormond Beach, I called Chief Jamison and shared the news. Julianna called the restaurant but Samantha hadn't returned. Whatever it was she wanted to tell me, she was adamant about waiting until Samantha was available.

I dropped Julianna off at Café Lily. Jenkins was still in a patrol car outside. She invited me to come in to have something to eat, on the house. The offer was tempting. It had been a long time since I'd had a decent meal, but I was already approaching the line of getting too close to her. Instead, I drove to my apartment, ordered a pizza and popped open a beer.

19. Julianna | Saturday, July 10

I awoke and, for a brief moment, couldn't remember what day it was. Then I recalled the events of the previous afternoon, when I'd become so angry that I fired Alex. A pang of regret settled in my stomach. Maybe I'd acted too hastily, but who could blame me? He'd stolen from his last job, lost my restaurant key, lied to the police and disparaged Michael. How could Samantha stick by this guy?

I adjusted my pillow to form a cradle around my neck, a feeble attempt to relieve the tension. Michael used to massage my neck, rubbing the knots with just the right amount of pressure. His hand would eventually trace my spine until he playfully cupped my butt. He'd slowly walk his fingers between my legs, tantalizing me to the point that I'd flip over and pull him on top of me. If only he were here now.

Instead of a massage with benefits, I'd have to settle for a walk on the beach. The sunshine, sand between my toes and fresh air usually lightened my mood. I rolled out of bed and walked to the kitchen for some coffee. Now I mostly used the Keurig—there was no point preparing anything fancy when I was the only one around. As I leaned against the marble countertop, waiting for the coffee to dispense, I glanced into the family room where my father's shotgun was mounted above the fireplace. After he died, I sold several of his competition guns. They were just collecting dust, but I couldn't bear to part with the Beretta, his favorite. The conversation with Detective Grant played in my mind. It had been a long time since I'd been to the range.

Still in my pajamas, I went to my bedroom and into my closet. Buried behind my suitcase was my mother's GTM leather range bag. I pictured her loading it into the back of Dad's truck, her routine on mornings of his skeet competitions. I lifted the bag by the thick handles and hugged the soft outer shell against my chest. The scent of leather, mixed with the faint trace of her perfume, triggered so many memories. I shut my eyes and imagined myself hugging her.

"I miss you," I said, out loud.

I wanted to cling to the sensation of her embrace, but the feeling slowly dissipated and I was left clasping her bag. I opened my eyes and forced myself to get on with the day. I found my pair of 5.11 Tactical pants and a camouflage T-shirt. When I slipped on the pants, they draped around my hips. No wonder Samantha was always trying to feed me. I guess I hadn't realized how thin I'd become. I scrounged through Mom's bag for ammo but didn't find any. Dad stored most of his ammunition in a metal box in the guest room, which was now Jasper's room.

I went into Jasper's closet in search of the metal ammo box, but stopped abruptly. Where Michael's polo shirts used to hang, empty hangers dangled on the rod. I'd given Jasper nearly all of Michael's casual shirts because he said he'd wear them, but now they were gone. Was Jasper discreetly moving out? Or was the offer to wear them just another lie, a ploy to get rid of his father's belongings? My temper flared at the thought of Jasper tossing out Michael's clothes.

My dad's ammo box was in the back of the closet, just as I'd remembered. There was another metal box next to it, a lockbox I didn't recognize. Out of curiosity, I pulled on the handle but it didn't budge. The lid was locked shut. Why did Jasper need a lockbox?

I tried to lift it but it was too heavy to move. Then I paused and questioned my own integrity. Was trying to break into Jasper's personal property as bad as him lying to me? I didn't care. The lockbox was in my house, so technically, it was my property. Not that it mattered as I couldn't open it anyway.

I packed my things for the range, placing several boxes of Dad's ammo into Mom's range bag, along with my ear and eye protection. To retrieve the shotgun, I had to step up on the raised hearth of the fireplace and lift it off its mounts. I'd forgotten how heavy the gun was. I checked that it was unloaded, just as my dad had taught me, and packed it into a fabric case.

Everglades Gun and Hunt Club was about twenty miles from my home. It was the only outdoor range nearby and drew people from all over Volusia County. The range bordered the Ocala National Forest. My dad used to add a fifth rule for gun safety: watch out for the alligators.

I pulled into the gravel lot and parked next to the main building, which resembled an overgrown shed. Down the hill were the skeet fields. For the big competitions, Mom and I used to pack a cooler and set our folding chairs at the edge of the parking lot, close enough to see everything below but far enough away to let the noise abate. This was the first time I'd been to the range without them. There was a comfort in being there, yet I felt out of place, like visiting my childhood home once new owners had moved in.

I walked inside to rent a bay. The room smelled of metal and leather. There was no air-conditioning and the heat hung heavy in the air. On the left side of the room was a long counter with a display of rental guns under glass. On the right side was a small shop selling accessories. A unisex bathroom was at the back. I immediately noticed a large glass vase filled with pink stargazer lilies on the checkout counter. I'd always been drawn to lilies, and a vase of flowers at a gun range was especially peculiar. As I approached, their sweet scent permeated the air.

"So, you come here, too," I said as I thought of my sister. I always felt that she strategically placed lilies in my path as her way of letting me know she was watching over me.

"Excuse me?" the woman behind the counter asked. She was middle-aged, with short gray hair and warm brown eyes.

I shook my head, realizing I had been thinking out loud.

"I'd like to rent a shotgun bay."

"Are you a member, dear?"

"Oh," I replied. We had a family membership, which surely had lapsed. "We used to be members. It's been a while."

"Wait a minute," she said. "You're Norm's daughter, aren't you? Of course, you are! You have his green eyes."

She reached out and took my hands. "I'm Becky Condon. I'm so sorry about your folks. They were good people. I meant to come to their memorial, but it's so hard to get time away from this place. Maybe I could bring flowers to their graves. I love to garden," she said, pointing to the lilies.

"We don't..." I paused, worried she'd think I was heartless and disrespectful. My parents hadn't planned ahead for their funerals so I had no burial instructions. In the accident, the car had caught fire and was totally consumed by the flames before the firetrucks ever arrived. So fate had decided for me. With no need for burial plots, we'd held a memorial service instead.

I cleared my throat. "We just have a plaque at the restaurant."

"I always meant to come over to your folks' restaurant. Norm promised he'd fix me a special plate so I could try a little bit of everything. And now, well, it just goes to show you. You gotta seize the moment when you have the chance. Tomorrow isn't promised."

"You can still come," I told her. "I'll make you that plate."

She placed her right hand over her heart. "That's so sweet, hon. They sure raised you right."

It was a little odd to be called "hon" at my age, but I knew it was a term of endearment. I expected her to ask about the murder, a topic I hadn't been able to avoid for the last week, but she didn't. Instead, she handed me a clipboard with the usual waiver and signatures.

"You planning to shoot skeet?" she asked.

"Oh, no," I said. "I'm not that skilled. I just want to try out my dad's gun."

"Sure thing. Shotguns are on Range B. You can have Bay 5. Don't worry about the membership, dear. I just need a copy of your license." I gave her my driver's license and signed the waiver form. In exchange, she handed me a bunch of rolled up paper targets.

Back at my car, I gathered my gear and put on my safety glasses and ear protection. Range A was down a dirt path in the opposite direction of the skeet shooting. Range B was just beyond it, separated by a large dirt berm. There were eight shooting bays. The first four were already occupied, leaving me the fifth slot. Each bay had a dusty wood table to be used for set-up. An RSO, range safety officer, stood behind the shooters to observe and to call the range commands. "Hot" meant we could proceed to shoot and "cold" meant to immediately stop shooting, unload, and put down your firearm. Only then could you go downrange to place or reclaim your target.

Once the RSO shouted the cold command, I walked downrange and clipped one of the targets onto the stand. When everyone was safely in place behind the firing line, the RSO called the range hot.

I unpacked the shotgun and loaded one shell into the bottom barrel. As my dad had taught me, I left the safety on until I was prepared to shoot. The sound of gunfire made me feel like I was lagging behind, but I was out of practice and needed to proceed with caution.

I adjusted my stance—legs apart, knees bent, shoulders leaning forward. Next, I extended my left hand to hold the fore end and placed my right hand on the grip, careful to keep my finger off the trigger. I could hear my dad's voice, providing step-by-step instructions. When I'd first learned to shoot, he'd put his hand on my back to help me brace for the recoil. I looked up, almost expecting him to be standing there, but of course he wasn't.

Adrenaline rushed through my body as I anticipated the gun's power. I knew the jolt would be strong, but I couldn't remember exactly how strong or how much my dad had helped me.

I took a deep breath and pulled the comb of the gun to my jaw. Then I moved the polished wood surface against my face until it nestled just under my cheekbone. I tucked the butt of the gun against my body, in the pocket between my shoulder and breastbone. With the gun in position, I looked down the barrel, aligned the sights and focused my eyes on the target. I wasn't entirely confident that I was in the correct position or that I'd remembered all the steps—it had been such a long time. The RSO was all the way down the bay. Besides, his job was to ensure everyone's safety, not be my personal instructor.

I slowly disengaged the safety and moved my finger to the trigger. The weight of the barrel made my arms start to shake. I instinctively focused on the sights and had to remind myself to look at the target, the opposite of how I'd trained with the pistol. Finally I squeezed the trigger.

B O O M!

The shot sounded like an explosion. Smoke spewed into the air. I staggered back, taking a few steps to regain my balance. My cheek stung. The scattered pellets hit the target, slightly to the right and above the center of the bullseye. Not terrible, but not exactly precise.

My dad had so loved this gun, which is why I wouldn't part with it. He'd enjoyed skeet shooting and wild turkey hunting. Maybe it was being here alone, or maybe it was feeling so unsure and out of practice, but I wasn't finding much pleasure being at the range.

I loaded another shell and attempted another shot, this time with more trepidation. Now I knew how loud it was and how much it was going to kick. I leaned forward a little further and widened my stance, hoping to offset the recoil. The extra preparation time made my arms tremble with fatigue. I slowly pulled the trigger, more hesitantly than before, and fired the gun. This time I wasn't knocked back as badly as before but my accuracy was worse.

After two shots, I'd reached a conclusion. This gun was not going to work for me. I could manage a pistol much more easily than a shotgun. I re-engaged the safety and placed my father's prized Beretta on the wood table.

My dilemma was that my pistol was still with the police. I needed it back. Also, I didn't know if I was allowed to carry it from the restaurant to my house without a permit. I was fairly sure I could have a gun for protection at home, in my car and at work, but what about the in-between points, like the parking lot? The last thing I needed was to get arrested in the parking lot of my own restaurant for illegally carrying a firearm. I could always buy another pistol for the house, but with business so slow, I was trying to avoid any extra expenses.

All of a sudden, I felt a hand on my left shoulder. I jumped and turned. It was Detective Grant.

"I didn't mean to startle you," he said. "You couldn't hear me." He pointed to my ear protection.

"What are you doing here?" I asked.

"Call me crazy, but since I carry a gun, sometimes I like to practice shooting it."

I smiled, slightly embarrassed. It wasn't like I had exclusive rights to the range. Detective Grant looked different today. Maybe it was the jeans and gray T-shirt, or maybe it was his demeanor. He seemed more relaxed.

"That's a beautiful gun," he commented. "Isn't it the one above your fireplace?"

I nodded. "It was my dad's. And it's a beast."

"I bet it is," he agreed. "Probably not your best option for home defense."

"Why not?"

"Well, it's designed for sport. The barrel's long, which makes it more accurate, but imagine trying to clear your house with that barrel. Defensive shotguns are typically shorter and aren't nearly as pretty. They look like badass black sticks."

I laughed. This gun was far from a black stick. It was an ornate masterpiece.

"I probably should have kept the 20-gauge instead of this one," I said.

"Not necessarily," he replied. "Women are told to shoot a 20-gauge or a youth model, but you can shoot a 12-gauge if you get one that fits your body. Have you ever tried the Beretta Vittoria?"

I shook my head. "What's that?"

"It's a shotgun designed for women." He paused and looked around. "Becky has one for rent up front. Want to try it?"

I tilted my head. "I thought you said you couldn't teach me."

He shrugged. "It's Saturday—my day off."

I wondered if our run-in had been by chance. He probably did practice at this range, but wouldn't he have gone to Range A, with the handguns? Frankly, I didn't care. I was glad to have the company. I repacked my bag and put the unloaded shotgun in its case.

As we walked down the dirt road back to the main building, I asked, "Do you think I'll get my pistol back soon?"

"I'll see what I can do."

"Am I allowed to bring it home from the restaurant at night?" I asked. "I don't have a carry permit."

"You don't need one. In Florida, you can have a loaded firearm at your home, place of business and in your car without a carry permit."

"But what about the parking lot of the restaurant?"

"It's your property, right?"

"Yes."

"That's covered, too. Now if your restaurant were in the strip mall next door, that would be different. That parking lot is public property. Or if you lived in an apartment complex, the parking would also be public property. But you have your own home."

"So I can take the gun from the restaurant, to my car and home without any issues?"

"Yep. Just be sure it's in a case in your car, or put it in the glove box or the center console. Or you can get the concealed carry permit. There's a course you'd have to take first, but then you can carry your pistol almost anywhere."

My dilemma for home protection was solved. I'd leave my dad's shotgun on the mantel for decoration and take the pistol home at night, once I got it back. When we reached the main building, Detective Grant had Becky show me the Vittoria. I no longer needed to try it, but he offered to give me some instruction and Becky waived the rental fee so I thought, why not?

As we walked down the dirt road back to the bay, I remembered I had something for Detective Grant. I reached in my purse and pulled out a slip of paper with nine digits written on it.

"I looked in our employee records after you dropped me off yesterday. I found McQueen's social security number."

I handed him the slip which he studied carefully.

"You'll look into him?" I asked.

He didn't reply which made my spirits sink. I couldn't blame him for having second thoughts. Lily's case wasn't his priority or concern.

"It may take some time," he said, making me realize I'd misjudged his reaction.

20. Grant | Sunday, July 11

Normal people take the weekends off, but not me. Even if I tried, I couldn't turn off my brain. Time at the range with Julianna had been my short reprieve. Under different circumstances, I might have asked her to go again, but these were not different circumstances. I had an unsolved case on my hands and a new boss to impress, so I was back at my desk continuing my research.

I'd finally gotten a copy of Brittany's birth certificate and researched her parents. Her mother died when Brittany was five. She was raised by her single father. I questioned if she'd been sexually abused—I'd seen it before, but I didn't find any signs of mistreatment: no hospital visits, no calls from neighbors, no reports from teachers. It appeared Brittany and her electrician father lived a modest existence in a small house off Grandview.

Things for Brittany changed when she lost her dad, who died of cirrhosis of the liver when she was sixteen. Still a juvenile, she was put into foster care and taken in by a family in Ocala. Not only did she lose her only parent, but she was ripped away from everything and everyone familiar. Being in foster care explained why she was on the streets at age eighteen. Up until then, she'd been a ward of the state, receiving social security survivor benefits from her father. When she aged out, she lost her free place to live and her financial support, which happens to many foster kids, often with dire consequences.

I had the address of the family in Ocala and added a visit to them to my list. Although the majority of foster parents are decent human beings, I didn't have a good feeling about these people. Brittany's murder was state-wide news. If a kid you'd helped raise was shot to death, you'd think they would've called the police to learn more, or offer to help. Unless maybe they had something to hide?

I put Brittany's birth certificate away and pulled McQueen's social security number out of my wallet. Lily's case was cold—ice cold. I didn't hold out much hope, but figured I'd see what I could find.

When I ran McQueen's criminal history, charges in both Florida and Georgia spanned several years, mostly for minor assault and possession of drugs. His final arrest, in Georgia, was for aggravated assault and pimping in the late 1990's. He was sent to prison for thirty years.

I was cautiously optimistic I may have found something. The teenage daughter of Norm and Frances Sandoval disappeared and the family friend, who Samantha suspected, was later arrested. That couldn't be just coincidence. Now I had to connect the dots between McQueen and Lily.

I called the Fulton County District Attorney's office to try to find out the particulars of McQueen's case. Being Sunday, no one was there so I left a message that I was following up on an old missing person's case. I added that there was a possible connection to a guy the DA's office had prosecuted and left McQueen's information on the voicemail.

21. Julianna | Sunday, July 11

I sat in my office at the end of the dinner shift, looking at the upcoming activities for the week. I'd put a reminder in my calendar for July Fourteenth, our Bastille Day celebration. Last year, Samantha had made raclette. The melted cheese over sliced meats, potatoes and crusty baguettes was a big hit. We'd decorated the restaurant in French flags and Michael danced around in a beret pouring Kirs, a French aperitif of white wine and crème de cassis.

I smiled at the memory. This year, I could think back to Bastille Day and remember happier times, but what about next year? When I looked back a year from now, my memory would be of unanswered questions about Michael's disappearance. That realization hit me hard, as if I was suffocating. I only had one year of happy memories before they ran out.

The staff were leaving for the night. Usually Samantha poked her head into my office and asked if I wanted her to wait. Since the shooting, the rule was that no one stayed at the restaurant alone. But for a second night in a row, Samantha had left without checking in. We hadn't yet talked about Alex. We'd just gone about our work with minimal interaction and a major elephant in the room. I knew she was torn. She loved Alex, but he'd made some serious mistakes. She also loved me. At some point, hopefully soon, we'd talk it over and get back to normal.

Outside my office, everything became eerily quiet. Had they all broken the rule and left me alone? I stood at the edge of my door and listened.

Silence.

I pictured the scene that was etched in my mind: the girl at the front of my restaurant, the unexpected blast from the gun, the shattering of glass and her strangely contorted face. I shook my head, trying to erase the image.

To my right was the delivery door. I could make a dash for it and escape to my car. I didn't know if anyone had locked the front door, but I was too panicked to care. I could call 9-1-1, but how long would it take for help to arrive?

All I could do was stand in my doorway frozen and listen.

Without making a sound, I reached in my pocket for my keys. I threaded each key between my fingers, creating a makeshift brass knuckle. Then I tiptoed down the hall, past the kitchen and peered into the restaurant.

Jasper was behind the bar.

A flood of relief filled my body.

He took a small stool and placed it in front of the liquor shelf. He stepped up, reached to the top shelf and snatched a bottle of whiskey. Next, he advanced the bottle behind it so that the shelf appeared full. Jasper stepped down and stuffed the bottle into a duffle bag, which was on top of the bar.

I watched in disbelief.

"Jasper, what are you doing?" I demanded. My restaurant wasn't his free liquor store. I already let him take food—a lot of food—but this was going too far.

He flinched at first, not realizing I'd seen him. Then he smirked. "Take it out of my pay."

"Well, I would if I knew you were doing that." My nostrils flared. "How many of those bottles have you taken?"

He shrugged. "It's not like anybody else is drinking them. We probably had ten people here tonight."

"That's not the point! What's wrong with you? Stealing from my restaurant...and lying straight to my face!" I was on a roll and didn't stop. "Jasper, I know you helped Michael with the preflight. Why did you say you'd dropped him off and left?"

His back stiffened. "Did I say that?"

There was no way he was going to squirm out of this. I knew what he'd told me and I knew what I'd seen on the video. Now I wanted the truth.

"You did say that," I replied firmly.

"I guess I forgot." He shrugged.

"You forgot what happened on the day your father disappeared?" I gathered my courage. "Did you do something to his plane?"

Jasper squinted. Anger brewed in his face. He shoved the bottle deeper into his bag and started walking toward me.

"What happened at the airport?" I demanded.

He stopped and faced me with a look of rage I'd never seen

before. Only then did I realize it was just him and me in the restaurant. I took a step back.

"You seriously think I fucked with the plane?" He looked at the ceiling, shaking his head and rolling his eyes as if he could barely stand to be in my presence.

I backtracked. "Maybe not on purpose."

He didn't respond and wouldn't look at me.

"Jasper," I said. "I know you've had a rough time. You lost your mom. And…" I paused. "With each day we don't have an answer, it's more likely we've lost your dad. I know what it's like to lose your parents."

"You don't know shit!" he exclaimed. Jasper turned toward the back entrance, charged down the hall and slammed his palms into the metal door release. The hinges rattled as the door swung open and crashed against the outer wall.

Before I could say anything else, he disappeared into the night.

22. Grant | Monday, July 12

Hall was sitting in my office when I arrived on Monday morning. He was tapping his pen and drumming his foot as he read through my case folder. It didn't appear his vacation had relaxed him much. I could've been pissed that he let himself into my office without permission, but I had to respect his initiative. He'd already familiarized himself with my work over the last week, but I briefed him anyway. It was always good to hear a fresh perspective.

"Where do you want me to start?" he asked.

There were still a lot of time-consuming tasks that needed to be done. I handed him discs with the phone records I'd subpoenaed. We had the recent call history of everyone related to the case and I needed Hall to look for any unusual relationships or connections. Brittany had a burner phone, but sometimes people slipped up and used one that was traceable.

"Are the cell tower records in here, too?" he asked.

I shrugged. I hadn't looked at them in detail yet. "Not sure, why?"

"We should look at the towers to see which phones pinged off of them. If I can get the three closest towers to the restaurant, I can triangulate the location of every phone in the area at the time of the murder."

"Have at it," I said. "I also need you to review the surveillance video again. I watched it, but take another pass."

I tossed him a thumb drive. "These are the witness interviews with the restaurant owner, her stepson, and the chef and bartender. Have a look and let me know what you think." I was about to add that I thought Alex and Samantha were lying, but wanted to see if Hall would pick that up on his own. If he caught their unusual behavior, great. If not, it would be a teaching moment, which is what the chief expected from me.

"What else?" he asked.

I'd given him a lot, but if he wanted more, I'd pile it on. "I didn't find anything on social media for Brittany, but she could've been using an alias. You have a way to check that out?"

"Sure, I'll look into it."

"And the stepson's juvenile records are due in. Keep an eye out for them. If we don't get them soon, reach out again."

"Got it," he said.

"And lastly," I added. "Can you look into Ms. Sandoval's missing husband? Maybe talk to the charter company where he worked."

Hall's eyes widened. "You think he could be involved?"

"I think he's dead, but let's cover all bases."

As I was finishing up with Hall, my desk line rang. It was the chief. "Yes ma'am?"

"You busy?" she asked.

"Just briefing Hall. We're about done."

"Good. Can both of you come to my office?"

When I relayed to Hall that Chief Jamison wanted to see us, all of his nervous energy came to an abrupt halt. "Did she say why?" he asked.

This wasn't like school. The professor wasn't going to grill him on his knowledge of the case, but he'd see that soon enough. "Come on, let's find out," I said.

As we entered her office, Hall started to rattle off the tasks that I'd just assigned to him. I could see the slight amusement in her eyes, but when she realized I'd noticed, her expression turned blank. She'd be a very hard person to interview, given her ability to instantly control her emotions.

While Hall talked, I casually looked around her office. Nothing gave a clue about the real Michele Jamison. The awards and diplomas highlighted her exemplary career, but nothing shed a hint about her personal life. She never talked about her family or dating, and I never pried. For me, it was good enough that our department was in capable hands. She was a strong yet private force.

"Hall, we're glad to have you back," she said, allowing her smile to return. "How was your cruise?"

"I'm sorry I wasn't here. I offered to stay."

"No need to apologize," she told him and then looked at me. "Grant, I need you to handle something. I've kept the Daytona news updated over the past week. Interestingly enough, the most tenacious reporter is Gage Holloman from the Ormond Beach News, although I think he's genuinely concerned. Can you give him an interview?"

I understood her desire to cultivate our relationship with the local media, but I didn't like it. I had more important things to accomplish.

"Here's his number," she said, handing me a Post-it note. "Give him a call. You know what to say and what not to say."

Hall chimed in saying, "I'll do it."

In unison, the chief and I both replied, "No."

Dejected, Hall set off to tackle his long list and I went back to my office and called Gage Holloman, to get it over with. He offered to stop by within the hour, and thirty minutes later, reception buzzed me.

Holloman was a skinny black kid with dark rimmed glasses. He wore a navy suit with a pink bow tie. Not a bead of sweat shown on his face even though it was ninety degrees outside. I led him back to my office and we both sat down.

Looking around, he asked, "Did you just start working here?"

"No," I replied.

"You planning to stay?" he asked.

I chuckled. "At least until I close this case."

"So you're confident that you'll solve this murder?" He placed his iPhone on my desk. "Do you mind if I record our conversation?"

"Not at all," I shrugged. Truth was that I did mind, but it was one of those things where you had to pretend not to care.

He leaned forward and asked, "Can you tell me what you've learned about Brittany Jones?"

I answered by sharing what was already publicly available through open records.

"Yes," he replied, pursing his lips. "I have all of that from the incident report, but can you tell me why you think Brittany Jones was shot?"

"That's what I'm investigating," I said. We both knew I was talking in circles. The question was how he'd react. To his credit, he pressed on undeterred.

"Have you identified anything in Brittany Jones's background that might have made her a target for murder? I really want to update our community if this was an isolated event, so they don't think we have a serial killer on the loose. Unless you think we do?"

His tone was curious but not aggressive. I was used to being badgered by reporters barking question after question. In comparison, he was fairly civil. I understood what the young reporter was trying to do: reassure the community. I decided to throw him a bone. It wouldn't jeopardize my investigation to admit that Brittany was targeted, but I didn't want to give away too much.

"I can tell you at this point in the investigation, we do not believe this incident was random. We have some promising leads that we're currently following up. As soon as I'm able, I'll provide you with more details, but I can't give you anything else right now."

If he was clever, he'd realize that I'd already told him more than was customary. He had enough to calm his readers, which he'd said was his goal.

Holloman quickly followed up. "Do you have any idea when you'll have more details to offer?"

I replied with a firm, "No."

He sat back in the chair and crossed his skinny legs, revealing a pink plaid sock. "One of the servers at Café Lily said you were testing a key to the front door."

My back stiffened.

He added, "I spoke with Ms. Sandoval, the owner of the restaurant. She said she was fully cooperating with the investigation. Maybe she can tell me more about that key?"

"Look, Mr. Holloman, you've read the incident report. You know that Ms. Sandoval's been through a lot. She doesn't need this right now."

I paused, still holding eye contact, daring him to upset my witness. "And I know you wouldn't want to do anything that would jeopardize some leads I'm chasing."

Holloman got my message and relented. "Okay, I'll hold off talking to her for now. When can I expect to hear from you about these leads?"

"As soon as we have something, I'll keep you informed."

He didn't seem satisfied, and I didn't need him harassing Julianna.

"You have my word," I added. "Lay off Ms. Sandoval and you'll be the first to hear anything new."

My phone rang. I stood. "I've got to take this."

"No problem," he replied. "I'll show myself out."

The woman on the phone, a special prosecutor from Fulton County, was returning my weekend call.

"Detective, you were inquiring about a Keith McQueen?" she asked. I heard pages flipping in the background. "This guy's a real beauty."

"I appreciate the call back. What do you have?"

"Sextortion. Appears he charmed his recruits into meeting with him privately. Then he drugged them, took compromising photos and blackmailed them into prostitution."

"Where's he now?" I asked.

"Still in prison, based on his sentence."

I thanked her and immediately contacted the Georgia Department of Corrections to find out where McQueen was serving his time. After an online check and a few phone calls, I received disappointing news: McQueen had died in prison.

23. Julianna | Monday, July 12

Monday marked a week since the shooting and we weren't any closer to knowing who did it. Jasper's blow-up weighed heavily on my mind. He'd never before spoken to me that way. He'd been so stoic since Michael's disappearance. Maybe all of his pent-up grief had finally bubbled to the top, or maybe there was more to it.

Then there was Alex. He'd lied about his alibi and lost the key to the restaurant—two reckless mistakes that put himself and the rest of us in jeopardy. What if Alex hadn't lost his key? What if he'd given it to Brittany? Was it possible he knew her? If only I could've talked to her for just a few more seconds, long enough to find out who she was talking about. I considered the men in my life: Michael, Jasper, Alex, Ed, even my father. Could she have been talking about any of them?

With the restaurant closed on Mondays, I had too much time to think and to worry. Mid-month payroll was a few days away and I was short on cash. I'd already given Jasper an advance for the month, but everyone else was counting on a paycheck in three days. With no other choice, I had to consider selling the boat.

Michael had a red waterproof plastic box where he kept all the paperwork for the boat. He brought it every time we took her out, but I'd been unable to find the box. I'd searched all over: the house, the restaurant, his car, but had come up empty. The only place left to look was the marina, although I dreaded going there. The marina threatened to dredge up more memories than I was prepared to face.

I drove in silence down US-1 towards Daytona Beach. Before, this trip always held the promise of a carefree, relaxing day. Michael and I would select a playlist, usually Kenny Chesney or Jimmy Buffet, and drive with the windows down and music blaring. On Monday boat days, I'd roll out of bed, no need to shower, slip on a bikini with a cover-up and gather my hair in a ponytail. Michael, dressed in bathing trunks and a T-shirt, would sing loudly, tapping the steering wheel to the beat. In the back seat we'd have our cooler with ice, beer and white wine. I always brought Pringles for a snack. If we were going out to sea, we'd pick up sub sandwiches on the way, but if we were just going to cruise the Intercoastal, we'd stop for lunch along the waterway.

"Michael," I spoke out loud. "Please give me a sign that I'm doing the right thing for the restaurant. You understand, don't you?"

Just then, I passed a billboard for Barber Yacht Sales. Our twenty-one-foot Yamaha cruiser was by no means a yacht, but it was the sign I needed that selling the boat was the right decision.

I arrived at the Halifax Harbor Marina, parked next to the office and stepped out of my car. A warm salty breeze swathed me as if to say, *welcome back, where've you been?* A few of the larger boats moored quietly in the water, giants hibernating until their masters returned for the winter. Normally, our boat would've already been in the water, fueled and ready to go. Michael would've called ahead to have it pulled from dry dock. For this trip, however, I didn't need it in the water. I just needed to look inside.

The marina manager, Gus, greeted me at the front counter. His face was cheerful until that inevitable switch went off, the one that reminded people they should be somber around me.

"Julianna," he said. "I'm so sorry."

I nodded. I didn't need another *I'm sorry* or *How can I help* or *Do you have any news*? I knew people were sorry, they couldn't help and I didn't have any news—not today, not yesterday and probably not tomorrow.

"I need to look in the boat," I said. "Would that be possible?"

"Of course. I'll have to get it down. Will be about fifteen minutes."

"That's fine."

"Are you taking it out?" He clenched the counter with both hands.

I shook my head which seemed to make him relax. I probably could manage the boat on my own. Michael had been a thorough and patient teacher, but I had no interest in trying.

Gus retreated to the warehouse and I waited on a bench in the front office. Outside, I recognized the Bentleys. He was loading fishing poles and a bait box onto their boat. She was standing on the dock spraying her legs with sunscreen. Sometimes we'd meet up with them, an impromptu invite for a casual lunch or we'd anchor right off the beach and have a floating party. Funny, I never heard from them when Michael went missing.

I gazed past the couple and the Intercoastal waterway toward the ocean. At the horizon's edge, the dark blue water met the pale sky. The sun's rays cast a streak of light that looked like white glitter dancing across the surface. I pictured Michael at the helm of our boat and me reclining on the bow. The front passenger side was my spot, the best place to sunbathe while enjoying a cool breeze. Every once in a while, I'd open an eye ever so slightly and catch Michael staring at me.

What are you looking at, I'd say playfully.

My golden girl, he'd reply with a wink.

A few minutes later, Gus emerged from the warehouse to let me know the boat was staged outside. I walked to the side of the building, in front of the parking area, to find *The Sea Lily* propped on a metal brace. Michael had renamed her in honor of my sister. She felt like an old friend from a lifetime ago.

Gus had placed a ladder next to the gunwale so I removed my shoes and climbed onboard. The glove compartment was next to the steering wheel. I opened it, but there was no red box. I searched under the seat cushions, where we stored the life vests, but found nothing there either. The boat was my last hope of finding the title and registration—documents I needed to begin the sales process. And even if I found the paperwork, I still had to find someone who wanted to buy a used boat.

Gus appeared on the starboard side. "Can I help with something?"

"You didn't happen to see a red plastic box, did you?"

He shook his head. "I didn't. Maybe your lawyer has it?"

"What?" I asked.

"A man came by here a while back. Said he was your lawyer and was asking about the boat." Gus pointed to the large yachts mooring in the marina. "He was checking them out until I told him yours was inside, in dry dock."

"Ed Harrigan was checking out our boat?" I asked.

"Sorry, I can't remember his name. Come to think, I don't recall him telling me. He was an older white guy, gray hair parted on the side, dressed in a suit."

"What did he want?"

"He wanted to know which one was yours. I couldn't let him in the warehouse. Safety rules. He said he'd just talk to you and left."

Ed had never spoken to me about the boat, and I couldn't fathom why he'd be snooping around the marina.

"I can ask if anyone has seen that box," offered Gus. "Does it have your name on it?"

I didn't want to admit that the boat's title might be inside, but I could at least tell him about the registration.

"I believe so," I said. "I think the registration is in that box and I need a copy."

"Oh, if that's all you need, just go to the county tax collector. Titles, registrations, they have copies of all of that stuff." He pointed south. "Closest one is about fifteen minutes from here."

I thanked Gus, looked up the Volusia County tax collector's address and made the short drive to their office. Fortunately, I kept Michael's POA in my purse. I took a number, waited until I was called and presented the POA to the clerk.

"I need a copy of the title and registration for our boat, please."

The clerk handed me a blank piece of paper and a pen. "Name and social security number of the owner."

I wrote Michael's information on the paper and passed it back to her. She typed on her keyboard and scanned the monitor.

"I don't have a boat registered under that name."

I took the paper back and wrote the vehicle ID number.

"Can you try the ID number?"

More typing and scanning.

"I see the boat," she confirmed. "But it's not under that name."

"Who changed it?" I asked.

She shrugged.

"Well whose name is it under now?"

"Ma'am, I can't tell you that." She seemed to take pleasure in withholding information.

"Why the hell not? It's my husband's boat."

She shrugged with that *I'm a minimum wage government worker and I don't have to help you* kind of shrug. Being in the service business, I was infuriated by her attitude, but I knew getting testy would get me nowhere.

"Okay," I said, trying to appease her. "You don't have to give me the name. Can you just confirm if the new owner is named Harrigan?"

She smirked.

"Is that a yes?"

Her reply shocked me. "You're making me very uncomfortable. If you continue, I'm going to have to call my supervisor."

"Yes, please," I said. "Let me talk to your supervisor."

"She's not here today."

"For the love of…" I stopped myself. There was no point dealing with this woman.

I called Ed on my drive home, reached his voicemail and left a message for him to call me right away. I'd never questioned Ed's expertise or motives, but couldn't understand why he was asking about the boat instead of just talking to me. And if he'd somehow changed the title from Michael to himself, why would he have done that?

Once home, I began researching how to get a copy of a boat title. An email popped up from a bride who'd booked the restaurant for her wedding reception in September. My heart started pounding. She was requesting to cancel the venue in light of recent events. Furthermore, she wanted her non-refundable deposit back. Then I saw another email that made me gasp—a message from the testing center.

I stared at the email header, reluctant to open it. Once I knew the answer, there'd be no going back. Before I could change my mind, I clicked on the email, which had a link to a secure website. I entered my user ID and password. The paternity test results were in a summary paragraph with a table of numbers at the bottom. I read the results out loud, in a low whisper.

Subject 1 is excluded as the biological father of Subject 2, with a Combined Parentage Index (CPI) of 0 and the Probability of Paternity of 0%.

I reread the results.

A probability of zero.

Michael was not Jasper's father. I let that reality register. All of a sudden I panicked, fearful that Jasper might come home. I wasn't prepared to face him. What were the possibilities? First, that neither Michael nor Jasper knew. Only the mother knew, and she'd lied to Michael. She was a desperate, dying woman who needed someone to take responsibility for her son. The second possibility was that Michael knew but hadn't told Jasper. No, that couldn't be true; even if he never told Jasper, he would've told me. Lastly, Jasper knew but Michael didn't. I shook my head, feeling like I was trying to play a game of chess without all the pieces.

24. Grant | Monday, July 12

Hall barged into my office, half out of breath.

"I was just up at Flagler Airport," he said. "Wait until you hear what I learned!"

I could feel my blood pressure rising. Of all the things I'd asked him to do, checking into Julianna's husband was last on the list. Was I going to have to painstakingly prioritize his work?

Hall took a step forward, rocking up on his toes as he spoke. "The charter owner, a guy named Chet Huff, didn't want to talk. Said he'd already covered everything months ago. I thought about threatening to bring him in to the station."

"You didn't," I cautioned.

"Of course not," he said. "I wanted to—he was a real smartass. But once I got him talking, he wouldn't stop."

"Hall, I need you on the phone records," I said, through gritted teeth. If he was going to be a distraction, there was no use having him back. Before I took this job, the chief said I'd be training the "brightest of the bright." Did that include Hall?

"I'm on them," he replied. "I loaded the numbers into a computer program I wrote that'll show any correlations. It's running now. And the phone company didn't give us the towers, so I drew up a new subpoena for the three towers closest to Café Lily."

My irritation subsided.

"But get this," he added. "When I asked Huff if Michael Sinise was a good pilot, he got real touchy. He went on about his policy of being fair and that everyone deserved a second chance. I didn't know what he was talking about, so I just shut my mouth and listened."

My shoulders, which had been up to my ears, relaxed. Listening was not an instinctual move for Hall, but maybe he was learning.

He continued, "Turns out that Sinise got a DUI, which got him fired from the airlines. The FAA suspended his pilot's certificate for a year. Huff thought I already knew and was defending his decision to employ a pilot with a DUI."

I recalled the background check I'd done on Michael Sinise. I'd seen the DUI, but didn't realize it had gotten him fired. Julianna said her husband had *chosen* to leave the airlines to work for the charter company. Was she lying to me or had he lied to her? This was another potential knot to unravel.

Hall paced in front of my desk as he referred to his notes on his iPad. "Sinise's charter plane was a Cessna Caravan C-208. It's been in production since 1982 and is the largest single-engine turboprop utility aircraft made. It generally has nine passenger seats but can be configured for fourteen. He was flying solo to an island in the Bahamas, North Eleuthera, to pick up four guys who were on a fishing trip. When I asked why there wasn't a copilot, Huff said it wasn't required. I mean, would you get on a plane with just one pilot? What if the guy had a heart attack? You're screwed."

"What's your point?" I asked. "You think Sinise had a heart attack?"

He shook his head and continued. "So, everything was normal about how Sinise left. He filed a flight plan at Flagler Airport and followed normal protocol. Daytona Departure cleared him to take off and then he checked in with Jacksonville Center as he headed south. Next, he was handed over to Miami Center, who were the first people to notice him missing. He just dropped off their radar. I asked Huff how low you had to be to drop off the radar and he said about 3,000 feet, give or take. He said drug smugglers fly just above the waves, like about 100 feet."

I pictured a plane skimming over the ocean to avoid detection and wondered if Hall had found some connection between Michael Sinise, Brittany and the running of illegal drugs.

Hall's pace quickened as he relayed more of his findings. "Huff said that Miami Center tried to contact Sinise but kept coming up empty. When he didn't respond to the radio, they called his cell phone. It went to voicemail, so they started calling nearby airports to see if he had landed somewhere else. That's when Huff's phone starts blowing up, first from Miami Center, then from the guys waiting to get picked up on the island. They were supposed to get picked up at four-thirty in the afternoon and called him around five, pissed as hell. There's not an airport on the island— just a landing strip with no control tower. And get this, there's just one guy who works customs when flights arrive, but you have to call him in advance. How backwoods is that?"

"Where are you going with all this?" I asked.

Hall lifted his hands, palms forward. "Hear me out. Miami Center doesn't waste any time calling the Coast Guard. They dispatch a boat and a few planes. I asked how they knew where to search, and here's the interesting part. They took Sinise's last known location, which was his check-in with Miami, and drew a circle from that point based on the fuel he had on board. They searched the entire area looking for signs of a crash but didn't find anything."

"And?" I said, still waiting for the headline.

"They only searched for a few days. For the Coast Guard to continue any longer, Huff's company would have to pay, which he refused to do. And when I asked if Julianna Sandoval offered to pay for the search, Huff said she also refused. I mean, would you refuse to pay for a search if your spouse was lost at sea?"

"You ever met my ex?" I said.

Hall stood motionless, completely missing my joke.

"Maybe she couldn't afford it," I added.

"Maybe she wanted him gone," he suggested. "You said it yourself—she's the beneficiary of his life insurance. She's the one with motive."

Just then, my phone rang. It was FDLE. More precisely, it was Sheila at FDLE.

"Hi Paul, how are you?" Her voice was an attempt at casual sexy, and I stress *attempt*. My jaw clenched. No one other than my mother called me Paul.

"I'm well," I said.

"I'm calling because we've finished with your audio evidence. Chief Jamison had us put a rush on it."

I was the one who'd put a rush on the evidence, not the chief, but I shrugged it off. Sheila was probably just trying to get a rise out of me.

"When can you come pick it up?" she asked. "If you can do it today, you can get it directly from me. If not, I'll have to submit it back into evidence. I assume you'll want it sooner rather than later?"

Sheila was back to her old manipulations, this time using evidence from my case as bait. She wanted to see me, but that wasn't going to happen. I replied, "Investigator Hall will come by today."

In a clipped tone, she said, "Well, I'm not going to be able to hold it. He'll have to go through the normal process."

My nostrils flared. Two seconds ago, she'd offered to hold the evidence. Now Hall coming by today wasn't good enough. I thought of the old saying, "Hell hath no fury like a woman scorned."

Then it hit me.

It hit me like the proverbial ton of bricks.

A woman scorned.

Brittany wasn't at the restaurant to help Julianna.

She was scorned. She was there to get even with someone else.

"Thanks for your work on this case, Sheila," I said into the phone and hung up.

Hall already had his car keys out, ready to go. I barked, "Get over to FDLE as fast as you can and pick up that audio evidence."

"I'm on it!" he said as he rushed out the door.

I glanced at the clock. If he hurried, he could be there before they closed for the day and we could start back fresh in the morning.

I thought about driving to Ocala, to interview Brittany's foster parents, but I was beat. Instead, I decided to take one night off, order take-out and go to bed early. I swung by the chief's office, gave her a quick update and packed up.

I was halfway to my favorite Chinese restaurant when my phone rang. It was Hall.

He asked, "Have you left the office yet?"

"Yeah. What's up?"

"You need to turn around. You gotta hear this. We need to move on it tonight."

25. Julianna | Tuesday, July 13

Because we were closed on Mondays, Tuesday's lunch crowd would be telling. Would people start to come back, or would they stay away until the case was solved?

I arrived at the restaurant around 9:30 a.m. Samantha and the kitchen staff were already at work. The bar looked empty without Alex. I had an ache in my stomach over how things had gone down. I'd let people go before, but there had always been an escalation—poor performance, repeated warnings. No one was ever fired on impulse. Until now. The only silver lining was a financial one. Having him off payroll meant I had one less salary to pay. If we remained slow, I could hold off on replacing him for several weeks, even months.

When I poked my head into the kitchen, Samantha was scream-ing at Justin, one of our newer staff members. In all of our years working together, I'd barely heard her raise her voice, so seeing this behavior was quite a shock. Apparently Justin had poured grease down the sink, which could cause a clog. It was an amateur mistake, but not something that deserved this kind of beratement.

I called out to Samantha, motioning for her to join me at the door. When she approached, I put my arm around her and we walked down the hallway toward my office.

"Do you want to talk about it?" I asked, knowing what really had her upset. Since Friday, she hadn't said a word about Alex. Surely she had to understand my position, although it had put both of us in an uncomfortable spot. I'd known her longer than she'd known Alex, but at the end of the day, she shared her life with him.

Samantha deflected. "This new guy's an idiot. I can't deal with him." She ducked out from under my arm.

"I've seen worse mistakes than a bit of kitchen grease down the drain," I said. "Remember the time Jesse used expired meat and we had to trash an entire main course? Now *that* was worth some harsh language."

She smiled faintly as she turned toward me. "You did lose your cool that time."

"Luckily you thought up Vegetarian Night, as if we'd planned it all along."

That story usually made us laugh, but not today. We stopped in front of my office door.

"How's Alex?" I asked.

Samantha grabbed her ponytail and pulled her long black hair out of its fastener. She raked her fingers through it, gathering the loose strands into a knot and refastened them. Unhappy with the first attempt, she loosened it and tried again. She finally stopped fidgeting, looked me straight in the eyes and sighed. "He's gone."

"What do you mean?"

"We got into a fight and he stormed out."

I stepped inside my office. She followed and I shut the door behind us. I couldn't help but feel responsible for their fight.

"What happened?" I asked.

"He was so angry. I have no idea where he went."

I was feeling more guilty by the minute.

"I found something," she started to explain. "We were cleaning out the garage yesterday and I found an open carton of cigarettes, like the kind you get from duty-free."

I tilted my head. What did cigarettes have to do with anything?

She continued, "The night of the shooting, Alex said he went out for cigarettes, but it turns out he had a carton of them in the garage. He didn't need to go out." She grabbed my forearm. "Julianna, I covered for him because I believed him. I didn't want the mistakes of his past to haunt his present, you know?"

"But now you think he lied?"

"I don't know. When I found the cigarettes, I asked him about it." She paused. "He got so angry. It was like he flipped a switch. He said I was accusing him of murder, and if I had that kind of doubt, I didn't know him at all. He stormed out and I haven't heard from him since."

"Since yesterday?" I clarified.

She nodded. "He hasn't responded to any of my texts. He didn't take the car, so I thought he'd just gone out for a walk to calm down, but he never came home." Samantha unknotted her hair again. "Did Jasper go out last night? Maybe he picked Alex up?"

I shook my head, realizing I was even more in the dark about Jasper than she was about Alex. "I'm not sure," I replied. "He's been staying with friends. Should I try to call him?"

"Alex or Jasper?" she asked.

"Alex."

"Probably not a good idea," she said.

We sat in silence. For a brief moment, Samantha's drama had made me forget about my own. Later that morning, Jasper would be coming to work. I was uncertain how I'd feel. A lot would depend on how he behaved. If he apologized for his blow up and explained why he'd lied about the preflight, I was willing to listen. If he didn't, I was ready to confront him with the video and ask about his name change. As far as the paternity test, I hadn't decided if I was willing to go that far. That knowledge could destroy him.

For now, there was one thing we had to do.

"Samantha," I said. "We have to call Detective Grant. You need to tell him the truth about Alex's alibi." I started to reach for my phone.

"No!" she exclaimed. "Just because I found those cigarettes doesn't mean Alex did anything wrong. And think of the trouble I'll get in for lying."

I shook my head. "Nothing good comes from lying. Better to come clean now."

"Let's wait," she begged. "Let's see if he comes home tonight."

I didn't want to betray her trust, but I couldn't withhold details about a murder investigation. In my gut, I knew I had to call Detective Grant. I could reason with him to go easy on Samantha for covering for Alex, but we owed him the truth. She gently put her hand on my phone. It wasn't a forceful gesture to prevent me from making a call, but more of a plea for me to wait.

26. Grant | Monday, July 12

When I got back to the station, Hall was already there, pacing in my office. Before I could sit down, he set the small recorder he'd picked up from FDLE on my desk and pressed play. I listened as Hall continued to pace. It didn't take long for me to comprehend what it meant. Before the recording ended, Hall blurted, "We've got to find Jasper!"

I agreed, although my first thought was of Julianna. Where was she, and was he anywhere near her?

"I could track his cell phone," Hall suggested.

I shook my head. It was a good idea in theory, but it wasn't practical. Getting a court order could take days, and we didn't have that kind of time. I grabbed the case file, flipped to my research on Jasper, and found his car make, model and license plate number.

I immediately issued a BOLO, or "be on the look out," for Jasper Sinise, providing his description and that of his car to our local patrol units. I warned them not to make contact, but to notify me immediately. We couldn't risk spooking him and having him bolt.

Next, I called Julianna. She was at the restaurant. Jasper wasn't there. I sent an unmarked car to Café Lily and another to her house, with instructions to apprehend Jasper on sight. She sounded worried, but I wouldn't let anything happen to her. She also said she needed to talk to me, but there was no time for that right now.

Hall and I each jumped in our own vehicles and began the search. We drove up and down the strip for hours, pulling into restaurants, bars, night clubs and any other place we thought Jasper might frequent. I even checked Brittany's deserted condo; I didn't expect to find him there, but stranger things have happened.

At around 3:00 a.m., I felt myself giving way to exhaustion. *Just ten more minutes*, I bargained with myself, knowing that we could find Jasper at any moment. When that ten minutes was up, I'd challenge myself to do ten more. Quitting simply was not an option.

Hall met me at a convenience store and bought a jumbo plastic cup, a Java Monster energy drink and a Mountain Dew. He mixed the drinks together and offered me a swig, but I stuck with my iced coffee. Then we were back on the road, continuing our drive up and down the main stretch of A1A and checking in with the patrol cars.

Three hours later, as the sun began to rise, I was thinking I should've tried Hall's energy concoction. I radioed him and we met up at a Waffle House for a quick breakfast. While we were eating, one of our patrol cars reported in. They'd spotted Jasper heading southwest on I-92. He'd pulled into a gas station and was filling up. I threw a twenty on the table; we left our half-eaten waffles and dashed out.

"Stay on him, but don't move in," I shouted into the radio to the patrol officer. I felt momentary relief, knowing Jasper was nowhere near Julianna. By the time we'd reached the gas station, he was on the move again, almost in Deland.

Once I had eyes on his car, I ordered the patrol car to back off and for Hall to stay farther behind me. Jasper was less likely to notice my unmarked Malibu than a squad car. We followed our suspect north, which led toward the Deland Municipal Airport.

"He's gonna take off," Hall called into the radio. "You've gotta get closer."

"Why gas up the car if you're flying out?" I said. "Let's keep our distance."

Jasper continued a short distance past the airport and turned onto a narrow dirt road with trailers on each side. A sign for "Chateau Deland" hung sideways from a rotting white fence. Weeds sprouted under a few dilapidated cars parked at the front entrance. A clothes-line with sheets billowed in the early morning wind. A graveyard of broken exercise equipment and old lawn mowers rusted nearby.

Jasper pulled up to the second trailer from the entrance and exited his car. He didn't bother to look around, apparently confident in the security of his hideout. He quickly scaled the rickety stairs and disappeared inside.

"Hall," I said. "Go to the county magistrate court. Get search and arrest warrants, and make sure they include the potential murder weapon and any property that belonged to Brittany Jones. I'll stay here and watch the trailer."

Once Hall was on his way, I pulled my car behind some trees next to the trailer park entrance, cracked open the window and turned off the engine. I quickly exited the driver's side, ducked into the back seat and crouched out of sight. With me hidden, the car looked empty, like the others.

Next, I called the sheriff's department and asked if they had a fugitive team available to hit a location I had under surveillance. They needed a few hours to assemble the team, which would give Hall time to secure paperwork at the courthouse.

Once everything was in motion, all I could do was wait. I lay across the back seat and tugged at my shirt for some ventilation. With the engine and air conditioning off, the car was sweltering hot. I wished I'd skipped that last cup of coffee, but I couldn't risk blowing my cover to take a leak.

Finally, Hall called with the warrants. I instructed him to park his car at the airport we'd passed and walk in. We couldn't take any chances of drawing attention. When he arrived on foot, I handed him my keys and we discretely swapped places. He took over surveillance from the back seat of my car and I headed on foot to meet the sheriff's squad, relieving myself in the bushes once I was clear of the park.

Six guys in three vehicles were waiting for me at the airport. They were dressed in full tactical gear, vests on and rifles out. As I was debriefing them, my phone rang. It was Hall…in a panic.

"Jasper came out!" he said, in a fast whisper. "He's loading a lot of stuff into his trunk! Looks like he's getting ready to leave for good."

"Just keep watching," I said firmly. "We're nearly in place."

"I can't let him get away."

"Stand down!" I ordered. "Don't compromise your position."

"If he tries to leave, I'll move the car and block the exit." From the shuffling in the background, I could tell he was already in motion.

"No! Hold your position!" I shouted.

I heard the car engine crank and nearly slammed my phone onto the concrete in frustration. I wasn't again going to have an impatient rookie destroy what I'd set up. I shouted, "Stand down, officer!"

Hall was about to jeopardize everything. We were prepping to do this takedown safely, tactically and without anyone getting hurt. He was about to blow it, putting himself and the operation at risk by showing our hand before the tactical team could get into position. He would drastically increase the chance of things going wrong. Very wrong.

"Let's move!" I commanded and jumped into the back of a Suburban with two of the deputies. We rolled in fast. Fortunately, the element of surprise was still on our side. Hall had listened to me—he hadn't moved the car. I took cover next to him while the tactical team advanced.

One minute, the park was empty, and the next, the place was completely surrounded. The team of six moved like ninjas, seamlessly taking their posts—three at the trailer front door, two around back, one under the window. The lead kicked in the front door.

I heard the deputy shout, "Get on the ground!" Two officers who'd entered the trailer with him called out "Clear!" as they searched each room. Within seconds, the raid was over. They'd moved in so fast and with such precision that the invasion was completed almost as soon as it had begun. It was an impressive thing to witness.

The lead deputy came to the door and waved to me and Hall, a signal it was okay to join them. I mounted the front steps of the trailer and went inside. Hall followed behind me. Two men were lying face down on the cheap linoleum floor with their hands cuffed behind their backs.

"We've got two in custody," the deputy said. "Found some suitcases by the door. Looks like they were packed up and planning to leave."

One of the deputies rolled Jasper on his side and pulled him to his feet. Standing there, Jasper looked shocked and hollow. The unexpected siege had him scared shitless. Any trace of his arrogance was gone, replaced with abject fear.

Another deputy rolled the second guy over and pulled him to his knees. He was bigger than Jasper and jerked his shoulder in an attempt to escape the deputy's grip. Unable to free himself, he scowled like a trapped dog.

"Good morning, Mr. Sinise," I said, as I locked eyes with Julianna's dead husband.

"What the fuck! Who the fuck are you? You don't know me. You can't just break in here," he spewed.

He thought I didn't know him, but I knew the man I'd been hunting long before I discovered his actual identity. He had no clue who I was, but I knew everything about him.

"I have a warrant for your arrest," I said. "And a search warrant for the premises."

"What am I being arrested for?" he quipped defiantly.

"Murder."

I watched Michael scan the room, searching desperately for his excuse, when his eyes landed on Jasper. "You don't know what you're talking about," he said. "You've got the wrong guy!"

The deputy pulled Michael from his knees to his feet. He was a tall man and heavier than he looked in the photos with Julianna. He had a grayish-brown beard and unkempt hair. His face looked pasty, the same pallor I'd seen on prisoners who never spent time outside. The months he'd spent hiding had taken a toll.

"Fine. Search the place. Take all the time you need," he scoffed. "You won't find anything here." Michael glared at Jasper as if daring him to speak, but his son was still shell-shocked.

I surveyed the small trailer. It wouldn't take long to search, but based on Michael's flippant comment, I doubted we'd find anything consequential. As I stepped forward, the deputy grabbed Michael by the arm and pulled him back to clear the way.

"Ow! You stupid fuck," he shouted. "I think you broke my arm. I'm going to sue every one of you. You'll have no job, no money, no life when I'm done with you!"

I walked in front of Michael and put my face inches from his. "You have a lot to say about life," I replied. "For a dead guy."

Michael lunged toward me, hissing and cussing, but the deputies yanked him back. He struggled to free himself, but he was trapped.

"Get him out of here," I ordered. Two of the deputies dragged Michael out of the trailer and put him in the back of one of the cars. Another deputy moved Jasper to the small kitchen table inside. Until the transport arrived, we needed to keep them apart so they couldn't coordinate their stories.

Residents of the park began to venture out, gawking at the scene and whispering to one another. Not long after, Michael and Jasper were hauled off to the station. Hall and I stayed at the trailer to conduct the search. Most everything the two owned was in Jasper's car or in the packed suitcases. For the next two hours, we combed every inch of the trailer, taking photographs and labeling evidence. As I suspected, we didn't find anything significant— not the murder weapon and not a trace of Brittany. Instead we found a lot of whiskey bottles, take-out bags from

Café Lily, rental paperwork for the trailer signed by Jasper, and a stash of cash and fake IDs.

By mid-morning, Hall and I headed back to the station. I grabbed an iced coffee, although by that point my adrenaline was keeping me awake. I updated the chief and talked to the officers who'd transported my suspects. Michael had nothing to say, but Jasper was asking a lot of questions.

The two were being held in different interview rooms. I decided to start with Jasper, the weaker link. As I walked into the room, he was a far cry from the cocky asshole I'd interviewed a week ago. He was ghostly white and still looked shaken from the takedown.

"Jasper," I started. "I don't have time for a whole lot of lies right now. Michael said you killed Brittany."

Of course I hadn't interviewed Michael yet, but Jasper didn't know that.

"That's not true!" he protested. "I didn't know he'd offed her until after he'd done it!"

"Hold on," I told him. "I want to hear your side of the story, but before you tell me anything or I ask you any questions, I need to make sure you understand your rights."

I went over the Miranda waiver form with Jasper. Without any hesitation, he waived his rights and started spilling his guts.

"I was in Miami when Michael called and told me what he'd done," he explained. "I gave you the flight, remember?"

"You did," I replied. "But you could've shot her around midnight and driven to Miami in time to catch a morning flight back to Orlando. Makes for a good alibi."

I was fairly certain this scenario wasn't true. Jasper's friends had vouched for him being in Miami on July fourth, and his phone had pinged from there. So unless he'd paid off his friends to transport his phone and lie for him, his alibi was pretty solid.

"Michael did it! I swear!" he shouted. "He followed Brittany to Café Lily and saw her talking to Julianna. Brittany was gonna blow everything. She was gonna tell Julianna he was still alive. So he shot her."

"Because Michael had faked his death?" I asked.

He stopped himself, probably realizing he'd said too much.

"Why'd he do it?" I asked.

Jasper clammed up.

If I couldn't get him to tell my why, maybe I could get him started with how.

"Look," I said. "We already know he disappeared three months ago on his way to the Bahamas. How'd he do it? How'd he manage to vanish without anyone knowing?"

"It wasn't like it was hard," he smirked. "He turned off the plane's transponder, dipped below 2,500 feet and tossed his phone in the ocean."

"How'd he hide the plane?" I asked.

He shrugged. "He'd already scouted a field in the Southern Glades with a deserted barn. After he landed, he hid the plane in the barn and Brittany picked him up."

"So she helped him?" I asked.

Jasper paused. "Yeah, for the insurance money. But nobody was supposed to get hurt. And I didn't kill Brittany. That was all Michael."

"Can you point out the location on a map where we can find the plane?" I asked.

He shrugged. "Maybe."

A *maybe* meant he knew more than he was saying, but I'd let him continue to blame everything on Michael.

"If what you're telling me is true, where's the gun Michael used to shoot Brittany?"

Jasper ran his fingers through his hair and looked around the room. "I don't know. He said he got rid of it."

I stared at Jasper, expressionless, although I believed that part. I doubted Michael was stupid enough to keep the murder weapon. Most likely, he tossed it in the ocean outside Café Lily or hid it somewhere we'd never find it.

I continued, "Michael said Brittany was your girl. Said you were the one who lost your cool with her. Look, Jasper, just tell me the truth. We may be able to convince the DA this was manslaughter, not murder. Heat-of-the-moment kind of thing."

His eyes bugged out. "She wasn't *my* girl! Michael was the one fucking her!" His eyes darted back and forth as he scrambled to think of any evidence to convince me, but he couldn't.

I grabbed a pad of paper and a pen. "Write down everything that happened," I instructed. "Every single detail. I'll be back in a little while."

I left the interview room, thinking it was almost too easy. Was it possible he'd rehearsed his story and was just delivering his performance? Was Jasper Sinise a step ahead of me?

I took note of his comment about nobody getting hurt. Little did he know, we had Brittany's recording, which definitely told us otherwise.

27. Julianna | Tuesday, July 13

Jasper never came into work and I was part relieved, part angry. I'd gone from having a bartender and a back-up to no one at all. He didn't even call in or reply to my texts, so I was forced to pour drinks all evening. I didn't get any of my own work done and there was no way I was staying at the restaurant alone to catch up.

At home, I took a steamy shower and debated what to do next. Jasper was eating my food, stealing my liquor, blowing off work and lying about the preflight. What did I owe him? He wasn't even Michael's son. He had an alibi for the night of the shooting, confirmed by Detective Grant, but something still felt off. Maybe he didn't pull the trigger himself, but what if he solicited help from someone else?

Someone like Alex.

What if Alex had come back to the restaurant that night? He'd already shown he was capable of stealing. What else would he do for money?

Still in my bathrobe, I rushed to the kitchen to find my phone. I needed to tell Detective Grant about Alex's fake alibi. As soon as I stepped into the hallway, I heard furious pounding on the front door, followed by the door bell ringing incessantly. When I looked through the peephole, I jumped back.

It was Alex.

My heart jackhammered inside my chest. I stepped away from the door and held my breath. I could pretend I wasn't home, but all the lights were on. The pounding continued, followed by him shouting, "Julianna, I need to talk to you!"

Finally I gathered the nerve to reply. "Go away, Alex! I have nothing to say to you!"

The pounding on the door continued, along with the continuous ringing of the doorbell. He was acting like a madman.

"Go away or I'm calling the police!"

The noise stopped. All was quiet, but I didn't think he'd left. He was plotting his next move. I hurried to the fireplace and lifted my dad's shotgun from its mount. I'd left two shells on the mantel, just in case. My fingers trembled as I attempted to ready the gun. With the shotgun at my hip, I stood quietly in the middle of my family room and listened. The terry cloth belt on my bathrobe had come loose, but I couldn't put down the gun to retie it. My breathing was shallow and I began to shake. I tried to convince myself that I had nothing to fear. I'd known Alex for years. Samantha lived with him. She trusted him. Then I thought about our last conversation. Maybe she didn't trust him after all. She already knew he was a thief. Maybe she'd figured out that he was capable of far worse.

A movement outside caught my eye. All of a sudden, Alex's face appeared at my back sliding glass door. I gasped. He looked like a bodiless head peering inside. I stepped back and raised the gun, pointing it at his invisible torso. Chills rushed like a current through my body. I pictured Brittany being shot through the glass window of my restaurant. How long could I wait before I defended myself?

His face disappeared.

I quickly side stepped to the kitchen while keeping the gun pointed at the back door. With a quick swipe of my hand, I flipped off the house lights. Everything went black, leaving me blinded for a few seconds. My eyes gradually adjusted to the darkness. Instinctively I ducked behind the kitchen counter, hoping he hadn't seen my hiding place. The only light in the room came from my cell phone which was charging on the counter and the small clock on the microwave.

"Julianna," he shouted. "I need to talk to you. I need you to talk to Samantha for me. She'll listen to you."

I couldn't tell where he was—maybe the side of the house. I inched my way to the phone and called Detective Grant. His line went straight to voicemail.

28. Grant | Tuesday, July 13

Next up was Michael. I grabbed another cup of coffee from the breakroom. I'd been awake for over thirty hours, and I needed to stay sharp.

My phone rang. It was Julianna. I wanted to answer so I could tell her Michael was alive, but this wasn't something I could do over the phone. Right now, I couldn't allow myself to be distracted. Knowing she was safe, I declined the call and prepared myself for the next meeting. I had to be careful not to mix up the facts of the two interviews, given that I was already tired. I needed to be confident, but not get into a pissing contest. With an alpha male like Michael, that wouldn't work. I grounded myself, put on my game face—neutral, not condescending—and opened the door to his interview room.

Michael was leaning back in the chair with his legs extended. His polo shirt stretched tight across his belly. When I entered the room, he didn't bother to look up, but continued picking at his finger nails.

"Mr. Sinise, I'm Detective Grant." I took a seat in front on him. "When we first met at the trailer, you indicated that I had some misinformation, that I didn't have the right suspect. I want to know more about that. But before you tell me what it is that you have to tell me, I need to inform you of your rights."

I went through the Miranda waiver, which Michael signed. Unlike Jasper, who cooperated because he was ready to confess, I assumed Michael signed because he thought he could outsmart me.

"So tell me what happened," I said, deliberately leaving my statement vague. I wanted to know where he'd start—killing Brittany, conning Julianna, faking his death or just denying everything.

"It was all her idea," he said.

It was Brittany's idea? That didn't make sense.

"She was running the restaurant into the ground. This was her way to save it. I took a fall for her."

I realized Michael wasn't talking about Brittany, but Julianna. I felt the blood pulsing in my neck but couldn't let him see he'd gotten a rise out of me.

"Who are you talking about?" I asked.

"I'm talking about my wife, Julianna. What kind of detective are you?" he said with a smirk.

I ignored the barb. "So your wife asked you to fake your disappearance?"

Michael crossed his arms but didn't say anything more. We stared at each other in silence. Typically, this tactic got the other person talking, but not Michael. He sat there, having a staredown with me, as if he had all the time in the world.

I needed to switch gears.

"Jasper was a lot more forthcoming about this whole situation," I commented.

"Jasper's an idiot," he retorted. "And he'll lie about anything and everything to cover his own ass."

"What would he be covering?" I asked.

"You're the detective. You tell me."

We were playing a verbal game of chess. Every move he made was done with the sole intent of trying to figure out what I knew. The trick was to listen without reacting, even when I knew I was hearing nothing but bullshit. I couldn't let on. I had to control my every word, my body language and my facial expressions. That's because as much as I was watching and reading him, he was doing the same thing with me. Criminals are good at reading people, especially cops. It was a high-stakes game to see who'd make the first mistake.

I responded, careful not to get baited. At the same time, I couldn't be too smug or he'd shut down. "Jasper said this was all your idea. He never mentioned Julianna knowing anything." Then I readied myself for the elaborate web of bullshit this con artist would spin.

Michael squinted. "You searched the trailer. I'm sure you saw leftovers from Café Lily. Who do you think brought them over? My wife was using me to save her restaurant."

He wasn't letting go of this farce about Julianna being involved, which was infuriating. No way was she part of this scheme. I'd spent my career reading people, and Julianna Sandoval was the real deal. I had no proof of her conversation with Brittany, but her testimony matched the evidence. And, of course, I had the recording.

"Okay," I played along. "But I didn't find anything from Café Lily at the condo on Myrtle Street."

He glared at me, realizing I knew more—a lot more. We sat there, our eyes locked, waiting to see who was going to flinch first.

"Why don't you get me a lawyer," he said.

I stood, gathered my case file and pushed the chair back. He had a smug look of triumph on his face, as if asking for a lawyer had somehow defeated me.

As I started to walk out, I turned and said, "For someone who says he's innocent, I find something quite interesting."

He raised an eyebrow.

I continued. "When I told you that you were under arrest for murder, you never asked me whose murder. You know why? Because you already knew. Because you killed Brittany Jones and I can prove it."

His reply was a single word, "Lawyer."

29. Julianna | Tuesday, July 13

I didn't leave Detective Grant a message. There was no time. I started to dial 9-1-1 when I heard a strange sound outside. It reminded me of a coyote howling, until I realized it was human. As I peered over the countertop, I could see Alex's silhouette, crouched on my back step, crying like a wounded animal.

I didn't know what to think. First he was pounding on my door like a maniac. Now he was sobbing like a baby. He was unstable.

He's not who you think he is replayed in my mind.

Brittany must have known Alex. The key she had must've been his. No wonder he'd tried to deflect the blame onto Michael. He'd been lying about losing it. What did I really know about Alex Walker anyway? Early on, he'd helped out at the restaurant so he could hang out with Samantha. It was a natural progression to bring him on staff. I'd never thought about doing a background check, which was a huge mistake.

I gripped my shotgun and listened. The crying stopped. I peered over the counter again but couldn't tell if he was still on the back steps. He was out there. That much I knew. I just wasn't sure where.

My phone rang making my heart skip a beat. I assumed it was Detective Grant—he'd seen my missed call. I snatched the phone and my body stiffened when I saw the caller ID.

It was Alex.

He was using my phone to pinpoint my location. I quickly dismissed the call, silenced the phone and crouched further behind the counter. In this location, I was shielded except for the window over the sink. If he peered through there, he'd surely see me.

The phone buzzed.

It was Alex again.

Feeling trapped, I answered and screamed into the receiver. "I'm giving you one warning, Alex. You need to leave. Now!"

"I didn't mean to scare you. I'm sorry. What do I have to do to convince you, Julianna? And Samantha? I didn't shoot that girl."

"I know you had Samantha cover for you."

"I went out, to get cigarettes, not back to the restaurant," he protested.

"You already had a carton of cigarettes. Samantha told me."

"I *did* go out for cigarettes. I forgot about the ones in the garage. I just thought it'd be easier to say I was home."

"Where'd you buy them?" I challenged.

"What?"

"The cigarettes. Where'd you buy them?"

"At the 7-Eleven on Nova Road," he replied. "Wait a minute! They'll have video of me there! I can prove it. Why didn't I think of that before? I'll get the video. Then you and Samantha will see I'm telling the truth."

Alex seemed genuinely excited at the prospect of getting this video proof. Would a guilty man make such an offer? Maybe, just maybe, he *was* telling the truth, but how could I be sure? There were only three men I trusted: my father, Michael and Detective Grant, and two of them were gone.

"Julianna, I just want my life back—my job, my girl. Give me a second chance; I promise I won't need a third."

I blinked, taken aback. When my father upset my mother, albeit rarely, he used to say the same thing, *give me a second chance and I promise I won't need a third*. Had Alex heard my dad say this?

"That's an interesting promise," I commented.

"Your dad said it to me. He gave me a second chance."

My thighs were starting to burn from squatting behind the counter. I slowly repositioned myself to kneeling on the floor while still gripping the shotgun.

Alex continued, "Your dad knew what I'd done at Kelly's Pub. I guess he'd called my old manager before you hired me. He confronted me and made me promise to never steal again. And I haven't. I swear."

I listened in amazement. Leave it to my dad to catch everything. Here I was, thinking we'd never vetted Alex, but my dad had. Even more, he hadn't told me. He wanted to avoid tainting my opinion of the guy. He'd truly given Alex a fresh start.

"You know what's worse than being caught stealing?" he asked. "Being accused of murder, and having the people closest to you ready to believe it's true. I could never shoot anyone, but you and Samantha think I could."

His words weighed heavily on me. He'd lied about where he was when Brittany was shot, but it appeared to be out of fear. How could I be certain? Then I had an idea. I'd tell Detective Grant about Alex's alibi and see if he could pull the video from the 7-Eleven. Only then could I really know.

"Alex, I want you to go to the Marriott by the restaurant," I said. "Go there, book a room and don't leave until I call you."

I heard him exhale. "Okay. So you believe me?"

"Just stay there until we sort this out."

I wasn't sure if I believed him or not, but most of all, I needed Alex away from me and away from Samantha.

30. Grant | Wednesday, July 14

I got home after midnight emotionally drained from five hours of interrogation, but it was a satisfying exhaustion. Brittany's murder had consumed me for over a week. I'd been wrapped up in the case, unable to relax. Now I felt an enormous release, almost like having sex. Not much else comes close to the feeling you get when you've solved a crime. You've put in the legwork, you've stayed awake at night thinking about it, you've rehashed what you know and what you think you know. Then, all of a sudden, you have the answers you've been chasing. You have your suspects in custody.

I became a cop because I don't like predators, thieves or bullies. What I didn't expect to enjoy was the thrill of the hunt. I only discovered that after getting into investigations. You're given bits and pieces and are supposed to figure out the who and the why of the crime, and sometimes you never understand the why. I knew this case had a fifty-fifty chance of unfolding quickly. I also knew that if we didn't solve it in a few weeks, it could become a cold case, maybe taking years to solve, if ever. But yesterday, after the first tile tipped, the dominos just kept falling.

Julianna had called while I was in my interviews. She didn't leave a message. Made me wonder if she'd already heard the news. Someone at the trailer park could've posted on social media or a journalist could've been tipped off about the raid. I texted her that I would come by her house first thing in the morning and then hit the bed. I hadn't slept so soundly in a week.

The next morning, my feeling of triumph quickly faded as I thought about the job ahead of me. I was about to deliver a blow to someone I'd come to care about. That part definitely sucked. I parked my car across the street from her house and repeatedly popped the lid on my coffee canister as I gathered my thoughts. Julianna had been through so much already. She was a strong woman, but how much more could she take before she reached her breaking point? Not only did I have devastating news regarding her husband and stepson, but I'd hit a dead end with her sister's case. At some point, definitely not today, I'd have to tell her that McQueen was dead and so was any chance of linking him to Lily.

The sound of a passing vehicle made me look up. A news van was parking in front of Julianna's house. A female reporter hopped out, smoothed back her wavy brunette hair and positioned herself in front of the camera.

"Fuck!" I shouted. I thought I had a little more time before the story broke. I expected the media at the restaurant, but not at Julianna's home. Nowadays, with the internet, it was too easy to discover where people lived.

Where people lived.

A random idea struck me, as they often did, regarding McQueen. I could check his residential history to find out where he was living the year Lily disappeared. It was a longshot, but might provide the link I needed to connect them. For now, reaching Julianna before the media was my priority. I exited my car and approached the van. The reporter extended her microphone. "Good morning, detective. We have reason to believe there's been an arrest in the murder of Brittany Jones."

I looked at the house. All seemed quiet.

"Call Gage Holloman with the Ormond Beach News," I told the reporter. "Once he's here, I'll give you both a statement."

I turned away ignoring her follow-up questions and hastened my stride to Julianna's house. Before I could knock, the door opened and I quickly stepped inside.

31. Julianna | Wednesday, July 14

I'd barely slept, too agitated by Alex's surprise visit and anxious about confronting Jasper. I hadn't seen him for three days, since his outburst on Sunday evening. Since then, I'd been uneasy, not knowing when he'd appear. He never called or texted—my only warning would be hearing the garage door open. He had every right to come and go as he wished, but knowing I could be intruded upon at any moment had me on edge.

Detective Grant was coming over. I needed to tell him about Alex's false alibi and see if he could check the video from the 7-Eleven. I also planned to share what I'd discovered about Jasper's paternity test. The more I thought about it, Brittany had to be talking about him. Jasper wasn't who I thought he was. He wasn't Michael's son, but why that mattered to her I wasn't sure.

I peered out the front blinds and gasped when I saw Detective Grant talking to a reporter. This could only mean one thing—bad news. He started walking to the front door so I quickly opened it, mindful to stay out of the camera's prying lens.

"What's happened?" I asked, as he stepped inside.

"Let's sit down and talk." He motioned to the kitchen table. I'd prepared his favorite coffee, but he declined a cup, another omen. I joined him at the table and braced myself for what was to come next.

"Have you ever heard of the term 'love bomb'?" he asked.

His question threw me. Why mention love when I was certain we were about to talk about death? "I don't think so."

"It's when someone overwhelms you with attention, sweeps you off your feet, but their intentions aren't pure. They're really just trying to manipulate you."

I wasn't sure what he meant, although the word *manipulate* lingered in my mind. Detective Grant opened his hand to reveal a small digital recorder, which he placed on the table between us. "I need you to listen to this recording," he said. "We recovered it from Brittany's belongings. But I need to warn you, this isn't going to be easy for you to hear."

He pressed Play.

I heard Jasper's voice. "I've got news."

Then a second voice, also male. "What's up?"

My heart jumped into my throat. I knew that voice. It was as familiar as my own. Detective Grant pressed the pause button and asked, "Do you recognize who's talking?"

I nodded. "It's Jasper…and Michael. When was this taken?"

He didn't answer. Instead, he pressed Play again and I heard the rest of the conversation.

Jasper: I tried to convince her, like you said, but she won't do it.

Michael: Why the hell not?

Jasper: I don't know. I guess she's still holding out hope.

Silence.

Michael: Look, get Julianna to hold a memorial service. Tell her to do it for you, if not for herself, and that you need closure.

Jasper: I'm telling you she won't do it. Doesn't even want to talk about it. Her lawyer, this old dude, came by and talked to us. I agreed to have you declared dead, but she wants to wait.

Michael: We can't wait. We can't do anything until she has the insurance money.

Jasper: Well, we're screwed, and it gets worse. She used her power of attorney at your bank. They gave her access to your account, no questions asked. Let her withdraw everything. She wiped out the account, paid off your credit card and the boat slip. Now I don't have any money.

Michael: She can't do that!

Jasper: You made her your fucking power of attorney.

Silence.

Jasper: We should've just offed her. This two-step thing is way too complicated.

Michael: Don't be an idiot. I would've been the prime suspect. This way, you'll have a clear alibi, and no one will question you being her beneficiary. Go back. Convince her.

Jasper: I can't keep pushing her. She'll get suspicious. Sometimes she looks at me funny, like she already knows something. I can't stand being around her.

Michael: Being around *her*? Try hanging out with Brittany all day. She's driving me fucking nuts. Threatened to go back to that used car loser if things don't break soon.

Jasper: You picked her.

Michael: As a side piece of ass, and 'cause she had this place, but for fuck's sake, she's making me miss Julianna. At least that bitch gave me money.

Jasper: So cut her loose. I've already got the new paperwork.

Silence.

Michael: Yeah, that's right.

Jasper: You don't need Brittany anymore. We've got this place for another year. That dude from Jersey isn't coming back. And if that bitch is making threats...she almost blew it for you before.

Michael: Let me think about it.

Jasper: Stop being a fucking pushover. You want her getting ahold of your phone again and calling Julianna?

Michael: I handled that. I'll deal with Brittany. You just get Julianna moving.

Jasper: Let's take her out now, sell the house and the restaurant.

Michael: That's a fraction of what the insurance will pay. We do this right and we're set. You have the new IDs?

Jasper: Not yet. Found a guy in Miami. I'm going there over the Fourth, but I'm out of cash.

Michael: You're getting paid by the restaurant. Ask for an advance. Look, you don't kill the golden goose till you get all the gold.

Detective Grant reached forward and turned off the recorder. "There's more, but you get the picture."

I doubled over, my arms cradling my stomach as if I'd been kicked hard in the gut. My insides were twisting so tightly, I felt like they'd implode. I couldn't catch my breath.

Finally, I whispered, "This is real?"

"Afraid so." Detective Grant winced and looked away.

"Michael's alive?" I asked, still in shock.

He nodded.

"But how? Why?"

He didn't reply. I let what I'd just heard sink in. "This was some sort of scam?" I asked.

As I said the word *scam*, I knew what it meant, but couldn't wrap my mind around it. The dichotomy between the Michael I knew, the man I loved and missed, and the vile voice I'd heard on the recording didn't register. My brain was splitting in two, one part refuting what I'd just heard, and the other part slowly coming to terms with the truth.

"Can you play it again?" I asked. Somehow I must have misunderstood.

He hesitated. "I can, but you heard it correctly."

My throat tightened. I became acutely aware of the need to throw up, and thought I'd choke if I did.

"Can I get you something? Some water?" he asked.

I shook my head as I searched for clarification. "Michael faked his death for money?"

"Yes," Detective Grant replied.

And then the unfathomable part. "They were planning to kill me?" I rocked in a circle as I cradled my belly. He shifted in his chair and extended his arms, as if he was readying himself to catch me. I'd understood him correctly. Michael was not dead. He wasn't even missing. He was hiding intentionally. He and Jasper had concocted a plan to betray me. They just hadn't pulled it off—yet.

"How'd you find out?" I asked.

"When we got the recording back, we followed Jasper. He led us straight to Michael, at a trailer park in Deland. They're both in custody."

"What will you do now?" I asked, barely able to speak.

"That's up to the prosecutor. Jasper is cooperating. He isn't going to take a murder rap when it was Michael who pulled the trigger."

"You think Michael killed Brittany?" I asked with a gasp.

"Yes," he confirmed. "Michael must have followed Brittany to your restaurant. When he realized she was going to expose their plan, he stopped her. It explains why the cameras never caught a glimpse of the shooter. He knew how to avoid them. It also explains how Brittany got into your restaurant. She took Michael's key."

My mind was racing. The key. Michael's key. Not Alex's. Alex was telling me the truth, but I couldn't think about that right now.

"How will you prove it?" I asked.

"At this point, Jasper is already a witness against Michael. He's in a lot of trouble and probably hoping for a plea deal."

I sat there, stunned. I'd always prided myself on being such a good judge of character. Other people, naive people, got duped. Not me.

"How could I have been such a fool?" I asked.

How could I have let such a deceitful man into my life? He'd so quickly won my heart and moved into my home and my bed. At one point, I'd thought he was too good to be true, but told myself that I deserved my Prince Charming. I'd waited long enough to find him. Yet all this time, he was just using me. I'd provided for all of his needs—food, shelter, money, sex. All he had to do in return was pretend to love me, but he couldn't even do that. He was planning to take my life for money, and he talked about killing me as if it was just another task on a checklist. What kind of sick person could look at another human being as nothing but a source of funds?

I could feel my body shaking. Anger, confusion and shock ripped through me. Maybe somewhere, deep down, I actually recognized this truth, that Michael wasn't all that he seemed to be. Maybe I'd chosen to ignore it, but it was there, lurking under the surface all along.

And what about Jasper? I'd taken him in, treated him like a son, and paid him a salary, even though he hardly worked. These last few months, he'd seen me plagued with grief over Michael, all the while knowing it was a lie. What kind of psychopath could watch someone else suffer like that?

I'm not sure how long these thoughts pin-balled around in my mind. Time stood still as I tried to dissect each bit of information and then piece it back together. I slowly recalled some of the red flags I'd chosen to ignore: the quick courtship and marriage, the strange call from Michael's phone when he was with me, and the suggestion to put them both on the restaurant payroll, although neither Michael nor Jasper had a real job. If it hadn't been for Brittany, they might have succeeded.

"How was Brittany able to record them?" I asked.

"Apparently she left the recorder on at her condo, where Michael was hiding out. Something must have made her suspicious."

"Why me?" I asked. "Don't people like them target rich women? I mean, I make a decent living, but I'm certainly not wealthy."

He shrugged. "Guys like Michael and Jasper look for single women with property or an inheritance and no family. I know it sounds sick, but I wouldn't be surprised if they were scanning the obituaries and learned about your parents' deaths."

I shook my head, which made it throb. This whole situation was surreal. Had I been so lonely and grief-stricken that the first man who paid me any attention was able to dupe me?

He added, "They seek out women who are vulnerable. You'd just lost your family. Don't beat yourself up, Julianna. You're too kind to fathom people like them."

I recalled how Michael had appeared in my life just after my parents' car accident. He'd played the single dad, new in town and ready for a meaningful relationship. He'd showered me with praise, which, at the time, seemed genuine. Now I understood what Detective Grant meant by a "love bomb." The Michael he pretended to be was nothing like the foul-mouthed, greedy man I'd just heard on the recording. It must have taken every ounce of his energy to put on such an act. And what about the sex? Was that an act, too? But how? How could he have been so tender, so completely infatuated with me, like he could never get enough? He made me feel so desirable, so special. Had that all been an act, too?

Detective Grant spoke. "You mentioned that Michael left the airlines by choice. Did you know he was actually fired?"

"Fired?"

"He'd gotten a DUI."

My mouth dropped open. "He said he liked the charter flights better." I could hear Michael's happy-go-lucky voice in my head.

Who wouldn't want to fly to the Bahamas all the time? He acted like he'd won the lottery, getting to fly the best routes possible.

"Wait," I said. "Did he lose his pension when he got fired?"

"Yes, he did."

"Wow." I exhaled and leaned forward, resting my cheeks in my hands. "We sort of had a deal. I'm not even sure how it came to be, but I covered expenses now, and he was going to take over when his pension kicked in." I took a deep breath. "There never was going to be a pension kicking in?"

"Afraid not." Detective Grant looked away as soon as our eyes met, which was so different from Michael. My "adoring" husband used to stare at me all the time. When I noticed, he'd give a quick wink or blow me a kiss. Was he really just sizing me up? The wolf watching the lamb? At the time, I'd felt so very lucky to have this man's attention. Maybe that's why I'd been so trusting. He made me feel so beautiful and treated me like a princess, at least in the beginning.

When we first started dating, I never paid for anything. Michael wouldn't hear of it. He played the well-off, generous pilot who was happy to have someone to spoil. But somehow, and I truly can't say how, things changed to the point where I was financially supporting him and Jasper. At the time I hadn't minded. I thought I was just taking my turn first. How had I not seen that it was just a ruse?

"This is so unreal," I said. "And Jasper is confessing but Michael isn't?"

"That's right. I guess blood isn't thicker than water, because Jasper's giving us a good case against his dad."

"They're not related!" I shouted. "I just found out. They aren't father and son."

Detective Grant raised an eyebrow. I explained how I'd done the paternity test and just gotten the results.

My head began to ache, like a huge vice was clamped around my temples. I didn't get this kind of headache often, but when I did, there was no relief. No medication worked—only sleep, and rest would be impossible. Too many questions were rushing through my mind.

"I have to get back to the station soon," he said. "Is there someone you can call? Maybe Samantha?"

I looked at my watch. She wouldn't be at the restaurant yet. I got up from the couch and peered outside. The reporter and van were still there.

"I need to warn you," he said. "This story is starting to break. You're going to have more media at your front door and at the restaurant. If you want to go somewhere else, you probably should pack a bag now."

I froze.

"If you don't want to leave, let's go ahead and close your curtains," he added.

I eyed the sliding glass door that opened to my back yard and pictured reporters dropping out of the sky, like paratroopers landing on my lawn. I hurried to the doors and yanked the curtains closed.

"I was planning on going to the restaurant today," I said. "Maybe I should tell everyone to stay home?"

"That's up to you, but might be a good idea."

I didn't know what to do. I felt like I needed to wake up from a crazy dream. At the same time, I felt like I needed to sleep for days.

32. Grant | Thursday, July 15

I went back to Julianna's house the next morning for two reasons. First, I wanted to check on her, and second, I'd sent Hall to get a search warrant and wanted to be there when he showed up. The news I'd delivered the day before had clearly been a shock. She'd gone from thinking her husband was probably dead to learning he was alive and plotting to kill her. I'd seen enough human depravity that not much surprised me, but Julianna Sandoval saw the good in people and wasn't used to this kind of malice. What Michael and Jasper had been planning was beyond her comprehension.

Several more news trucks were camped outside her front lawn. I'd given cursory details to the female reporter and Gage Holloman the previous day, but it was Chief Jamison who'd broken the full story later that evening. I didn't mind. Being in front of the news cameras was never something I enjoyed. As I approached Julianna's house, I dodged the reporters. This time, however, Julianna didn't hide when she opened the front door. I got the impression she was numb to the circus that had overtaken her front lawn.

When I stepped inside, I smelled smoke. The fireplace was smoldering with what appeared to be pictures and other memorabilia. Frankly, I was glad she was reacting this way. I'd rather see her rage than curled in a fetal position.

"How are you?" I asked, a stupid question.

Her eyes were puffy and she was wearing the same pants and top as the day before. She shook her head as she collapsed on the couch. Her words were fast, a manic sputtering that typically comes from sleep deprivation.

"How did I not see this? I've been thinking about it all night. Here I was judging Samantha for being so forgiving of Alex when his offenses don't even compare!"

"Don't beat yourself up." I spoke slowly, trying to calm her. "When you're ready, in a few days, we can talk." In reality, I couldn't provide many more details beyond what I'd already told her. She was still a witness; one we might need at trial. Plus, she was clearly in no frame of mind to absorb more information.

"Go ahead," she said quickly. "I want to hear it all."

I hesitated.

"Tell me!" she demanded.

The fire popped and a log shifted as it burned. I sat down in a chair next to the couch which was farthest from the fireplace. The heat didn't seem to bother her. I had to walk a fine line between what I was allowed to share, what would satisfy her and what would overwhelm her.

"Well, as you know, Jasper confessed. He was certain Michael would try to pin everything on him and wanted to get a jump on a deal, if there was one to be had."

Her eyes widened. "Are you giving him a deal?"

"That's not for me to decide. The prosecutor will make that call."

"He doesn't deserve one," she huffed. "What'd he say?"

I spoke cautiously, reading her face to gauge if I should stop. "The two of them met at a casino in Vegas. Jasper was living there and Michael was in town gambling. As you already know, they aren't related, but it didn't take long for them to figure out they'd make a good team. They concocted the story of father and son to be more believable—that's why Jasper changed his name."

"But Michael had this elaborate story about the flight attendant mother. Why even tell me that?"

I shrugged. "Part of the con, I suppose. Just before you met Michael, they'd been living with a widow in Jacksonville, but she kicked them out."

Julianna sighed and rolled her eyes. "She was smarter than me."

"I wouldn't say that. They stole her boat."

Her mouth dropped open. "Michael didn't own the boat?"

"That's correct. I spoke to the woman earlier today. She never reported it missing."

"That's why he was hiding the paperwork," she mumbled. "But why was Ed snooping around?"

She began to knock her forehead with her fist, as if beating herself for missing a clue. I leaned over, took her hand and gently pulled it away from her face.

"So who was the mastermind?" she asked. "Michael?"

I nodded. "Jasper doesn't have the patience or planning skills, although neither of them really thought it through. They didn't foresee that you'd wait to have Michael declared dead. When you delayed, it put a kink in their plan."

"What about Brittany?" she asked. "Was she in on it, too?"

"She knew they were pulling off an insurance scam, which is why Michael had to hide. She had a nice condo, paid for by a married man up north. It was a good place for Michael to lay low, but I'm guessing the close quarters started to wear on them. She must have suspected something was up and recorded Michael and Jasper. And she brought that recording to the restaurant to play for you."

"You don't think she knew their plan? I mean, what they were going to do to me?"

"Not at first. At some point they probably clued her in, likely with the promise of a pay day, or a threat if she told anyone."

"So Michael just killed her in cold blood?"

"I don't believe it was planned, at least not for that particular moment, which forced Michael to scramble. He had to find a new hideout, and fast. That's when he moved from Brittany's condo to the trailer park where we found him."

Julianna pulled her bare feet up on the couch and tucked them under her knees. "Okay, but there's still one thing I don't understand. Even if I had declared Michael dead and gotten the insurance money, I hadn't changed my will. Would the State of Florida just give everything to Jasper because he's my only relative?"

"I think they changed your will," I replied. "I can't prove it yet, but..."

Julianna jumped to her feet. "Jasper has a lockbox in his room. I thought it was an odd thing for a kid to have. It weighs a ton. Can you get someone over here to open it?"

She started toward Jasper's room when I motioned for her to stop. I definitely wanted to see what was inside that lockbox. In fact, I wanted to search his entire room, but I needed to wait for Hall with the paperwork, which was due any time now.

"As soon as I have the warrant," I replied.

Julianna paced in front of the fireplace. She needed something to give her purpose, to settle her mind.

It wasn't long before my team arrived. Hall was holding the search warrant and White had a crowbar and a few other tools. We started in Jasper's room. White would have made an adept thief because he had the metal box open in no time. Inside we found a treasure trove: fake IDs for Jasper and Michael, an ID with Julianna's information but Brittany's photo, cash, title papers for the boat and, as I'd expected, Julianna's forged will.

On Brittany's recording, Jasper confirmed that he had the "new paperwork." It was a subtle clue but had stuck with me. That comment, along with the copy of Julianna's driver's license and the pages of practice signatures at Brittany's place, told a story. Brittany must have pretended to be Julianna and used the fake ID to have the new will notarized. The notary stamp was real, but nothing else about the document was authentic.

My team began to load our vehicles with evidence from the house, skirting the incessant questions from the media. An older man took advantage of the open front door and walked right in. I blocked him before he could reach Julianna.

"Sir, you can't be in here," I said. I grabbed his arm to escort him out.

"It's okay," said Julianna. "He's my lawyer."

"I just heard the news," he said. He opened his arms and she fell into his embrace. She mumbled something, then lifted her head and repeated her question.

"Did you know Michael had stolen the boat? Is that why you were at the marina?"

He shook his head. "Forgive me. I should've said something to you sooner. How are you doing?"

"What about the boat? What'd you know?" she asked.

"After Michael went missing and you showed me his life insurance policy, I was perplexed. I couldn't fathom why he had such a high amount. His son was grown, he didn't own property and you weren't leveraged. Being insured for two million dollars didn't make sense. The only reasonable explanation was to cover his boat. But when I saw it was just a small speedboat, I was still puzzled. Now it makes sense."

"Ed, none of this makes any sense," she replied.

He put his arm around her and led her to the couch.

"Do I have to see them?" she asked.

"No, I don't think so. Not until their trial, which I imagine will be a ways off."

As she silently considered his advice, I took the opportunity to let her know I was leaving. "We'll be taking this evidence back to headquarters now."

"You're going?" she asked.

I nodded.

"Will you come back? Later. If you have time?"

What could I say? Professionally I had no reason to return. Personally, I wanted to check on her again.

33. Julianna | Friday, July 16

My cell phone rang.

I didn't recognize the number, but assumed it was one of our suppliers, inquiring about a late payment. When I answered, a robotic voice asked if I'd accept a collect call from the Volusia County Corrections Facility. Static interrupted the line, distorting the caller's name, but I immediately recognized the voice.

My throat tightened. A searing flash of fear and rage struck me, leaving me short of breath. Over the last two days, I'd imagined the many things I wanted to say to Michael: Why me? Did he meet me by chance or did he deliberately target me? Did he ever love me? Did he love Brittany? How was he planning to kill me? Was he going to reveal his plan or just shoot me in the back, like he did to her?

Mixed in with all my questions was intense hatred for the chaos he'd brought into my life. Reporters camped relentlessly at my front door and the restaurant. A barrage of questions accosted me every time I tried to leave the house. No one was this interested when Michael went missing. A couple days on the news and it was over. I'd begged for more media attention, to raise money for the search to continue, but was ignored. Now, however, they couldn't get enough of this salacious story of a man faking his death so he could kill his wife and have his fake son cash in.

The phone crackled. Would I accept the call? I knew I'd have to face Michael one day, but I wasn't prepared for that day to be *now*. My first thought was to hang up. He had no right to contact me and I didn't want to speak to him, even though I had so much to say. I doubted he'd be contrite. More likely he'd try to deceive me further, as if he could. I was on to him now. With a fresh sense of boldness, I accepted the call.

"Julianna," Michael began. "It's so good to hear your voice."

He was talking as if we were about to have a normal conversation, as if circumstances beyond his control had kept us apart.

I didn't respond.

"I need to see you," he said, his voice urgent. "I put you on my list so you can visit."

My silence turned to rage. "Are you fucking insane! You were planning to kill me!"

"No!" he protested. "I can explain. I know it seems bad, but it wasn't my fault. Jasper cooked up this plan so we could get money from my life insurance. I couldn't tell you about it. I didn't want you to have to lie for me."

I let his words sink in, but my gut knew they didn't make any sense.

"You're lying. I heard the recording," I told him.

Static filled the line for several long seconds. I heard him take a deep breath and exhale.

"Julianna, please, you have to believe me. Oh God, I'll lose my mind if you don't believe me."

"You just wanted my money!" I screamed into the phone.

"No! It was the opposite of that! I didn't feel like a man, taking your money. I didn't feel worthy of you. I was trying to secure your financial future, but Jasper took it too far."

"Why should I believe you?" I snarled. "You let me think you were dead." Tears started to pour down my cheeks, the rage seeping out of my body.

"I had to. To protect you. So you'd be blameless. I didn't expect it to go on this long, then Jasper got out of control. He and that girl, Brittany, cooked up their own plan. I didn't know what they were doing until now. I swear. Julianna, I love you."

For a moment I heard "my Michael," the man who loved me, but what he was saying didn't match the recording. It was as if I was dealing with two people instead of one: the Michael I wanted to trust and the one I knew I couldn't.

"I heard the recording. I know what you and Jasper were planning. And I know you were sleeping with Brittany."

"No I wasn't! She's Jasper's girl. Ask her. She'll tell you."

My mouth dropped open. He didn't know she was dead? How could he have killed her if he didn't know that?

"What recording are you talking about?" he asked.

I didn't reply.

"Julianna, sweetie, you have to believe me. I don't know who's told you what, but it sounds like they're filling your head with lies. Come see me. Please. I'll explain everything. I was wrong to try to get the money, the life insurance, but I wanted it for you. Everything I did was for you."

"I don't want your money," I shouted, and then wondered why we were even having this conversation. This wasn't about his life insurance. This was about him deceiving me. Somehow he was twisting the conversation to get me off track.

My voice grew cold. "You and Jasper were planning to kill me. I know that."

"Julianna, I would never hurt you. I would never let anyone hurt you."

There was no way he was telling the truth. Detective Grant had told me what they'd planned. Even worse, I'd heard Michael's voice with my own ears. Yet something felt off. Then I realized what it was. Michael didn't know Brittany was dead. Was it possible he wasn't the shooter? Was he being set up? Could the recording have been a fake, deliberately planted on Brittany so it would be found? Detective Grant was making his case based on two things: Jasper's confession and Brittany's recording. What other evidence did he have?

My mind reeled. I felt unstable, like the floor below me would collapse and I'd descend into a dark abyss. The same driftlessness had haunted me after my parents died. Then Michael came along and made me feel anchored again. His disappearance had ripped away that sense of security, and I desperately wanted it back. I wanted to feel grounded again.

"Julianna, please, if you'll just come see me, I'll explain everything. Jasper is trying to destroy me, destroy us. I need your help."

"I don't know." I was so confused. I'd spent the last two days accepting the worst. My marriage was a sham. He'd never loved me. He'd cheated on me, faked his death and was so vile that he was planning my murder, for money.

Finally, I asked, "Why would Jasper do that?"

"He's not my son. I just found out. He's known it all along. He inserted himself into my life, our lives, so he could use us. He convinced me to do something very wrong. I felt an obligation to him because I'd deserted him as a baby and it clouded my judgement. All along, he had a bigger plan. He's setting me up, Julianna, and he's going to get away with it if you don't help me."

I didn't know what to believe. I looked at my fireplace and all the memories I'd destroyed. Had I acted too hastily? Was there more to the story? Michael seemed sincere and he was confirming what I already knew: Jasper wasn't his son.

"I have to go," I said. I needed time to think and to hear all of the evidence from Detective Grant. I started to hang up when he said the one word that stopped me.

"Lily."

I froze.

Why was he bringing up my sister? My immediate thought was that he had something to do with her disappearance until I realized it wasn't possible. Michael would've been a child when she went missing.

"What about Lily?" I demanded.

"I know what happened to her."

My jaw clenched. He couldn't possibly know what happened to my sister.

He continued. "Remember the shelter, where we take the Sunday leftovers? There's a woman who comes there who knew Lily."

I recalled my own trips to the women's shelter, though it had been a while. I hadn't encountered anyone who could've been Lily's age. Most of the shelter women were young single mothers. Besides, wouldn't anyone who had information about Lily have come directly to me?

"Who is she?" I challenged. "What's her name?"

Static flickered on the line and the robotic voice broke in. "You have one minute remaining to complete your call."

"Tell me what you know!" I demanded, frantic that I was running out of time.

"I will. I'll explain everything, but I need to do it in person. Come see me. Today. I won't have visitation again for two weeks."

I felt trapped. I wasn't prepared to face Michael. I was almost certain he was lying, but if there was the slightest chance I could find out something about my sister, I had to know. I couldn't wait two long weeks to learn if he had anything real.

"Julianna, we don't have much time. Are you coming?" he asked.

The last few days had been agony. Sleepless nights and a growing list of unanswered questions. I didn't have to wait for his trial to confront him. I could do it today.

"You'd better not be lying," I said with ice in my voice and hung up.

🛞 34. Grant | Friday, July 16

People think once an arrest is made, that's the end of the case. In reality, it's just the beginning. Preparing the prosecutorial packet was time-consuming work. I had to write a summary of the entire case, from start to finish. Prosecutors typically don't have time to read the whole file, so my summary was a vital part. In the packet, I included all of my evidence: investigator notes, digital recordings, surveillance videos, phone calls, interviews, Miranda waivers, search warrants, subpoenas, photographs, medical examiner reports and FDLE reports. I described how we'd come to arrest Jasper and Michael, and included the video and transcript of Jasper in custody, along with his written statement.

Once I'd summarized what we'd done, I listed the work that was still outstanding in the investigation. We needed to return to Brittany's condo. First, we'd show a picture of Michael to the maintenance man. When I'd learned about Joe Ricci, I'd dropped that lead, but now I was confident Michael was the older man seen with Brittany. Second, we'd deliver subpoenas for surveillance video from the complex, particularly of the cameras in the parking lot. Most footage is only archived for thirty days, but I was confident we'd find Michael coming and going at some point, and potentially on the night of Brittany's murder. We also needed to follow-up on the surveillance video from the shops near Café Lily. It was critical to find evidence beyond Jasper's confession, especially since we didn't have the murder weapon or anyone who could link Michael to a firearm, not even Jasper. Any good defense attorney would try to put doubt in a jury's mind so our evidence had to be compelling.

Also outstanding was finding the plane. Jasper had identified the general area and we had the local Sheriff's department searching abandoned barns, which was like looking for the proverbial needle in the haystack. According to Jasper, Michael had falsified the fuel onboard in his flight plan, which limited the initial search radius. In reality, he'd had enough fuel to pick up his fishing clients in North Eleuthera and fly back. Instead, he'd diverted to a desolate field with a deserted barn where Brittany was waiting for him. From there, they drove back to Ormond Beach and he hid while he waited for

Julianna to receive the insurance payout. What he'd underestimated was Julianna's reluctance to take action and how long the process would take. He'd also misjudged Brittany's patience.

I had a meeting with the DA at the courthouse to deliver the packet and review the case. Hall joined me. We entered the courthouse lobby, stored our firearms in a locker before going through security and waited in the DA's conference room. I watched Hall take in the surroundings. It was meant to impress: a large oval table with ornate carvings, plush leather chairs, volumes of law books lining the shelves and a large-screen TV with a DVD player that covered the far wall.

When the door opened, I immediately recognized the DA's investigator, Chuck Werley. He'd been on the force in Daytona before "retiring" to a plumb job at the DA's office, where he had the luxury of a nine-to-five job. The downside was he had to tie up the loose ends of our investigation so we could move on to the next case.

The DA, Billy Reyes, was new to the job and looked fresh out of law school. He wore a pin-striped suit and his dark hair was slicked back with gel. After brief introductions, Billy puffed himself up and began to speak.

"Gentlemen, I want to thank you for meeting today. Obviously we have a very important case in front of us, one I'll be prosecuting personally. I've spoken to the public defender for Jasper Sinise and am planning to offer a deal: ten years for conspiracy to commit murder and insurance fraud, if he continues to cooperate. I know we can't nail him on Ms. Jones's murder..."

Chuck and I locked eyes. We each knew what the other was thinking. Jasper's attorney had obviously attempted to influence the DA before he could meet with us. It was an underhanded but not uncommon tactic. Fortunately this meeting gave us the opportunity to adjust his perspective. When Chuck didn't jump in, I realized the *education* was going to have to come from me.

"With all due respect, Mr. Reyes," I said. "You can."

Billy Reyes cocked his head, clearly surprised to be challenged so early in the conversation. "Can what?" he asked.

"You can charge Jasper Sinise with felony murder," I replied.

"It was Michael Sinise who we believe shot Ms. Jones. According to Jasper Sinise's attorney, his client was in Miami, which I believe you confirmed. He didn't know about the shooting until after it occurred."

"True," I agreed. "But we have a recording of Jasper and Michael conspiring to commit murder against Julianna Sandoval, Michael's wife. Brittany Jones was killed, by Michael, in the act of conspiring to kill Julianna. Therefore, we have transferred intent, which makes Jasper just as guilty. Also, he was an accessory after the fact, by housing Michael, and he obstructed the murder investigation."

Chuck smiled.

"I thought you were targeting Michael Sinise," Reyes said.

"I am," I replied. "But we have a lot of time between now and the trial. Just don't want to give Jasper any wiggle room to change his statement."

We spent the next several hours reviewing the evidence to ensure both Michael and Jasper received the appropriate and maximum charges. Though Jasper's lawyer was trying to secure a deal, he had an uphill battle because Jasper confessed prior to any arrangements being made, and he would soon be dealing with a DA who was much more informed. Billy Reyes decided to offer Jasper life in prison with the possibility of parole, provided he continue to cooperate. Michael, on the other hand, was facing the death penalty if the case went to trial and he was found guilty.

35. Julianna | Friday, July 16

I thought about telling Detective Grant my plans to visit Michael, but decided against it. He'd disapprove and maybe try to prevent me from going altogether. The restaurant was still closed so I didn't need to check in with Samantha. I'm sure she would've disapproved, too.

As I pulled out of my garage, a throng of reporters encircled my car like bees swarming a hive. Microphones tapped against my window as they shouted questions. I backed my car into the street and managed to speed away before any of them could follow.

On the drive to the Volusia County Corrections Facility, I reviewed the many questions that had tormented me over the last two days. I tried to imagine Michael's response and wondered if I'd be able to tell if he was lying. My stomach started to knot the more I pictured facing him.

Thirty minutes later, the voice on my GPS announced I'd arrived. I'd been so engrossed in my thoughts that I hardly remembered the trip. Of the many joyful reunions I'd pictured with Michael, this version was unfathomable.

I pulled off the main road and onto the driveway of the facility. A windowless, putty-colored building was situated behind a tall chain link fence topped with barbed wire. There were two entrances, one for law enforcement marked with a foreboding sign, "GUARD LINE - DO NOT CROSS," and one down the hill for visitors.

Once parked, I flipped down the sun visor and examined myself in the mirror. My cheeks were pale and taut and my shiny blonde hair had lost its luster. Boating with Michael had kept me tan and fit, but that look had vanished over the last few months. I didn't want to appear as damaged as I felt and, if I was being honest with myself, part of me cared that I still looked attractive, which was absurd.

I approached a set of double doors marked for visitors. A sign was posted prohibiting cell phones, weapons and contraband. I hadn't thought about my phone so I walked back to my car and left everything in the trunk except my ID and keys.

At the entry, I passed through a metal detector and joined a long queue of people at the visitor counter. When I finally reached the front of the line, a woman took my ID and asked who I was there to see. She typed on her keyboard and then wrote my name, the date and a six-digit number on a sticker. I was told to put on the sticker, have a seat and wait.

Like the other visitors, I sat in a plastic bucket chair that was bolted to the floor. A small television mounted in the corner played the weather channel with jazz music, which struck me as odd.

Without my phone, the wait felt like an eternity, and the longer I sat there, the worse my stomach cramped. Finally, a deputy called five of us, by number. We followed him through a set of double doors and were led down a nondescript corridor with harsh fluorescent lighting.

My heart raced faster at the thought of seeing Michael. I felt a strange combination of anticipation and dread. We were led to a large room and told to check in at the counter. I stopped and looked around while the other four walked ahead. They apparently knew the drill. The room was full of partitions with video monitors like you'd see at a school computer lab. Each visitor was assigned a stall number—I was given stall number five on the end.

I'd assumed Michael would be there in person, behind a glass barrier. I'd never expected that our visit was going to be via a computer. The knot in my stomach eased. I sat down at my booth, put my keys and ID on the table, and wondered what I was supposed to do next. With the partitions between us, I couldn't see the other visitors, although I could hear murmurs of conversations. The computer in front of me hummed, but the screen remained black. I leaned forward and looked for the switch to turn it on.

Suddenly Michael's face flashed on the screen, inches from mine. I jumped back in the chair.

He looked bloated and in need of a haircut and shave. In fact, he didn't look clean. The man on the screen was a ratty version of my handsome, charismatic Michael. Had he ever been that person, or was I only now seeing the real version?

Someone walked behind him, dressed in the same orange jumpsuit he was wearing. Michael appeared to be in a common area where inmates were free to move around. Every once in a while, he'd glance over his shoulder, probably to ensure the others were keeping their distance. As for me, I felt safer talking through a computer screen.

He reached forward and touched his monitor. "I had hoped to see you in person. I've missed you."

I didn't reply, but pressed back into the chair.

"You may not believe me," he continued. "But we were never supposed to be apart this long. It was so hard for me to stay away from you."

"So why did you?" I asked. My voice was flat.

"Julianna, I wanted to be a better husband and a better provider. After the airline screwed me over, I needed to find a way to make more money. The charter flights weren't enough, and I didn't want you supporting us. Jasper and I got to talking one day. It started as a joke, that I was worth more dead than alive, but then he became more serious."

"The airline screwed you over?" I said. "You're the one who got the DUI."

"You know me, Julianna. You know I'm not a drunk. I was dealing with a lot. Jasper's mom dumped a kid on me that I never knew I had. That night I was in a haze. I'd had a few too many and was just trying to get back to the hotel for a flight the next day."

Michael sometimes had a few glasses of wine with dinner, but I didn't consider him an alcoholic. I'd prepared myself to hear nothing but lies, but this wasn't one. I almost let my guard down until I remembered that the DUI wasn't the point. He was twisting things around again. We weren't here because of his drinking.

"What you did makes no sense," I told him. "We weren't hurting for money. I never asked you for anything."

Michael started to answer, but I cut him off. "You made me think you were dead. I was coming to terms with being a widow. I was deciding if I should plan a funeral without a body. If you cared about me at all, how could you have put me through that?"

"I didn't think it through. I was trying to protect you."

"Protect me?" The sarcasm flowed easily from my tongue. "I know what you and Jasper were planning."

"I don't know what they've been telling you, Julianna, but they're lying. Cops lie all the time. They don't know you. They don't care about you like I do."

He was trying to reframe things again, but I knew he didn't care about me. Thank goodness there was a recording. Had I not heard his vileness with my own ears, I might have been duped again.

"Julianna, sweetie, talk to me."

"Don't call me that," I snarled. "What do you know about Lily?"

He tilted his head and the crease on his forehead smoothed. Michael leaned in closer to the camera and spoke in a hushed voice.

"I met this woman at the shelter. She came over to me when I was delivering food and told me she knew what happened to Lily."

I crossed my arms. "What'd she say?"

"She said she was a classmate of your sister's. Lily had confided that she was being blackmailed by an older man. He'd drugged her, taken compromising pictures and was forcing her to prostitute herself or he'd share the photos."

I immediately thought about Keith McQueen. Older man. Blackmail. It was possible, but why would this woman confide in Michael instead of me? And why was he only telling me this now?

"Look, I'll tell you the rest once I get out of here. Can you do something for me? Can you visit Jasper? Find out exactly what he's saying. You know he grew up hustling in Vegas and now we're caught up in his scheme. It's critical that I know what he's telling the cops."

"What's the woman's name?" I demanded. "The one who knew about Lily."

"Look, Julianna, I get that you want to find out about your sister and I'll help you. I promise. But we have to deal with this first. That girl, the one who got shot at your restaurant. They're trying to pin that on me."

"What about that girl?" I asked. "Did you know her?"

"No. I was hiding out at her place, which was really, really stupid. They're trying to say I killed her."

And there it was. On the phone, Michael had suggested I talk to Brittany, to confirm she was Jasper's girlfriend. He didn't know that she'd been killed, or so he'd led me to believe. Turns out Michael did know Brittany was dead. The problem with telling so many lies is that you eventually get them crossed, and he just did.

"Strange," I replied, "that you didn't know that girl. You didn't bump into her while you were sharing a bed?"

He froze. "No, I was at a trailer park. In Deland. Ask the cop. That's where they picked me up."

I finally realized how he'd been able to fool me. Michael lied effortlessly and with such conviction. I knew he'd been hiding out at Brittany's condo. I was certain he was having an affair with her and had probably killed her. Yet he could deny it all with such ease. He was probably lying about Lily just to lure me here. I had loved him. I had believed in him. That had made me even more susceptible to his charm.

No more.

A strange calm came over me. The tension I'd been feeling began to fade, as if every muscle in my body relaxed in unison. Michael was making a list of things I needed to do for him: hire a lawyer, ask about bond, find out what Jasper was saying. He asked if I was writing everything down so I wouldn't forget. As he spoke, I watched his lips moving but tuned out the droning of his commands. For the first time since his disappearance, I didn't feel desperate. My world was not going to implode without him. I would be okay on my own.

I noticed a black cord that snaked from the bottom of the monitor to the wall. With a newfound sense of power, I reached forward, grasped the plug and yanked it from the socket.

The monitor flashed and then turned dark.

While the other visitors savored their precious time, I quietly stood and left the room.

36. Grant | Monday, July 19

I watched the jail video of Julianna talking to Michael, pissed as hell that he'd used Lily to lure her there. She should've checked with me first. Of course I would've stopped her which is exactly why she didn't. Watching him trying to manipulate her made me want to kill the bastard with my bare hands.

Michael needed Julianna as a source of information. He was blind to what Jasper was saying and she could provide those details. He knew he was facing insurance fraud—he'd admitted that much, but he seemed confident he'd beat the murder charge. He'd disposed of the weapon and evaded the cameras at Café Lily which made him smug. He was unaware, however, that Jasper was cooperating fully and we had Brittany's recording. He also didn't know that the owner of the high-end boutique next to Café Lily had finally supplied her surveillance video of the night of the shooting. Michael may have evaded the restaurant cameras, but he hadn't evaded hers.

I took pleasure knowing DA Reyes was charging Michael with conspiracy to commit insurance fraud, conspiracy to commit Julianna's murder and the murder of Brittany Jones. If convicted, he'd die in prison. His life was over, although I hoped a jury would see fit to stick a needle in his arm and end it sooner.

I heard a knock on my door. It was one of our clerks with an envelope from the morning mail. With all of my energy focused on Brittany's case, I'd forgotten about the request I'd made for Keith McQueen's residential history. I ripped open the envelope and rifled through the paperwork. McQueen was living in Warner Robins, Georgia, the year Lily Sandoval disappeared.

Then something strange caught my attention. He had two addresses in Warner Robins for the same time frame. One address was a house near the center of town, close to shopping centers and restaurants, which made sense given his line of work. The other was an apartment on the outskirts of town, close to I-75. I thought about how different prostitution was in the 1970's. There was no internet. Traffickers didn't use hotels. Instead, they typically found a cheap apartment next to a highway or military base and guys would come to them.

Every instinct in my body was telling me that Lily had been in that apartment. Still, I had to make the connection. I looked up the number for the Warner Robins Criminal Investigations Division and gave them a call. A female detective with a thick southern drawl answered. I explained that I'd tracked a person of interest to Warner Robins and asked if she could do a search of any incidents at McQueen's address on Oakview, the apartment he'd rented.

"I'm sorry," she said. "I can't search any of that. It's from before we had computers."

Another dead end.

She continued, "The only information in our on-site archives are homicides, missing persons and unidentified bodies. I can check what we've got there, but it won't be a lot. What exactly are you looking for?"

"I'm trying to solve a missing person case from Florida. I think she may have been at the address on Oakview."

"Let me see what I can dig up," she offered. "My dad retired from the force. He might remember something."

I thanked her and found Hall. Back in Daytona, we typically went out for lunch once a case was solved—a short break before the inevitable next one would come along. I also needed to get some air after watching the video of Michael with Julianna. That scum had to know I'd be notified of any visitors and that their conversation would be recorded. My one relief in watching the video was that he was trying to pin the blame on Jasper, not Julianna. I'd expected him to try to implicate her, like he'd done in our interview. I guess he figured he'd have a better chance at winning her over than trying to portray her as the mastermind of the insurance fraud.

Not long after we returned from lunch, I received a call from the Warner Robins detective. Her speech, though still thick, had picked up its pace.

"Detective Grant, we spoke earlier about your missing person case. Well, I went to the file room to see how many cases we have. There were so few back then that they're all in the same box. I think I may have something. We have a white female, between the age of thirteen and eighteen, height 5'4". Her death was ruled a suicide by hanging—they found a macramé belt around the neck. The body was quite decomposed and we were never able to make an ID."

When Michael told Julianna that Lily had been blackmailed, I didn't give it much credence. He was a desperate man ready to say anything to convince his wife to help him, but sometimes the most believable cons start with a shred of truth. If McQueen had been blackmailing Lily, she may not have felt she had any way out.

"I called my dad," the detective continued. "He misses the job and was all too happy to talk. He remembers Oakview Apartments because they were known for drugs and prostitution. He made a lot of arrests there. But get this—just behind those apartments was another complex that was boarded up. That's where they found the unidentified girl's body when the crews came in to start demolition."

"That could be her," I said. "Where are the remains?"

"They were sent off to the Georgia Bureau of Investigation decades ago."

I already knew my next step. "Thank you," I said. "You may have just cracked this case. I'll let you know."

I immediately called the GBI, introduced myself and gave them a rundown of the case. I asked if they had done any further investigation, particularly forensic reconstruction. With an unidentified body, the GBI's forensic artist would have interpreted the features of the skeleton to determine demographics and used tissue markers and clay to reconstruct the person's face. The technology started out fairly crude, but improvements over the years had made the digital representations almost lifelike. The officer at the GBI said he'd check and call me back.

My adrenaline was pumping. After so many dead ends, I felt like I was headed down a path that might yield an answer. I went to the breakroom to grab a coffee. The chief was refilling her cup.

"I may have found something regarding Julianna's sister—an unidentified body. Waiting for a call back from the GBI."

She raised an eyebrow. "Solving two cases within one week?"

"That's how it always seems to go—everything breaks at once."

I started back to my office when the chief asked, "Grant, if this unidentified body turns out to be her sister, do you think she's pre-pared for this outcome? She's dealing with a lot right now."

I considered the chief's question. It was a fair concern. Julianna had just lost the husband and son that she believed she knew. Leav-ing her with the hope of finding Lily, at least for now, was potentially the kindest thing I could do.

The chief added, "And are you prepared to be the one to give her the news?"

I nodded. "I am."

Chief Jamison placed her hand on my shoulder as she passed by. "You're a good man, Paul Grant."

On the way back to my office, I received a call back from the GBI. The officer had found the Warner Robins case and confirmed a digital reconstruction had been completed. I provided my email address and stared at my Inbox waiting for the file. When the message arrived, I clicked on the attachment which opened to a full-size, black and white sketch on my screen. I recalled the photo of Lily that Julianna had shared on our drive to Orlando. This drawing had no color, but I imagined her blonde hair and green eyes. If I didn't know better, I would've sworn I was looking at a young Julianna.

But I knew who this was—I'd found her.

My shoulders slumped forward and I bowed my head, overcome with the most unsettling kind of closure. It was a hollow victory. We'd have to confirm Lily's identity with DNA or dental records, but to me, that was a formality.

I considered the chief's comments. Should I hold off saying anything right now? Give Julianna some time to heal from Michael's betrayal. I thought about the other missing persons cases I'd worked over the years. For the families, the not-knowing was a constant ache. Either they were continually thinking about their lost one or, if they happened to go a day without remembering, they'd feel guilty. At least for Julianna, she'd be able to bring her sister home and give her a proper burial. It wasn't a happy ending, but I didn't think she'd ever expected one.

I sent her a text message: *I may have a lead on your sister's case. You free to meet?*

Of course I had more than a lead, but my message would put her in the right frame of mind to hear the rest.

I pushed away from my desk and stretched my arms. There, in the corner of my office, the stack of cardboard boxes from Daytona sat collecting dust. I stood, walked over to them and unclipped my knife my belt. With the flip of my wrist, I opened the blade which ʒd into place. Slicing the masking tape on the top box, I pulled the lid and started unpacking.

37. Julianna | 2 Months Later

Café Lily looked like a picture from a fairytale: white linen tablecloths, sparkling candles and beautifully scented lilies in crystal vases on every table. After a few months of planning, the night was finally here. We were hosting a charity dinner, with all proceeds going to Florida Cares. Everyone was there—Chief Jamison, Detective Hall and his wife, Lynnette, Officers Phelps, Jenkins and White, and several other officers from the Ormond Beach Police Department.

Ed Harrigan had sponsored a table for his firm and Gage Holloman with the Ormond Beach News had invited some of his young friends. Emily Pickett and the staff and counselors from Florida Cares sat up front. Almost all of our regulars had each bought a $100 seat for charity, even Myra and Gene Cohen.

Samantha and the kitchen staff were busy preparing the Beef Wellington and baked salmon for dinner. Alex and an additional bartender could barely keep up with the drink orders. Yes, I'd rehired Alex. I wasn't good at holding a grudge and it meant a lot to Samantha. He was on serious probation—if he ever lied, cheated, stole, or omitted telling me anything, he'd be out and he knew it.

Detective Grant had a seat at my table. He'd told me I could call him Paul, and I was trying to adapt to using his first name, but it felt a little strange. We'd gone to the range a couple of times over the past few months. I was glad to see someone getting enjoyment out of Dad's shotgun. I'd invited him to the restaurant to try Samantha's cooking; he'd declined three times before finally changing his mind. I got the sense he was concerned about any appearance of impropriety with Michael's case still pending. If we weren't busy, I'd sometimes join him so he didn't have to eat alone which he seemed to enjoy.

"Julianna," a voice interrupted my thoughts. It was Alex asking where to put the hostess stand. I motioned to a spot just beside the bar so it could serve as a podium. We had a very special guest speaker, Angelle Rodriquez, the sex trafficking survivor who had known Brittany. Her ordeal was both heartbreaking and inspiring, and after she'd shared it with me and Detective Grant, I mean Paul, I wanted others to have the chance to hear her story.

Once the guests were seated and the salads were served, I approached the stand and picked up the microphone. I briefly thanked everyone for coming and introduced our guest speaker. Angelle stood and walked toward me. She wore a flowing turquoise dress with tan heels. A necklace made of chunky blue stones glistened against her dark brown skin. Her wavy brunette hair curled around her shoulders and her eyes were a warm brown. Had I not known her background, I would've assumed she was like any other pretty, stylish twenty-year-old.

She took her place at the podium, her voice calm and steady as she began to share her story.

"At fifteen, I lost my virginity to our landlord. My mother sold me to pay the February rent because she didn't have enough money. From that day on, my family 'contribution' was to cover the monthly rent for me, my mom and my two younger brothers. I remember getting panic attacks as the end of each month drew near. Afterward, I would feel a short reprieve, during the single-digit days. By the tenth, my anxiety would rise, and by the twentieth, the panic was in full bloom and wouldn't subside until it happened. Then the clock would reset and the cycle would repeat.

"Over time, he was no longer satisfied with a monthly payment. Whenever my mom was gone, he'd use his master key to come into our apartment and find me. He threatened to kick my family out on the street if I told anyone. The strange thing was that if he'd kept the bargain, the 'monthly payments,' I might've tolerated it. In my adolescent mind, they were part of the deal with my mother. Though I dreaded them, those days were somehow allowed. But the in-between rapes were different. It was like he was cheating. Of course, now I know all of it was wrong.

"By the time I ran away, his visits were happening several times a month, and his threats had escalated from kicking us out to killing my family. The only way I could escape was to leave, so I did. I spent a few nights on the street, lost and hungry. I almost returned home, where at least there was food, when a woman befriended me. She said I was beautiful and could earn a lot of money dancing. I liked to dance, so it sounded like a great idea. She brought me to a house, gave me food and clothes, and put me in a room with two other girls. Neither of them talked to me that first night. They were either too scared or too doped up or both.

"I never saw the woman again, the one who'd recruited me. The next day, a guy named Romeo came to the house. He took me into a private room, raped me and beat me unconscious. I was locked in that room for several days, without any food or water. When I cried out for help, no one came. I started to believe they were going to let me starve to death. What they were really doing was breaking my spirit.

"Three days later, Romeo came back. He gave me a cheese sandwich and medicine for the pain. He even bandaged the cut on my face. I remember thinking I was going crazy. Why was the man who'd inflicted these injuries now trying to nurse me back to health? I now know that it was one of his tactics to manipulate and control me. Every girl in that house cowered around Romeo. We never knew who would show up, Jekyll or Hyde.

"I was given a new name, Crystal, and told that if I ever said my real name, I would be punished worse than what he'd already done to me. I was given a new birthdate that made me eighteen years old, two years older than my real age. Then, with bruises still on my face and body, I was taken in a van to a motel, along with the other girls. I was put in a room with two double beds. I was on one bed and another girl on the other.

"Before I understood what was happening, men started coming into the room, two at a time, all night long. At one point, I looked over at the other girl and she was lying there, lifeless, while the guy thrust himself into her and moaned. I shut my eyes and resigned myself to the fact that this was my life now. In some way, I felt that I deserved it because I'd run away. I became complacent, and my will to fight back was gone. I believed the only value I had as a human being was the use of my body for sex.

"And do you know, not one time did any of those men ask me my name. Not one of them ever asked my age or if I wanted to be there. A few tried to be romantic, but at the end of the day, it was all about their fantasy, not my reality.

"Each night, it was a different hotel. Some were nearby and others had us in the van for hours. We worked seven nights a week. If we missed a nightly quota there were beatings, starting with the girl who rotated between the rooms and collected the money. I slept a lot during the day and started using marijuana because it dulled my senses and helped me to disassociate from the rapes. Weed was abundant in the house because it was cheap. Romeo used to ration our weekly allotment of toilet paper, but we could have all the marijuana we wanted. Sick, right?"

Angelle paused and took a sip of water from the bottle that had been placed on the podium for her. She took a deep breath and continued.

"The girl that was shot here was named Brittany Jones. I didn't know her as Brittany. The name she went by in the house was Cici. She wasn't there long, and we didn't talk much, but this is what I can tell you about her: she was a fighter.

"As I mentioned, Romeo rationed our supplies, including giving us a weekly allocation of toilet paper. Cici started taking extra rolls from the hotels and hid it in her room. If we ever ran out, we could always go to her for more, and she would share her stash with us. It was just a little thing, but it showed me her character, that she had a good heart. I suppose I could've done the same thing, stolen toilet paper from the hotel bathroom, but I didn't dare. I was too afraid Romeo would find it and beat me, but Cici—Brittany—was different. She still had some fight in her.

"I don't know if Brittany was sexually abused before she ended up at our house. I suspect she was, because about seventy percent of victims of sex trafficking have a history of sexual abuse. I remember at one point telling Brittany that I never knew my dad, but that I liked to imagine he'd miraculously show up and save me. She told me that her father couldn't save her because he was dead and then she left the room. I remember that specific conversation because it was one of the few times I saw her look so sad.

"I don't know how Brittany managed to escape. One girl thought she'd snuck out of the van. Another thought she found an adjoining hotel room and hid there. By the time Romeo discovered she was missing, she was already long gone. There were consequences to her leaving, though, starting with beatings for the rest of us.

"Just after I turned eighteen, I worried that he would kick me out because he was always finding younger girls. Instead, I was promoted to being a handler. That meant I'd take the cash from the men and assign the rooms. I couldn't keep any of the money. I was still a slave, just doing a different job. Up until then, I had no clue how much money Romeo was making. I never did the math. But let's do it now. If one girl worked nearly every night for a whole year, and she had sex with eight to ten guys per night, which is conservative, and each guy paid a hundred dollars, that's two-hundred and fifty to three-hundred and fifty thousand dollars per girl, tax-free.

"Romeo was making a fortune off of us, and we were thrilled if we got a night out at McDonald's. In treatment, I learned that what I'd experienced is called 'trauma bonding,' where cycles of abuse are interspersed with a reward—like the beatings followed by the bandaging, or the starvation followed by a lavish dinner at a fast-food joint. This type of behavior actually made me more attached to my captor and less likely to leave."

Angelle pulled back her hair to reveal the tattoo on her neck, a dagger interwoven with a vine of small flowers.

"There's a reason I'm showing you this tattoo," she said. "Romeo branded each of us like cattle—we were his property. And even though I was high on drugs, I remember the stabbing of the needle. That's a pain you don't forget."

She let her hair fall back in place.

"You may ask why I don't have it removed, since it's a reminder of a horrible time in my life. Trust me, at first I had every intention of removing it, as soon as I could afford to have it done. I wanted to erase that experience from my life and from my skin."

Angelle paused and looked around the room. Her eyes locked on one of the counselors.

"But as I went through my treatment with my amazing counselor at Florida Cares, I decided to keep the tattoo for two reasons. First, it's a reminder to me that I'll never go back to that life again. Even if I'm down to my last dollar, I won't ever sell my body for sex or allow another human being to think he owns me. The second reason has to do with how I was finally freed.

"One night, the police raided the hotel. Most of the girls were arrested. I bring this up because in these raids, the girls are the ones who get punished, not the guys who are paying for sex. If we really want to eradicate sex trafficking, we have to change our laws. We have to stop prosecuting the victims and levy heavy fines on the customers demanding sex-trafficked women, who are the real victims. I was very lucky that night. One of the police officers took pity on me because of all of the sores I had on my face—it was gonorrhea left untreated. She sent me for medical treatment, and soon after, I met my counselor from Florida Cares. That's when my real healing began.

"Months later, I went back to the house where I'd been kept for so long. By that point it was abandoned. I assume Romeo bailed his girls out of jail and moved on with them. That's the other reason I keep this tattoo: in case one of those girls notices it. You see, I didn't even recognize Brittany when her photo was on the news. Her driver's license photo didn't look like the same person I knew. It was only when Detective Grant showed me a close-up of her tattoo that I realized Cici was Brittany, the girl who'd been shot."

Angelle looked over at Detective Grant and gave him a nod.

"I keep this 'branding' in the hopes that some other girl who is still imprisoned sees it. I hope she'll dare to speak to me, but even if she doesn't, we'll have an unspoken sisterhood, and I'll do everything in my power to save her. Thank you."

For a moment, everyone sat motionless, riveted by her horrific yet triumphant story. I dabbed my eyes as, one by one, people began to rise and applaud. The emotion of the night and Angelle's poignant speech had brought Lily to the front of my mind. Though generations apart, both girls had been preyed upon in a similar way. What was it going to take to make the next generation safer? We'd raised seventy-five hundred dollars for Florida Cares to continue their good work—that was a start.

Paul leaned over and whispered, "You've done a good thing here, Julianna."

I looked at him and smiled as a tear rolled down my cheek. He raised his hand and softly caressed my face, wiping away the tear. The gesture was so tender and natural.

Without hesitating, I grasped Paul's hand, holding it tightly in mine. In that moment, his touch felt so familiar, like I'd known him all my life.

AFTERWORD BY MICHELE SARKISIAN

Board Member of ECPAT
(End Child Prostitution and Trafficking) International

Board Member of BEST
(Business Ending Slavery and Trafficking)

Many thanks to Liz for bringing forward such an accurate depiction of a horror that occurs around us all the time. It's in our communities, schools, neighborhoods, businesses, hotels, organizations, churches and more. To say it simply, human trafficking is the exploitation of individuals, not their movement from place to place. This exploitation starts early, in the form of forced sex or labor, through coercion, deception and manipulation. In the dozen years I've worked in anti-trafficking, I've not met anyone who started in the sex trade as an adult, although it happens. Most often children are the ones targeted for trafficking.

My interest in sex trafficking prevention primarily has been directed toward helping young people. I've served on the Advisory Board of ECPAT (www.ecpatusa.org) because of its laser focus on the travel industry, where I spent a significant portion of my career.

Hotels, airlines, taxis, ride sharing and related businesses have a natural connection to trafficking. This is because sex requires a location, usually away from the customer's home, and so it involves moving victims from place to place. Events such as conventions, sports competitions, trade shows and conferences are attractive targets for exploiters because it allows them the opportunity to arrange multiple lucrative transactions per day.

Sex traffickers make a significant fortune for very little investment. In my city, Atlanta, I'm told an average "pimp" makes over thirty-five thousand dollars per week. Unlike drugs or other consumables, humans can be "sold" over and over again, and they are relatively easy to move without detection. And unless ordinary people learn to look for behavioral clues and oddities in the actions of the people around us, exploiters face very little risk of being noticed and apprehended.

The sad news is that kids are moved into the United States from many places, particularly across the southern border. Regardless of anyone's political views or feelings about our current administration or their positions on various issues, there is absolutely no question that unaccompanied minors cross the border. Coyotes bring them in with falsified documents, all the while deceiving the children's parents back home.

Families are promised that their children will reach the land of opportunity and that their "sponsor" will ensure their training in English, gain a position for them in a trade, continue their education and/or obtain many other benefits. Families pay dearly to transport their children, sometimes giving the "sponsor" the title to their home, which supposedly will be returned once the child has earned enough to pay back the sponsorship.

In actuality, once the young boy or girl arrives in the United States, often suffering physical and emotional trials along the journey, they immediately are put to work performing sex acts, pornography and other tasks for their handler. Drugs are often involved, particularly in the beginning, simply to ensure the victims' compliance. Drugs may or may not continue, but threats of retaliation against the family back home, including keeping the home's title, hurting a brother or sister, and deceiving more family members, are constant. In short, the child is now trapped.

There are certainly U.S. based victims, too. Typically, exploiters troll shopping malls, bus stations and other common places where a runaway, a loner, or an abused or depressed child might hang out. Exploiters know what to look for and how to play on these children's emotions; offering a meal, comforting words of affirmation, gifts and friendship so they gain their prey's trust.

Kids also are "groomed," especially if they fit the description of a high demand profile—such as virgin, wholesome or untouched beauty. These exploiters may work at a local smoothie shop after school, or may be a familiar face such as a crossing guard or a regular volunteer at events that kids typically attend. In these cases, exploiters become regulars at the location or event until they've earned the trust of the young person.

In one case, a grandfatherly type frequented a local restaurant in the mall where a young girl worked. He eventually gained her trust to the point that she started making his order as soon as he walked in the door. Not long after, he introduced his target to his "grandson," an attractive young man who took an interest in the girl. She immediately assumed the grandson was safe because he was related to her friend. The grandson invited her to grab a soda and she eagerly accepted. They "dated" a short while, until he invited her on a day trip to the beach. Without telling her parents, she accompanied the young man. And before she could understand what was happening, she found herself drugged, in a new city and without her phone.

It is ugly, but progress is being made to counter these kinds of nefarious efforts. Sunshine is a great disinfectant and the sun is shining in every city, in all industries and from our government and border patrol.

We're learning to observe; to say something when we see something. We're teaching kids to steer clear of unknown people online. We're asking kids what's going on when they act out of character, have unexplained wealth and lavish purchases or gifts. We take notice when a teen on an airplane is accompanied to the restroom by someone who does not use the restroom themselves. And we notice when a child looks different, unclean, and without their own documents or luggage when they are accompanied by an adult who speaks on their behalf.

States are posting "Not Buying It" and "End It" signs and placing signs in bathrooms outlining where a victim can call for help. Hotels also are posting signs, airports are broadcasting announcements over their public address systems and Uber drivers are being trained on what to look for. Police who make routine stops are learning the signs of someone being trafficked against their will and so are hotel front desk agents and housekeeping staff.

School nurses, doctors, clergy, hospital and medical staff, psychologists, teachers, coaches and others who work with kids are being trained in detection and gentle probing techniques to use when they sense trouble.

Lawyers are offering pro bono legal support for victims of trafficking. There are Lobby Days when the public converges on their legislative houses to support or oppose bills that affect victims and exploiters.

Companies also are implementing zero-tolerance policies when their own employees or vendors exploit others. For example, if an employee arranges a transaction for sex using his company phone or computer, or while on a company trip, severe consequences result for violating company policy and values.

The same rules can be applied to vendors who employ slave labor. One resource for sample policies and help in situations involving both employees and vendors is BEST, Businesses Ending Slavery and Trafficking (www.bestalliance.org). They offer templates for companies to use to refine for their own policies, and these templates can be applied to human resources (e.g. zero tolerance of exploitation by any employee using company resources or while performing work or services on behalf of the company) and to supply chain vendors (e.g. Tier 1 suppliers agree to no human trafficking or indentured servants and they require same of their suppliers).

There is increasing work on the demand side of trafficking as well. An organization called Streetgrace (www.streetgrace.org) in Atlanta has implemented tools that enable them to capture incoming transactions for sex with minors and communicate directly with the customer/exploiter. That opens up all kinds of possibilities: to address an addiction, to instill fear of exposure and of apprehension in the customer/exploiter, and to simply capture repeat offenders. I've seen phony ads placed in various promotional arenas where interaction between parties can be tracked and reported. Social media is getting much attention for how they aid and abet many types of nefarious activity, perhaps unknowingly. With the public's growing awareness of the situation they are beginning to demand that these social media companies take a stand and do something to curb the exploitation.

So, what can people like us do in our everyday lives? Lots of things. First, be aware of what's going on around you and be prepared to do something when you are concerned.

The Polaris website, www.polarisproject.org, is a good site to review. The Polaris hotline phone number is a good one to have on hand: 1-888-373-7888. It is also helpful to call 9-1-1 when you see abuse. I know of a specific case where a bruised young girl was noticed by a server at a restaurant. The girl displayed other signs of abuse. She was fearful, dirty and looked different from the adults with her. The server contacted 9-1-1 and snapped a photo of the car and license plate, which led to the apprehension of the abusers and rescue of the girl.

We can also commit to patronizing and applauding those companies and communities which are doing something about trafficking. For several years, I refused to stay in one brand of hotels because they did not sign the code (www.thecode.org). The Code of Conduct for the Protection of Children from Sexual Exploitation in Travel and Tourism is a multi-stakeholder initiative with the mission to provide awareness, tools and support to the tourism industry to prevent the sexual exploitation of children. Industry leaders who sign the code agree to take actions including training their employees on how to detect potential trafficking of children and what steps to take if they see something suspicious. I always ask individual hotels if they signed the code and have been trained in anti-trafficking when I make a reservation.

When I was working in corporate America with numerous large company clients, I asked my employer, as well as my clients, about their humanitarian policies and we had substantive conversations and efforts to combat trafficking. You can do this, too.

We can ask our communities and city councils about businesses that seem suspicious and request investigation. My city has closed multiple massage parlors for violating ordinances that were created to prevent exploitation. Ordinances include rules such as operating only within published hours, e.g. cars and customers should not be there at 2:00 a.m. when the business is only open until 9:00 p.m., no closed drapes on the front windows, no minors employed, e-verify used, and so on.

Above all, we must have conversations about trafficking and exploitation with those we care about in our families and communities, workplaces and social circles. In reality, many are victims of exploitation themselves who've developed a hard shell and lack of trust in humanity because of what they've endured. We must refrain from passing judgment on individuals who appear to have made poor choices, and instead use our humanity to come to their aid.

ACKNOWLEDGEMENTS

Thank you to...

Heather Stockdale and Georgia Cares – How lucky was I that the CEO of Georgia Cares stepped in as our substitute trainer on the day I took the sex trafficking education class. I went from knowing almost nothing about DMST (domestic minor sex trafficking) to knowing enough to write the fictional stories of Brittany, Angelle and Lily, which are composites of many real stories and facts. Like you, I hope that one day you'll work yourself out of a job.

Michele Sarkisian – You give so much of your time, passion, intelligence, network and integrity to the cause of fighting human trafficking. I could not be more honored and proud to have your afterword for this book!

John Requarth – I'm grateful to have found an experienced airline and charter pilot who was so giving of his time and so knowledgeable about all things aviation.

Mark Anglin – Although I could never do your job working at the medical examiner's office, I respect and admire the knowledge and skill it takes. Thank you for hosting our Citizen's Police Academy and for allowing me a return visit and many follow-up questions.

Claude Werner – Many thanks for your incredibly thorough and patient firearms instruction. I'm proud that my first shotgun lesson came from "The Tactical Professor."

Vicki Farnam – Thank you for your time and patience. Every woman should be so fortunate to learn from you, a master instructor and expert on human nature.

Christa Forrester – I recommend Confident Carry Firearms to anyone interested in exceptional training by an exceptional woman. Proud to call you my instructor and one of my best friends.

Anne Mauro – I could not be more appreciative that you were willing to share your experience and expertise with me! As a competitive shooter, coach, designer and overall firearms expert, you brought perfection to the range chapter. You're too young to be called a legend, but to me you are one.

Esther Schneider – You inspired Chapter 1, which launched this entire book. Thanks for taking me under your wing like a protective big sister. The Julianna character was modeled after you – grace under pressure and too fiery and smart to be deceived or underestimated.

Julianna Crowder and Robyn Sandoval – Need I say more? As you know, I name my characters for people I want to honor. Thank you for letting me "borrow" your names.

Debbie Holt, Judy Myers and Angela Beck – I'm honored that you would bid to add a name in my book, with proceeds going to great causes: Debbie, Judy and Lynnette are for you!

Holly Kiely – Your willingness to share your pain at the loss of your husband gave this book an authenticity I struggled to find. God bless you and dear Joe Kiely's memory. We all love and miss him.

Barbara Ray – Thanks for being my boat expert and lending me Gus's name. That chapter was my missing link, then you came along and provided such great content.

Christopher Schneider – Only someone with your talent could go from years on the SWAT team to overseeing a major brand. I admire your zest for life. Some people are naturally the "life of the party" and it makes the rest of us relish your company.

Claudia Chisholm – You are a pioneer and a powerhouse, taking over your father's company long before that was the norm for a young woman. Now you've turned the business into the mega successful brand of Gun Toten' Mamas (GTM). I'm so honored to call you a friend and to feature your range bag in this book.

George Weinstein – You are such a generous author! I marvel at how you find the time to write your own fantastic books with all you do for everyone else, including leading one of the best conferences I've attended. May what you do for others come back to you tenfold!

Maegan Clark & Christian Kazanjian – Thank you for facilitating phone calls and video chats so I could read my book to my mother. Not only did it help me with proofreading, but it gave us hours of enjoyment together!

Carrie Ailes, Amy Allen, Josette Chmiel, Elaine Edwards, Laura Evans, Christa Forrester, Heidi Kortejarvi, Andy Nunemaker, Dirk Swanson, Barbara Thompson, Sheli Walters, Ashlee Weeks, Mike Werley and Judi White – Your astute feedback allowed for so many improvements to the novel, and you know I'm a stickler for accuracy and eliminating inconsistencies! #bestbetareaders ever!

Heidi Brakewood Adamek – You're exceptional at everything you do, whether it's a corporate leader, daughter, sister, wife and now mother. With your busy schedule, thank you for tackling book #3.

KJ Howe – Every apprentice needs a master. I appreciate your generosity and steadfast support. You are my hero…well, you and Thea Paris.

Evelyn Fazio – I wonder why we even "track changes" because you know I'm going to accept your edits…they are perfection! And beyond your incomparable expertise and wisdom, you are such a dear person! Kisses to Creamsicle and loving memories of Butterscotch, Caruso and Oreo.

Rebecca Faith Heyman – Just when I thought this novel was ready, you came along and challenged me to do more. What I needed and you absolutely provided was a relentless pursuit of perfection. The edits, though difficult, took my writing and storytelling to a new level.

Richard Brakewood – *Always* my rock of support and soft place to land.

SUPPORT FOR LIZ

If you enjoyed this novel, we would so appreciate you taking a moment to tell others:

- Share with a friend or book club—Liz will often visit or Zoom/Skype with book clubs if requested

- Write a review where you purchased the book—it's the best way to both thank and encourage the author

- Post about the book on your favorite social media site: Facebook, Instagram, Twitter, Pinterest

If you would like to stay in touch with Liz, she can be reached at:

Website: www.lizlazarus.com

Facebook: www.facebook.com/AuthorLizLazarus

Instagram: www.instagram.com/AuthorLizLazarus

Twitter: www.twitter.com/liz_lazarus

BOOK CLUB DISCUSSION QUESTIONS
FOR *SHADES OF SILENCE*

www.shadesofsilence.com

For a visit by the author, Liz Lazarus, at your book club
please contact liz@lizlazarus.com.

In order to provide reading groups with the most thought-
provoking questions possible, it is necessary to reveal important
aspects of the plot of this novel. If you have not finished
reading *Shades of Silence*, we recommend that you
wa it before reviewing this guide.

1. OVERALL Would you recommend *Shades of Silence* to a friend? Why or why not?	**6. DNA & PATERNITY TESTING** Julianna uses a paternity test to find out if Jasper is Michael's son. Have you ever done a similar test – for paternity or ancestry? What did you learn?
2. LOSS & GRIEF In this book, Julianna loses her parents to a car accident and her husband's plane goes missing. What did you notice about the way she processes her grief? Have you been in her situation—losing a parent or a spouse?	**7. HOMICIDE INVESTIGATION** We follow Detective Grant through the process of a homicide investigation. What did you learn about how an investigation is conducted?
3. HUMAN SEX TRAFFICKING We learn about the myths and realities of sex trafficking and the ways to spot a child in danger. What else did you learn about domestic minor sex trafficking in this novel?	**8. GUNS & SHOTGUNS** Have you ever been to a shooting range or shot a shotgun? If not, is it something you'd like to try? Why or why not?
4. FIRST IMPRESSIONS When we first meet Brittany, she is trespassing and swearing. Once you learn about her background, do your feelings about her change?	**9. ENDING** Were you surprised by the ending? What different ending could you imagine for this book? What other elements of the book surprised you?
5. MISSING PERSON Do you know anyone who is dealing with a missing person's case? How has it affected his/her life and family?	**10. MOVIE CASTING** If *Shades of Silence* were made into a movie, who would you cast for Julianna, Grant, Samantha, Alex, Jasper and Michael?

Excerpt of

PLEA FOR JUSTICE

by Liz Lazarus

⚖ 1. Jackie — Last Year

On the coffee table next to my *People* magazine sat a Papa John's pizza box with day-old grease stains. Except for the garlic packet, I had eaten everything, even the limp jalapeno peppers. Beside the cardboard box were six napkins, one for each Krispy Kreme I had devoured. I had kept the donuts in the freezer as a way to ration them, but 15 seconds in the microwave took care of that. As if in a trance, I thawed them one at a time until they were gone. Besides, once the floodgates were opened, what was the point of restraint?

In hindsight, I should have joined the other paralegals for happy hour instead of spending my Friday night binging on pizza and Net-flix. But after a long week at the law firm, I looked forward to vegging out alone on the couch.

I surveyed the aftermath of my mindless indulgence. Maybe it wasn't as bad as it looked. I headed down the narrow hall to the small bathroom of my one-bedroom apartment. As I stepped onto the cold tile floor, my guilty eyes fixated on the oval white scale in front of the bathtub.

Holding my breath, I stepped on it and looked down.

My spirits sank.

I stepped off, let it reset and tried again. But the number didn't change.

Dejected, I trudged into the bedroom and flipped on the TV. A skinny blonde with perfectly coiffed hair and sparkling white teeth was robotically reading the morning news on CNN. If the camera added ten pounds, then she really had to be anorexic. How I wished to be her just for a day, to be seen as beautiful, attractive and perfectly put-to-gether. I was sure people didn't sneer at her when she bought a cup of coffee with extra cream and a few donuts.

The reporter continued in her cut-glass voice, "We have breaking news in the case of the Snapchat Killer. Local artist Aaron Slater was arrested last night for the murder of Catherine Snow. Slater was at his residence and art studio, where authorities made the arrest. We're told they've found compelling evidence and expect to have DNA results in the coming weeks."

I gasped, seeing the familiar face of the boy I knew in high school, though his sunken eyes and weathered face were a much older version of the Aaron I remembered. Still, not even a police photo could mask his curly brown hair and chiseled jawbone. His ever-present dimples, the ones that had made every teenage girl swoon, enhanced his good looks. Besides Lindsay Lohan, Aaron was the only person I'd ever seen who managed to look like a movie star in a mug shot.

By contrast, my appearance was hardly as glamorous. My XXL T-shirt draped like a tent from my neck and shoulders, my red hair was starting to frizz and the inflamed blemishes on my jawline looked like a mild case of chicken pox. What a cruel joke that my acne still flared in my late twenties.

The anchorwoman cut to a live feed of the local reporter bundled in a winter coat and scarf outside Aaron's art studio in Decatur, Georgia. Several vans, camera crews and other reporters were all trying to get a jump on the story. The reporter on the scene provided some details of Aaron's biography, one I knew well.

In our small hometown of Columbus, Georgia, everybody knew everybody. My high school graduating class had only sixty students. Aaron had been my best friend and the only kid in our class who had treated me with a shred of decency. Well, decent in his own way. When some of the "mean girls" had spread rumors that I had lice, *which wasn't true,* Aaron brought a bottle of lice-killing shampoo to school and slipped it to me in front of my locker.

"Even if you don't use it," he had said softly, "just show them the bottle and maybe they'll stop saying that stuff."

I had thought only the girls were talking about my alleged lice so I was doubly devastated when I learned that the boys were gossiping about me, too. But Aaron was different. Although he didn't advertise or acknowledge our friendship, not in public anyway, he had always helped me in private, like with the shampoo.

How could Aaron Slater be guilty of murder? He couldn't hurt a fly—could he?

⚖ A. Me — Before Conviction

You don't notice me at first, but I notice you. Let's start with your clothes—the hiked-up miniskirt and yellow tank top. You're going to freeze your ass off. Legs streaked with fake tanner, you look like a zebra. A refined lady sips her liquor, but not you. You slam the free booze from a secret admirer. Sure, you look around the bar to see who might have sent it. That's when I take a piss, to stay out of sight. But the more the shots keep coming, the less you care who sent them. Spoiled bitch. Daddy's princess.

Is your ugly sidekick going to stay sober and stick with you? Why the loyalty, ugly girl? Hoping to get the leftovers from Birdie? Sure enough, ugly girl lasts awhile, but when she can't convince you to leave by midnight, she bails. My move—chicks can't resist these dimples.

You're drunk but you don't refuse another shot. You like the attention of a real man, not a college boy. You casually rub my forearm, admiring my muscles and my expensive TAG watch—both are appealing. You like to flirt, and when I play it cool, you try even harder, probing the bottom of the shot glass with your tongue. Yeah, I noticed.

That's when you make your first mistake. I ask to take a selfie of us using your phone and you foolishly let me. My digital infiltration begins.

Now the tricky part. I have to jailbreak your smartphone. You wouldn't understand how to download outside applications, but I do. I shift from taking selfies of us to pics of just you. You imagine you're a Victoria's Secret supermodel and I'm your prize photographer. As I rapidly snap your picture, you eat it up. In reality, I'm not taking any photos at all. I'm working my magic to invade your life.

"Excellent," I encourage. It doesn't take much. "Now give me your best sexy look. You got it. Don't stop."

You continue to giggle and pose like a slut while I download and launch my spyware on your phone. You writhe like a worm, wrapping your leg around the brass bar railing. You think you're so hot. I play along, all the while pretending to take pictures of you.

For my invasion to be complete, the phone must be rebooted. I deliberately turn it off and then stare at the device as if it has betrayed me.

"Your phone is crap," I say, as I hand it back. "It just died on me. I hope I didn't lose all those great poses."

You take the phone and gape at the dark screen. I wait. Can you possibly be this dense? You finally figure out the obvious solution to try the power button.

"It works fine for me," you slur. "Must be user error."

"Must be," I admit. And with the finesse of a world-class thief, my spyware is live. Not that it was a particular challenge—you don't even use a password, you stupid girl.

With my monitoring software installed, I'll track your calls, look at your photos and read all of your texts and emails. With access to your calendar and GPS, I'll watch your every move and know exactly where you are, all without leaving the comfort of my favorite chair.

You continue to flirt, leaning in closer and placing your sticky fingers on my leather jacket. Sloppy bitch. You want me to kiss you, to whisk you away to my bed, but that's not the plan, not tonight. First, I need to invade your digital life.

I grab the nape of your neck and whisper that I have to go. You lean in more, expecting me to ravish you right there in public, but I don't. Instead, I leave you at the bar—horny, intoxicated and rejected. I almost offer to drive you home, just to be sure you're safe, which is the ultimate irony.

⚖ 2. Jackie — Prison Visit 1

Other than the TV mug shots, I hadn't seen Aaron since the summer after our high school graduation. I was working the concession stand at our local movie theatre and he showed up with a group of kids. They were going to see "Batman Begins." I remember it clearly because Aaron and I had talked about seeing that movie together—I had a free employee pass and could get him in for half price.

But he acted as if he didn't see me. Sometimes he was aloof like that when he was with the popular kids, but he would always call me later. This time he never called. A few days passed, but I still didn't hear from him. Days turned to weeks, weeks turned to months—and still nothing. I had texted him early on, but he didn't reply. That wasn't unusual. He never liked to text, but he would always call. Yet my phone never rang; my pleading voicemails were never answered.

I racked my brain, wondering what I had done to offend him. But I couldn't think of a single thing. I couldn't understand how we could go from hanging out nearly every week for the last four years to nothing. Sure, we had graduated, but that shouldn't have changed things.

At first, I told myself he was busy and would call soon. When I realized he was never going to call me, I felt so betrayed. I took his number out of my "favorites" so I wouldn't have to keep seeing it. I thought about deleting all of his information from my phone but just couldn't bring myself to do it. For the rest of that summer, I worked the concessions, consumed buttered popcorn and cherry Coke, listened to sappy songs on the radio and eyed the door, hoping to see him again.

That fall I was off to Agnes Scott College on a partial scholarship. I heard occasional snippets about Aaron—that he played minor league baseball for a few years and later opened an art studio. I lost track of him eventually, and frankly, I didn't want to think about him. He'd dumped me without a second thought after we'd been so close. And it wasn't as if I'd been his girlfriend. We didn't have a fight and break up. I'd always thought that was my one advantage—*not* being his girlfriend. They would come and go, but I'd always be part of his life.

When the time came, I didn't go back to my five-year high school reunion. There were no good memories for me in Columbus. I did wonder if he would be there, and later saw all the party pictures on

Facebook. Aaron didn't have an account but everyone else did, and he was in a lot of the photos—drinking and dancing. As always, he was the center of attention, with pretty girls draped all over him.

Now, our ten-year reunion had just come and gone. I didn't go to that one either, but I'm sure the buzz was all about Aaron's arrest, his plea deal and the shock of it all. Those pretty girls, the ones who'd tried so desperately to win his affection, were probably the same ones saying they'd always known he was a bad egg. As for me, I tried not to think about him. Any time something would trigger a fond memory, it would invariably lead me to the same place, that hollow feeling of betrayal and confusion.

My reconnection with Aaron started with repeated, annoying calls to my mobile phone from "No Caller ID." I ignored them at first, but they became more persistent. When I tried to block the caller, it didn't work. I even tried creating a contact called "No Caller ID" so I could add it to my blocked numbers, but that didn't stop the calls, either. I was just about to pay for an app that guaranteed to block the number when my phone rang once again with no ID. I answered in frustration.

"Stop calling this number!" I shouted. "Or I'll report you to the police."

"Jackie, wait! It's me, Aaron," the voice on the other end said.

"Aaron?" I was stunned.

"Yes. Please, Jackie, I need to talk to you."

"Wait. Aren't you in prison? How are you calling me? How'd you get my number?"

"I'll explain that later," he replied in a hushed voice. "Look, I can't talk for long, but I need to see you. It's important. Please come and visit me."

The nerve of this guy! He blew me off ten years ago, killed a woman, admitted to killing her, and he now thinks I'm just going to waltz down to the prison to visit him.

"Don't call me again!" I shouted and hung up, staring at my phone as if I didn't trust it to remain silent.

Little did I realize that "No Caller ID" could also send me text messages.

> Jackie please I didn't do it just let me explain

Once the initial shock wore off, I began to feel guilty. Here he was in prison, reaching out to me in apparent desperation, and I was ignoring him. My anger started to fade and the good memories resurfaced—hanging out at his house, going to the lake, admiring the sketches he was always doodling. I read somewhere that pain is the hardest emotion to retain. I guess that's true, judging by my changed attitude.

So, after initially ignoring the string of text messages and voicemails, I finally picked up the phone. Aaron had been able to "ice" me for years. I, on the other hand, could only ignore him for a few days.

"Hello," I said.

"Jackie, is that you? It's me, Aaron."

"I know."

"Thank you for answering." He sighed. "I've been praying that God would whisper in your ear."

That struck me as a really odd thing for Aaron to say. He had never been religious. I guess prison could put the fear of God into anyone. He explained that he'd bartered for a phone by painting a portrait of a guard's wife from a photograph. His first call was to his parents, but they refused to speak to him. Next, he tried his uncle, friends from high school, and even friends from baseball, but nobody would have anything to do with him.

After a few brief phone conversations, I caved and agreed to visit him. Maybe it was out of pity. Or maybe I wanted him to explain why he'd abandoned me. Maybe I just wanted to hear the truth from his lips. Was he really capable of murder?

Once I agreed to go, there was a whole process involved in getting to see him in prison. It wasn't as if I could just drive up and ask to speak to Aaron Slater. The only people allowed to visit were family members who were on a pre-approved list and his lawyer. I toyed with the idea of mailing a letter to the prison on my firm's letterhead, saying our senior partner was his new counsel and assigning me as his assistant. That approach would allow me to visit without any hassle, but what if I got caught? In junior high, I wrote crib notes for a history test in tiny print on my palm. Ironically, the process of writing the "cheat sheet" helped me to memorize the information. I never once needed to look at my hand during the exam. That evening, my brother saw the notes—I had forgotten to wash them off—and ratted on me. I was grounded for a month. Instead of getting an 'A,' which

I actually earned, my mother forced me to take a zero, breaking my straight A average.

Rather than risking this deception and failing, I mustered the nerve to talk to Mr. Rubin, the managing partner at our law firm. I asked if he would agree to nominally represent a high school classmate of mine who was in prison so I could visit him. I assured him that he'd have no obligation toward my friend nor any repercussions from doing this favor for me. To my surprise, Mr. Rubin agreed. Luckily, he didn't ask for more details because I left out the fact that my friend was the confessed Snapchat Killer.

With the legal details settled and the official paperwork processed, one Saturday morning I made the hour-long drive to rural north Georgia and the Wheeler Correctional Institute. When I reached the exit ramp to the prison, there was nothing but rectangular patches of farmland as far as the eye could see. I turned down a long driveway leading to a group of gray cinder block buildings behind reinforced metal fences that were topped with barbed wire. The American, State of Georgia and Department of Corrections flags rose from the top of a lookout post, rippling in the slight August breeze. There was not a single human being in sight.

I parked in a gravel lot reserved for visitors. Wearing the only suit I owned, the same black one I'd worn for my job interview at the Sterling, Martin & Rubin Law firm, I approached a metal gate. Clutching my purse and briefcase, and hoping that I looked official, I took a deep breath and pressed a large red button, my heart racing.

"Wheeler Correctional," a female voice announced. "May I help you?"

I hadn't asked Mr. Rubin what I was supposed to say at the gate, not wanting to pester him too much. I was playing at being a lawyer but had no idea what I was doing. Not knowing how to respond, I momentarily considered running back to my car.

"May I help you?" the voice repeated.

I took a deep breath and forced myself to speak. "I'm Jackie Siegel. Legal counsel for Aaron Slater."

I waited, half expecting the voice to call me out and say, "No, you're not. You're an imposter and you have no right to be here!"

Instead, a loud electronic buzzer sounded. I pushed the huge metal door open to find myself in a fenced corridor, but still outside. The grass could have been a putting green—it was that well-manicured. I walked about twelve feet to a second metal door that led inside the facility. By now my heart-rate started to get back to normal—I'd made it past the first gauntlet.

The large room I entered had shiny linoleum floors that looked as if they were waxed every day. Several vending machines hummed in the far corner, and two rows of brown plastic chairs created a small waiting area.

I stepped up to an enclosed counter, behind which the guard, a hefty ebony-skinned woman sat, looking bored. Sometimes other large women were nice to me, kind of an unspoken sisterhood. Sometimes, especially if they were bigger than me, they could be the meanest of all. This one was just indifferent.

"ID please," she said.

I handed her my driver's license and wondered if I needed to show her the letter from my law firm, the same one I'd mailed the previous week so I could be added to Aaron's legal team. Or would doing that just give away my inexperience? I decided to follow her lead. She typed on her keyboard, squinted at her computer screen and, after a few moments, handed back my license.

I jumped at the sound of another loud buzz, then hurried to open the door she pointed toward.

"Purse and briefcase," she said, once I was on the other side of the door and facing her. I handed them over and she motioned for me to pass through the metal detector. Before I could reach the archway, she ordered me to wait. I looked back, wondering what I had done wrong.

"You better take off those heels," she suggested.

I nodded and braced myself on the side of the detector so I could pull off each shoe without losing my balance.

Once I was through the metal archway, I wobbled as I stepped back into my shoes. When it became clear that I didn't know where to go next, the guard pointed to the end of the hall and said, "Attorney booths are over there."

I felt as if I'd entered a world with a different set of rules and that no one had given me the handbook. As Mr. Rubin's paralegal, most of my work involved research and notetaking. Rarely did I go to court, and I'd never been to a prison.

I walked down the hallway, my heels clicking like tap shoes on the linoleum, and headed for a pair of bright yellow doors. I'd noticed a faint, unpleasant odor when I'd first walked in, but now I got a full dose of the stench that could best be described as a mixture of bleach and excrement. I thought I might vomit. Instead, I covered my nose and mouth with my hand and kept walking.

As I approached the yellow doors, yet another buzzer sounded, allowing me inside the visiting area. The walls were light gray cinder blocks and the floors were just as glossy as the waiting room. On my side, brown plastic chairs faced cubicles that were separated by metal partitions. A counter and glass barrier ran the length of the room, physically separating lawyers from inmates. At the base of the glass barrier, there was a narrow slit with just enough space to pass papers back and forth.

I sat down in a flimsy chair that sank toward the floor as its legs splayed and then finally steadied. For a moment, I was afraid the legs might snap under my weight. With the extra pounds I'd put on since high school, I wondered what Aaron would think. Would he notice? Would he care? And why was I even concerned about this right now?

Setting my purse and briefcase on the floor, I retrieved a blank legal pad and pen, assuming that's what a lawyer would do. Within moments, I heard heavy footsteps and a cacophony of chains rattled behind locked doors.

I had spent so much time planning my access to the prison that I hadn't prepared myself for what was next. In a few seconds, I would be face-to-face with Aaron the inmate. My stomach knotted and I felt my body flush with heat. Would it be awkward? Would we feel like old friends, or had we completely lost that connection? What if our childhood bond was gone and he was now nothing more than a stranger?

The door opened and two barrel-shaped black guards escorted the inmate into the room on the other side of the barrier, each guard holding one of Aaron's arms. He was dressed in a bright-orange jumpsuit, white socks and tennis shoes with the laces removed. His head hung down, so all I could see was a mop of curly brown hair. His ankles, wrists and waist were bound with chains. A separate, heavier chain held his wrists close to his slender waist. One of the guards unlocked the wrist cuffs and reattached the right cuff to a clamp on the metal partition.

The guard looked me up and down through the glass barrier and commented, "Hey A, you got yourself a nice lawyer."

Aaron slowly sat down on a wooden stool that was bolted to the floor. He faced me, but his head still tilted and he didn't meet my gaze. His left hand rested in his lap. His right hand, the one attached to the barrier, rested on the counter. He was so pale now, unlike the boy I knew who'd always sported a golden tan.

I expected my anger at Aaron to resurface, along with the buried resentment from his decade-long silence. I thought I'd feel repulsed by him—after all, he'd killed a girl and admitted it. But somehow that didn't happen. Instead, all I felt was overwhelming pity at how diminished he looked. To my surprise, it felt like no time had passed at all, and that I was reunited with my long-lost friend.

Aaron licked his left thumb and started rubbing what looked like a purplish-blue bruise on his right hand, all the while avoiding eye contact.

"We'll give you some privacy," the guard said. "You be good to him, young lady." He winked at me and the guards left the room.

There were old-fashioned wall-phones hanging on both sides of the barrier. I reached over, picked mine up and held it to my ear. Aaron did the same.

"I'm glad you came," he exhaled, still not looking at me. "You didn't have to."

I nodded, not knowing what to say.

He lifted his head slightly, as if he wanted to look at me but couldn't quite find the courage. He'd begged me to visit, but he now seemed so embarrassed. Of all the emotions I'd ever felt toward Aaron—friendship, admiration, protectiveness, love, and then resentment—pity had never entered the equation. I didn't know what to do so I tried to lighten the mood a bit.

"I'm so sorry, Aaron. Of all the people I know, you're the last person I'd expect to see here. You were voted most likely to win the lottery, remember?"

But then I realized how inappropriate this comment was in light of his predicament. Being in prison was no joking matter and reminiscing about high school couldn't have brought him any pleasure. It had to be crushing for him to think about his former life and his lost future.

What was I thinking when I agreed to come in the first place? I wasn't helping anything by being there.

After a brief silence, Aaron spoke. "I can't believe I'm in here, Jackie. I know everyone thinks I'm guilty, and I know you may not believe me, but I really didn't do it."

For the first time, he looked directly at me—his dark brown eyes intense and still alluring. Even in these somber surroundings, Aaron retained his elusive charm. It was what made all the girls want to be his girlfriend and all the guys want to be his pal. With the cliques, turf wars and other drama that had come with adolescence, Aaron always seemed above it, never making enemies. It reminded me of the guy on *The Bachelor* who was everyone's friend, and while the other guys were duking it out, he quietly swooped in, won the girl and somehow had all of his rivals cheering for him.

My heart sank—not because I didn't believe Aaron, but rather because I did. I hadn't expected him to talk about the murder. I'd assumed he'd avoid the topic, which would be an unspoken admission of guilt. On the drive up, I'd wondered about how to forgive the man without condoning the behavior, and whether I could separate the two. I wasn't sure I could, but now I didn't have to. Still, if Aaron was innocent, why would he have taken a plea-bargain? And what did he want from me?

"I'm not sure how I can help you," I finally replied.

He had a sadness about him that I'd never seen before. Gone was the happy-go-lucky boy from my childhood. His voice had lost its cocky confidence, replaced now with a defeated whisper. "I honestly didn't know I was pleading guilty that day in court," he admitted.

"What do you mean?" I asked, surprised.

"There has to be a way to look into my case. If somebody could just do that, they'd see it wasn't right. I know they'd see I was innocent."

Now I understood. He wanted my brain, just like when we were kids. He somehow must have found out that I worked at a law firm and that I might be able to help him. But this wasn't like writing his term paper. This was a potential life sentence and I had no training or experience to draw upon.

When I didn't reply, he spilled out a half-coherent rendition of events. "My attorney, Ms. Jackson, she told me the evidence all pointed to me. She said my only option was to sign the paper. That would keep the death penalty off the table. But I had to do it that day or they'd change their minds. So I signed it. So I'd have a chance at parole. And then I thought I could testify at my trial."

I tried not to let my expression reveal my shock. All I could think was, *You can't possibly be that naive!* A flashback from high school popped into my mind—of Aaron swearing, on late Sunday evening, that he'd never heard the teacher say our book report was due on Monday. Without hesitating, I gave him my paper and stayed up all night writing a new one. Thinking back, I'd bailed him out a lot, to the point that it became normal for us. Ironically, he got an A and I got a B-, along with a reproach from our teacher, who wrote on my second effort, "Not your best work, Jackie."

I snapped out of the daydream to see Aaron looking at me expectantly, as if I'd have the answer to his predicament.

"Didn't your attorney go over your waiver of rights?" I asked.

"I don't know." He ran his fingers through his thick, curly hair, making it even more disheveled. "They brought me into court and she gave me a bunch of papers. She said I had to sign them or I'd be put to death, so I signed them. And then I was in front of the judge, and he asked how I pled, so I looked at her. She told me to say guilty so I said guilty, but I added that I didn't do it. I know for certain that I said that. The judge asked me something about a jury, so I thought the trial would come next."

"What did he ask you?"

"I don't remember exactly, but I know he mentioned a jury."

I spoke slowly and deliberately. "Did he ask you if it was possible that a reasonable jury would find you guilty?"

"Maybe. I don't remember." Aaron kneaded his hands together like he used to do when he was warming up for pitching practice. "The next thing I knew, I was signing another piece of paper and was sent back to jail. That's when I found out from one of the guards that I'd be in prison for the next thirty years."

He hung his head again, this time resting his forehead in his hands. Now I got a better look at the purple mark and could see that it wasn't a bruise, but more like a stain. The attached chain clanked as he rubbed his head. In an exasperated, defeated voice, he whispered, "Nobody will listen to me, Jackie. No one will help me."

My poor Aaron. I wanted to break through that glass barrier and wrap my arms around him. I wanted to find his incompetent public defender and smack her—she obviously hadn't explained things clearly to him. I also wanted to find that judge, who apparently had used

Alford language to nudge a guilty plea out of Aaron. How I wished I could take him by the hand and lead him out of that prison, but I couldn't.

"I'll help you," I volunteered, before I even realized what I was saying. Short of an embrace or prison escape, which were impossible, it was all I could offer.

He looked up—a small glimmer of hope shining in his eyes. "How do we fix this, Jackie? Can I change my plea?"

I didn't want to be the one to give him hope only to dash it. I didn't have the heart to tell him that the law only allows thirty days to withdraw a guilty plea. For him, that time was long gone. But then another idea struck me.

"I'm afraid it's too late to change your plea, Aaron. But you might be able to apply for habeas corpus."

"What's that?" His brows tightened in confusion.

I had studied habeas corpus briefly in college. Literally, it meant "bring the body before the court." I knew just enough to be dangerous but was by no means proficient. That would require a lot more research. For now, I could give him a short explanation, one that would keep his hopes alive.

I said, "Habeas corpus is a way for you to petition that you are being unlawfully held. I believe you would have to sue the prison, or I guess the warden, for illegally detaining you."

"And then they would let me go?" he asked.

"Not quite. After you write the petition, your defense lawyer would get subpoenaed and brought before a judge. At that point, you'd have the chance to state your position. You'd have to prove that your case is unfair, and as a result, detaining you is a violation of your rights."

"Can you help me?" he asked. "You know—write the petition?"

I should have seen that coming. For once, Aaron should do his own homework. Unfortunately, this wasn't the right circumstance to teach him a lesson.

"I need to research it, but let me see what I can do."

If nothing else, I was encouraged to see him progress from being the near-zombie who first sat in front of me to a slightly resuscitated Aaron. I glanced at the wall clock, wondering if our visit was timed or if I could stay there all afternoon.

"I guess I'd better get going," I said. "To start my research."

He nodded. "Can I ask you one more thing?"

"Okay," I said. He reminded me of a little boy who wanted just one more bedtime story. I supposed that as soon as I left, reality would hit him and he'd feel alone again.

He glanced around, and then reached into the vest pocket of his orange jumpsuit and pulled out a sheet of paper folded in half.

"What do you make of this?" he asked, as he slipped the paper through the slot in the glass barrier.

I reached across the table, unfolded the paper, which was actually parchment, to see the full sheet. It was a page torn from the Old Testament, apparently of the Ten Commandments. Commandments 5, 6, 9 and 10, were underlined.

Had Aaron become religious since going to prison? I recalled his unusual comment about praying that God would whisper in my ear.

Was this his way of covertly confessing to me?

1. I am the Lord, your God, who brought you out of the land of Egypt, out of the house of bondage.	5. <u>Honor your father and mother.</u>
	6. <u>You shall not murder.</u>
2. You shall have no other Gods before Me.	7. You shall not commit adultery.
3. You shall not take the name of the Lord in vain.	8. You shall not steal.
	9. <u>You shall not bear false witness against your neighbor.</u>
4. Remember the Sabbath Day and keep it holy.	10. <u>You shall not covet.</u>

"What is this?" I asked.

"Somebody mailed it to me. What do you make of it?"

That changed my perspective. This wasn't originated *by* Aaron, but was sent *to* him.

"Why would someone send you the Ten Commandments?" I asked.

His eyes widened for a brief moment before he looked away. He just shook his head.

I continued, "I suppose 'You shall not murder' makes sense, if someone is trying to chastise you. But why are the other three underlined?"

He shook his head. "What do you think?"

"Honor your father and mother. You shall not bear false witness against your neighbor. You shall not covet. Those don't have anything to do with your case, do they?"

He repeated my words slowly, as if he was trying to sear them into his memory.

"Have you shown this to your lawyer?" I asked.

"No, just you."

"I guess it could be from the girl's family, or from one of her friends, or from some loon who followed the case, right?"

Aaron's face hardened. I could see the anger slowly boiling inside him. "It's from the real killer. He's sending me clues. He's taunting me."

That thought had not occurred to me. If Aaron was innocent, there was a real killer on the loose. Even in the safety of a guarded room full of security cameras, I suddenly felt a chill.

"I wouldn't give it too much heed," I encouraged, as I started to slide the sheet of paper back to him.

"You keep it," he told me, pushing the paper back toward me.

I instantly pictured him as a teen, pushing a bag of salty pretzels toward me. Back in high school, he taught me to drink beer. We were sitting at his rickety kitchen table with the blue and white plastic checkered tablecloth. His mom was a nurse on third shift, so we had the house to ourselves. I took my first ever sip of beer from his open Miller bottle and cringed. Seeing the face I'd made, Aaron grabbed a bag of pretzels and slid them toward me, saying they'd help. He'd made the same sliding motion now, flooding my mind with images of our past friendship.

We had indeed been the odd couple. At school, our worlds didn't intersect. But in private, at his house when no one else was around, I was no longer the fat geek and he was no longer the cool jock. We were just friends. Well, we were friends until the summer after high school. I thought about asking him what I had done to make him abandon me, but given the current circumstances, that seemed trivial. I put the paper with the Bible passage in my briefcase and started to stand up.

"Have you been back to Columbus lately?" he asked, referring to our hometown.

I shook my head as I sat back down. "I don't go home much."

"Your parents, they're doing okay?"

I nodded.

"And your brother? He went to medical school, right?"

"Yes. He's a doctor. Married with two kids. How are your parents?"

Aaron turned his cheek as if I'd slapped him. When he finally looked up, his eyes looked wet.

"They divorced," he said. "Dad moved out West. But Mom's still in Columbus. I haven't seen her since…" His voice trailed off.

"She hasn't visited you?" As soon as I said it, I realized I was rubbing salt in the wound. I didn't mean to be cruel. I was just shocked that his own mother wouldn't visit him in prison. It had been over six months since he'd been locked up. Hadn't anyone else visited Aaron? He shook his head, too choked up to reply. My heart broke for him. How could his mom do this to her son, her only child?

"Maybe you could check on her for me—I mean, if it isn't any trouble or if you're already headed that way. But I guess you don't go back there much, like you said."

I didn't have plans to go to Columbus, but I took Mrs. Slater's number just to make him feel better. I didn't have any real intention to visit his mother, or so I thought at the time.

At that point, a guard stuck his head into the room and said, "Hey A, you gonna be having lunch? It's corn dogs."

I'd lost track of time. Apparently, as his "lawyer," I could stay as long as I wanted. It seemed odd how the guard treated Aaron like he was a guest at a hotel, rather than an inmate in a prison.

"Yeah, sure. Thanks, Cyrus," Aaron replied. Then the same two guards walked into the room, uncuffed Aaron's arm from the partition and reattached it to the chain at his waist. As the first one led Aaron out of the room, the other leaned toward me and said under his breath, "Hey, you seem like a nice lady. How 'bout putting some money on his account? He could use it. Ain't nobody else helping him."

The guard's comment struck me as odd. Why was he taking such an interest in Aaron's well-being? And if Aaron needed cash, wouldn't he have asked me? Then again, he probably was too proud. I nodded at the guard and added that task to my mental "to do" list—figure out how to credit money to a prisoner's account.

Just before he was out of sight, Aaron looked over his shoulder and asked, "So you'll help me?"

"I'll try," I replied, as he was escorted away.

Try what? Try to look deeper into his case? To see if habeas corpus was even a possibility? To visit his mom? I couldn't say for certain what I was going to try because I didn't really know myself.

⚖ B. Me — Before Conviction

You light up seeing me again at the bar, thinking it's a coincidence, maybe even fate. Stupid girl, I've been tracking your every move for over a week. This time, instead of sending shots from afar, I saunter right over. You try to play it coy, but I'm different from the other guys—mature, aloof, mysterious. Everyone says that boys like a chase. I'll let you in on a secret—girls do, too.

Your ugly sidekick isn't with you this time. You exchanged messages with her earlier to meet you at the bar. Not like her to be a no-show. You have no idea that I intercepted your conversation and diverted her.

How did I do that? Easy.

The spy software lets me see your phone activity but not act on it. For that, I needed your email password. I first try "password," but no luck. I would have been sorely disappointed if you had been that lazy. Rummaging through the text messages to your mom, I discover that all you talk about is your pathetic cat, Sylvester. So, I try "Sylvester" and bingo, I'm in your email on my second try. Not even a challenge. Then I send an email "from you" to ugly girl's phone with "@txt.att.net" at the end. She receives a text message appearing to be from you, bailing on the bar scene tonight.

I've also been reading all your emails and texts, not only from the last week but over the last few years. I know about every person you've called, every contact you've stored, every message you've exchanged. Thanks to you, we now have many mutual friends. You see, after I hacked your email, I sent a message to some of your friends with a link to a few "fun photos." Naturally, they clicked on the link. Why wouldn't they? Nothing suspicious there. As soon as your friends opened the attachment, I had access to their digital lives, too. Did you know that your sorority big sister, Lindsay, is secretly dating your boyfriend, Nick? Didn't think so.

I offer to buy you a drink and start the conversation by asking what you're studying. You proudly inform me that your major is art history. But I already know that. I know your whole course schedule and your latest grades—all B's and C's. Between a lame major and a disgraceful GPA, what were you going to contribute to society, anyway?

I suggest that you visit my art studio for a little "education," Miss Art

History Major. You giggle, twirling a long lock of blonde hair around your index finger. A boy standing nearby glances at me with disdain. He was planning to make a move until I showed up. Now he's eavesdropping on our conversation, watching the master in action.

Before I can prevent it, you snap a picture of me. Back at your sorority house last week, you couldn't find our selfies. You wanted to show your friends what a stud you'd met, but alas, you had no proof. I remind you that your phone crapped out and offer to take more, reaching forward, but you resist. Instead, you quickly review the image to ensure it's still there. Having my photo on your phone is not part of the plan. No problem. I'll just delete it later.

I pull out my Android to take a shot of you. You protest but I tease that it's only fair, since you have one of me. You tilt your head to the right, insisting I get your "good side," which works with my plan—to play on your vanity.

I take the photo, open the editing app on my phone and begin my digital plastic surgery. First, I widen your eyes and intensify the color—producing an unnatural, ocean blue. Then I lift your eyebrows, sculpting the perfect arch and symmetry. Your nose is decent, so I leave it alone, but every girl wants Angelina Jolie lips so I plump them and add some color. You watch with fascination as I turn a pretty girl into a knockout.

"How about your hair," I ask. "What would you like? Marilyn Monroe?"

You nod eagerly, and with a single stroke, I turn your mousy blonde hair to platinum. When you ask how I did it, I tell you it's easy and offer to show you how. Like putty in my hands, you don't think twice when I reach for your phone.

"Let me install the app," I say. I give you a quick demo, but also delete the spy software that's been on your phone since last week. I delete my photo, too—can't make it that easy for the cops. And for my finishing touch, I put your phone in airplane mode before handing it back. Apple should really require a passcode to disable the Wi-Fi and cellular connections, but they don't. Now your last known location will forever be this bar. Sure, the cops will eventually find your phone by tracing the last ping, but that will be days from now.

Around midnight, I suggest we go back to my place. You hesitate. Why? Last week you couldn't wait to fuck me. Maybe that pea brain of yours instinctively warns you that I'm not a good man. To nudge you along, I ask if you've ever heard the roar of a Maserati Quattroporte. Your eyes flash dollar signs and you hop off the bar stool, ready to go. I never said I *owned* one—that's your ignorant assumption. What would a man who owned a hundred-thousand-dollar car be doing in a dive bar in Decatur, Georgia, with a girl like you? There are higher class broads to be found, but I don't need high-class. I need a cute little bird who will tear at the public's heartstrings when she goes missing.

Arm in arm, I escort you to the door. At the exit, I look up at the surveillance camera, pause for a moment and kiss your neck so your face tilts upward. At the same time, I slip your phone from your bag and place it onto the wooden railing. Then we walk out into the autumn chill. Once we reach my car, I open the door for you like any gentleman would. I take off my coat and wrap it around your shoulders. You smile at being treated like the princess you know you are. As expected, you forget to check the model of my car. I ease into the driver's side, reach nonchalantly below the seat and unseal a zip-locked bag. My fingers grasp the soaked cloth. Pretending to lean in for another kiss, I lunge and cup the cloth over your nose and mouth, pressing firmly.

Unlike the first time I used chloroform, when I expected it to work instantly, I now know better. You struggle, but your strength is no match for mine. I wait. After a few minutes, you slump over, unconscious.

ABOUT THE AUTHOR

Liz Lazarus grew up in Valdosta, Georgia, known for its high school football and being the last watering hole on highway I-75 before entering Florida. She was editor of her high school newspaper and salutatorian of her class. Lazarus graduated from The Georgia Institute of Technology with an engineering degree and Northwestern's Kellogg Graduate School of Management with an MBA. She went on to a successful career as an executive at General Electric's Healthcare division and later joined a leading consulting firm as a managing director. In addition to writing, she also leads US Operations for an Atlanta-based medical technology start-up.

Interestingly, Lazarus initially ignored the calling to become a novelist. Instead, she tackled other ambitions on her bucket list: living in Paris and learning to speak French, getting her pilot's license and producing a music CD. But, as she explains, her first book "wouldn't leave me alone—it kept nudging me to write it to the point that I could no longer ignore it."

Though her first novel, *Free of Malice*, released in the spring of 2016, is fiction, the attack on the main character is real, drawn from Lazarus's own experience. It portrays the emotional realities of healing from a vicious physical assault and tells the story of one woman's obsession with forcing the legal system to acknowledge her right to self-defense.

Reader response to Lazarus's first novel was so encouraging that she embarked on a writing career, releasing her second novel in the spring of 2018. *Plea for Justice* is a thriller that depicts the journey of a paralegal investigating the case of her estranged friend's incarceration. As she seeks the truth, loyalties are strained and relationships are tested, leaving her to wonder if she is helping an innocent man or being played for a fool.

Shades of Silence is Lazarus's third novel, written with her trademark style of creating entertaining yet educational books with complex characters and unexpected, surprising conclusions.

Lazarus lives in Atlanta with her partner, Richard. When she's not working, she enjoys reading, traveling and spoiling their orange tabby, Buckwheat.

Made in the USA
Middletown, DE
27 November 2021

53561555R00163